About the Author

Lily's upbringing was deprived and brutal. Her education was minimal, leaving school with no qualifications. However, her thirst for knowledge ensured a professional qualification in her thirties and she became a successful businesswoman. She is immensely proud of her success and that of her children. She now enjoys retirement with her husband.

I would like to thank my husband Roger who always supports my ideas.

To Jill

Lily Graham

THE PHONE RANG

Lily Graham (signature)

AUSTIN MACAULEY
PUBLISHERS LTD.

A CIP catalogue record for this title is available from the British Library.

ISBN 978 1 78455 446 0 (Paperback)
       978 1 78455 448 4 (Hardback)

www.austinmacauley.com

First Published (2015)
Austin Macauley Publishers Ltd.
25 Canada Square
Canary Wharf
London
E14 5LB

Printed and bound in Great Britain

Acknowledgments

To the many brave women I've met who've fought back against the extreme violence they've suffered at the hands of the men who purport to love them, then aided and inspired other women to do the same – Thank You.

CHAPTER 1

Sheena Miller dropped heavily onto the sofa. She was totally exhausted. Leaning forward she held her head in her hands and sighed and struggled to hold back the tears that were so close to flowing. Another row with Tom, her husband, last night had resulted in a black eye. But she had no time for exhaustion. She had a five-month-old baby, Lucy to feed, who was at the moment fast asleep. As she glanced at Lucy lying in her pram, exactly as she had been since they returned from taking her other two children to school, Andy who was eight and Susie who was almost five, she was overwhelmed by the love she felt for her baby, not only for her baby, but for all her children. For Sheena was sure that without her children and her love for those children, she would surely have gone mad by now. But Sheena still had a half hour to an hour before Lucy would wake for her feed and so she let out a huge sigh and tried to relax. She would have to be calm and relaxed in order to successfully breast-feed Lucy as she was extremely sensitive to Sheena's moods. It was almost as though she worried with her. So taking in some deep breaths she did her best to calm herself.

It was a beautiful April morning and the sun was streaming in through the window and as Sheena looked up she couldn't help but notice how everything looked so lovely and peaceful. But the reality was that nothing that morning was lovely *or* peaceful in Sheena's life. The sun was shining directly onto the mirror over the fireplace. She instinctively got up from the sofa and found a cloth to wipe the dust from the mirror. The last thing she needed today was for Tom to find something else to be angry with her about. And dust was something he would *definitely* be angry about. Whilst wiping the mirror Sheena was shocked by what she saw, and for a moment it stopped her in her tracks. Not just the bruises on the face looking back at her, although they were bad enough, no, she'd seen those in the mirror last night, it was the fact that an old woman was looking back at her that shocked her. She leaned forward, closer to the mirror trying hard not to believe what she was seeing. *Where was that young woman with the sparkle, hope and excitement in her eyes? Was this woman looking back at her really only twenty-eight? Where did that lovely young woman go?* Sheena shocked and distressed at the reality of her reflection ignored the dust and sat down again on the sofa as the despair that was in danger of overwhelming her was threatening to reduce her to tears.

As she went over the incidents of the previous night she knew that she had deserved everything that she got from Tom. She had pushed him too far. Thinking about it now she wondered where she had found the courage to challenge him in the way that she had. But she had certainly suffered for it. But for now she would have to decide how to get him into a good mood before he got up. For there was no doubt in her mind that if he got up later today in the same frame of mind that he was in when he went to bed, then it wouldn't only be her who suffered, it would be the children too. She would have to do something to make things better by the time Tom woke up.

A wicked smile played across her mouth. Her face now a complete contrast to that of just a few moments ago. She knew what she would do. But the timing had to be right. Timing was everything. Tom may well be a bully. He may well frighten her. Whether he was physically abusing her, sexually abusing her, or simply verbally abusing her, there was no doubt that he frightened her. But he was also easy to fool and she would use all her cunning, lying, feminine wiles and anything else – within reason, to placate him and put him into a good mood. He might hit with his fists but he thought with his dick! She held her hands over her mouth as she laughed out loud at her own thoughts. Sheena hated sex and was at a loss to understand how anyone could actually *like* sex. But she had seen enough films and read enough books to know what she was supposed to do. Timing though, she must get the timing right.

Sheena would go up to wake him about fifteen minutes before she had to go and pick up the children from school. She would take a cup of tea up to him then quietly strip naked and slip into bed beside him. She could see it all now in her mind's eye. After all, she had done it often enough before – but still he never realised what she was actually doing! His 'Dick' would stand to attention the minute she got into the bed and the following scenario would be played out:

"Tom I've been thinking about you all day. I really couldn't wait." She would whisper to him as she climbed on top of him placing his 'Dick' inside her. "Come on Tom, quickly," she would say. "Oh you're so good. Do it quicker. I can't hold on," she would plead. Then she would 'pant' and 'moan' in all the right places – not that she knew where the 'right' places were – she just knew that he didn't seem to know the 'right' places either, so it didn't matter. What mattered was making sure he was happy and most of all, making sure of it quickly! And so she would praise him and tell him how 'good' he was. And it always worked. It never took more than a few minutes so the end result justified the means. 'Normal' sex for Tom only ever took a few minutes, once he had 'come' then he was finished – then she would give him his cup of tea and tell him that she had to hurry to get the children. He would complain of course.

"Why didn't you wake me earlier?" he would say.

"Are you sure we haven't got time for one more go?" Sheena would reply to the effect that she knew how hard he worked so didn't want to wake him too early and that she was also so, so disappointed. And she would sound perfectly genuine! She would normally wake him after she got home from picking up the children. Sometimes on these 'necessary early' occasions like today, he would say, "I'll stay here till you get back, then we can have another go." Sheena's reply would then be that she couldn't wait and would hurry back. But of course a teacher at school would hold her up over something or other. Or another mother would need to talk to her, perhaps to apologise for a mix up between her son and Andy. However it would occur, there would be something to delay her return, and as he had to leave for work at 5.30pm then there would only be time to quickly get his tea eaten before he left. On most occasions he would already be up when she returned. "Oh, Sheena, you can be so devious at times," she said to herself.

Sheena couldn't really understand why Tom should enjoy these experiences, because she knew very well that *her* 'enjoyment' meant nothing to him. There were many occasions when he would come home in the early hours of the morning and just climb on top of her. She would pretend to be asleep – she would hear his motorbike pull up onto the drive and then she would 'steel' herself against the cold that she knew she would feel when he came to her. Her heart would beat fast, but with fear rather than excitement, and she was scared, for she knew that if he realised that she was awake then the whole thing would last much longer and probably be much more involved.

It was really important to her that she showed no signs of being awake – not an easy thing to do, especially in the winter! The next thing she would hear would be his key in the door. Her heart beating even faster she got herself into the best position to make things as easy as possible for him. She would lie on her back with her legs slightly apart, probably with one arm on the pillow and the other just lying gently across her chest and, of course, her eyes firmly closed – but not in such a fashion that they looked closed with force or fear, nothing that would give her away! If he spoke to her then she wouldn't answer. Then he would just climb on top of her and get the 'business' done. As if she could possibly be asleep and stay asleep when he was cold and icy after coming off his motorbike! – But as long as she had no knickers on and her legs were apart, then that was all he needed. And he seemed to firmly believe that she *was* asleep, thank God! He would delight in telling her later in the day that he'd 'had' her that morning – his words – without waking her. And he would actually be pleased with himself for that. He would consider that to be the act of a good husband, not disturbing her. Sheena would have 'moaned' softly during the 'event' and so she would say in return to him, "Oh you're so considerate, Tom. I thought I was dreaming!" She shook her head at the thought of how easily he was to fool, and thought how stupid he must really be. If ever there was a case for a man thinking with what was between his legs, then that was surely it.

It was so funny that it was actually sad, for although Sheena didn't like sex, actually not *liking* sex was far too mild an expression, because in fact she *hated* it with a vengeance. Tom was the only person she'd ever had sex with and even on the first occasion he'd taken her by force and made her believe that no one else would ever want 'used' goods, and so he told her that she would now be his forever. But nevertheless, she did feel that somewhere deep down inside, deep in her heart, that with the right situation or person or whatever it was that was needed, then she felt she was actually bursting with love. She wasn't sure if she was a good person, because Tom told her often enough that she was ugly, stupid and lazy, but she had endless amount of patience and love for her children. She would go through anything for them and that made her feel that if she could give that love to Tom, then maybe he would teach her to be a better person, and then there might not be so many fights. But, facing reality, as she was forced to do, she knew in her heart that that kind of love would always evade her. In fact, that kind of love was probably just something that was made up for films. Just pure fiction and probably all women merely 'put up' with these things, because without sex then there would be no children. For instance, she knew for a fact that her own mother hated sex and just 'put up' with it. And she knew that her father was brutal in his attitude towards her mother as well. She had witnessed his brutality against her mother many, many, times and so she had lived with this behaviour all her life.

She was scared of her father and she was scared of her husband. But she adored her mother and was so very close to her. In fact, her mother was really her only friend and the only person who understood her. But even considering how close she was to her mother she'd never told her *all* that went on, *all* that Tom did to her. That sort of information would only hurt and upset her mother, and the last thing Sheena would want to do would be to give her mother even more to worry about.

So she wondered to herself: what sort of woman actually enjoyed being treated like that, for surely that's how all women were treated? And, of course, sex was expected of them. Men had their needs – as Tom frequently reminded her. Also, when they talk about 'orgasms' on films and did all that moaning etc., what exactly was that about? – which she herself did when it suited her – well she was absolutely positive that all that was a made up things for the films.

As for Sheena's plans to get Tom into a good mood and the mirth she felt at the thought of fooling him, well those plans and the idea that she was actually looking forward to fooling him, suddenly took on a different slant in her mind and the smile on her face turned to a look of terror when she thought about the possible consequences of what she was planning. Leaning forward she wrapped her arms around her legs and rocked slowly backwards and forwards saying out loud: "You silly, silly, stupid woman. Can you really be *so* stupid as to laugh when you know how much could go wrong with your plans?" she thought more about the dangers involved in her plan. He could realise what she was up to. He hadn't gone to work the previous night because of the almighty row that they'd had, and that could mean he could wake up early. Now she was physically shaking. Even the cheeks of her bum were subconsciously being held tightly together and her eyes were tightly shut. But still a tear leaked out and rolled softly down her cheek until she felt the saltiness of it as it touched her lips. She could feel sickness welling up in her as she recalled his 'special' sessions.

If Tom woke early he would know that she would be keen to make things right between them. He would know that the previous night was all her fault; he would know that she would go to almost any lengths to please him and so that could easily mean a 'special' session. There was a whole lot of danger to her plans but she just *had* to hope that he stayed asleep until she was ready to go up to him. He really mustn't wake up early. She quite simply *had* to make things better. If Tom woke up angry, he would be sure to tell the children that his mood was their mother's fault, and Sheena knew that they already suffered from nightmares. It was obvious to anyone who saw the children with their father that they were scared of him too, they always tried far too hard to be 'good' when they were with him, and so there was no other way for her, than to hope things went according to plan. But it was definitely no laughing matter.

***

Her thoughts turned to better times. Those first six weeks after Andy was born. Her body felt warm and comfortable just with the memories of those first few weeks of Andy's life and her face lit up. They were undoubtedly the *best* weeks of her life. Sheena adored her beautiful son, and in the evenings with Tom at work, she had had him all to herself.

She would've breast fed him, bathed him, cuddled him and danced around the room with him. The memory of his lovely warm body next to hers as she fed him and his little fingers softly stroking her breast was so strong she could almost feel those little fingers caressing her now. Afterwards there would be no television, just music to dance to. Andy had seemed to love it as much as she did and she was sure that was why he'd always slept well. But even so Sheena would always drink a bottle of stout whilst giving him his last feed of the day, and that helped both of them to sleep well. And now that Andy was older she was well aware that Andy still liked their 'alone' times. So when the other two were asleep and his dad was working, they would still put music on and sing or dance together. Totally out of tune, of course, but that didn't matter. Laughing out loud was what mattered. And they'd had such fun. She'd enjoyed the long summer days of that first summer with him as well, walking with him for miles, her talking, him listening – yes they were happy, in fact, very happy days when she was full of hope for the future.

Tom worked nights at that time, indeed he still worked only the night shifts. He would come home at about five-thirty in the morning then sleep for most of the day. Andy was all hers for most of those six weeks. But at that time she'd also felt like she had endless amounts of energy. She'd sleep when Andy slept and getting up in the night for feeds posed no problem at all for her. She would just pick him up and take him downstairs and he would nestle into her breast and feed till he was contented. Then she would change him, hug him and hold on to him for perhaps a little longer than strictly necessary, just for that extra cuddle. The feelings of love that she'd felt for him and the love that he gave back to her were wonderful. And those feeling were if anything even stronger now, now that he was growing into such an adorable young man. A love that was so much stronger and more special than she could ever have hoped for.

Nothing at that time had been too much trouble for her. Life was more than bearable, it was wonderful, and after the night feed she would go back to bed feeling warm and happy, so very, very happy. But despite broken sleep, Sheena would still get up before Tom and make him some breakfast on his 'rest' days, when he wasn't working, and she did all of that in order to include him in her excitement with Andy. Sheena had so, so wanted Tom to be as happy as she was, and she had thought that they were all truly happy. She'd had no idea that Tom was anything less than as happy as she was. They were a family now and she'd tried so hard to do all she could to make sure of that. But unfortunately, life as she now knew had not turned out the way she'd hoped for in those early heady days.

Not *having* to have sex and not having to *worry* about the sex had also had an effect on Sheena, and she was sure that that had contributed to her seemingly huge energy levels. She'd been so pleased that Tom was sticking to the doctor's orders to wait six weeks before resuming sexual relations. And although she'd been worried about sex starting up again, the fact that he *was* waiting and that he'd seen the pain of the birth had made her think that maybe the sex would be more gentle than before. Maybe being a father would make Tom more loving generally. She'd hoped so anyway. Tom had been tetchy at times, but Sheena had reasoned that his tetchiness was because his sleep was being disturbed, which is why she'd always taken Andy downstairs to feed at night in order to let Tom sleep peacefully.

The stout she used to drink whilst giving Andy his last feed had been a tip from her mother, who'd been a great help to her in the run up to the birth of Andy, but unfortunately Tom had made it quite clear that her mother had to go back to her own home when Sheena came out of hospital. He'd said that as she'd been there for two weeks that was more than enough for him. He'd insisted that she could cope perfectly well without her mother there.

And it was true, because she did manage, but she'd missed her mother at that important time in her life and she knew her mother was extremely hurt at having to go home before she'd even arrived home from hospital. Her mother had been so looking forward to helping Sheena with Andy, but she also knew that it was Tom's decision not hers. But Sheena had visited her mother often when Tom was in bed, even though it meant two bus journeys because at that time they didn't own a car. Tom had his motorbike for travelling to and fro from work, but Sheena had to either walk or get a bus if she wanted to go anywhere, and of course, she hadn't always told him about her visits to her mother's because she knew he wouldn't have approved. Mother and daughter though often shared confidences that neither of the men in their lives knew about.

The six-week Postnatal examination to see if all was well after Andy's birth was upon her in no time at all, and so Sheena went nervously to see the doctor at 10am on a sunny summer morning. She wasn't sure if she actually *wanted* all to be well for she knew what that would mean for Tom, what it would mean in regard to sex. She'd also needed an episiotomy because Andy was a big baby at 8lb 7oz and he was coming fast. As a result she was still sore around the area where she'd been stitched when she visited the doctor, but he'd assured her that all was well and it was safe to resume sexual relations with her husband. She recalled the doctor looking at Sheena's troubled face and saying, "That's a good thing. You have nothing to worry about, trust me. Just take things slowly, but remember you had a very quick birth and a very large baby, but both you and the baby are doing really, really well so don't look so worried."

He added that he could see that the episiotomy scar was still a bit sore, but that's to be expected, it will get back to normal in time. You'll forget you even had it. He'd laughed lightly as he'd said that, and she knew that he was trying to reassure her and she tried so very hard to smile back, but still it was a very nervous smile. "Thank you Doctor," she'd said as she left to make her way home. But Sheena was *extremely* nervous about resuming sex again. Still, she reasoned, Tom would be in bed when she got home and it would surely be the next day before she had to face that. Feeling reassured and happy she'd put a smile on her face and a spring in her step as she pushed Andy the five minute journey home. "Stop worrying," she'd said to herself. Tom is happy now. Things are different. She was trying her hardest to convince herself!

But as she'd pushed the pram around the corner towards their house she was shocked to see Tom waiting for her at the front door. From quite a distance she could tell from his stance and general demeanour that there was going to be trouble. He was standing with his arms folded in front of him and he looked worryingly impatient. Her mind had been quickly working overtime to think of the best way to deal with him. As she'd got nearer she looked at him, and she suddenly 'saw him' and he was ugly. He was thin, scrawny, short, untidy and most of all, scary. But he was stronger than her, physically anyway. What had she ever seen in him? she wondered. She knew that she'd married him because he was the first person to treat her well, reasonably well anyway, and that she'd been desperate to leave home. And he did treat her well at first and she did love him. She had also thought that he'd loved her. Well, all she could think of now as she approached her front door was that love really was blind! Well she tried to walk the last few yards with confidence, determined not to be bullied!

That confidence disappeared as soon as he'd opened his mouth. *"Get in here,"* he'd said, in a really angry and impatient voice. *"I've waited long enough for this."* He was right, he had waited. He'd waited the whole six weeks. The very same six weeks that had been the best of her life. Well they were over now! "I bet you enjoyed that doctor having a free 'feel' didn't you? You're not smiling now because I've caught you out. But I saw you smiling as you came round the corner and didn't know that I was looking." And with that he'd dragged her into the house leaving the pram at the front door and practically threw her up the stairs. Sheena was terrified, her body was shaking and trembling and she was crying.

"Don't rush me Tom please," she pleaded. "Andy will be due a feed soon and you need your sleep." Her heart was racing and she was panicking. "I'll come up and wake you early when we've got more time. Please, Tom," she begged. *"Don't rush you,"* he yelled at her. *"Don't fucking rush you?* I've waited six bloody weeks and I'm not going to wait any longer. *Don't rush you,* hah don't make me laugh. Get in there." And with that he'd thrown her onto the bed.

There were two big blue bath towels lying over the sheets. "What are the towels for?" Sheena had asked nervously. "Don't worry about the towels. And you shouldn't be crying, you're about to have the best time of your life. Get undressed," he'd ordered. "Can I just go and bring Andy in?" she'd asked him, her body now physically trembling with fear. Andy was still in his pram outside the front door.

"I Said GET UNDRESSSED. It's always Andy, Andy, Andy, with you. It's never me, is it?" He had suddenly changed. His face was contorted with rage and his eyes were full of malevolence. She obviously knew that he was expecting sex, but his look said that it was to be more than that. She knew that he could see the fear in her eyes as much as she could see the menace in his. She tried to put a brave face on. Tried to make him wait by telling him again and again that Andy needed feeding – which he did – but nothing made any difference. She could practically see his mind working as he stripped off and paced naked up and down the bedroom slowly, considering what to do to her.

She'd been slowly getting undressed, trying desperately to find a way out of what she was facing, but he'd suddenly grabbed at her and practically ripped her clothes off her body. The tears were streaming down her face but her cries were silent. She was in shock. Scared, terrified. Then surprisingly he gently laid Sheena on top of the towels. "What are the towels for?" she'd asked again. "We don't need them. Come on I've been waiting for today too." She'd tried to stifle her fears and sound interested, encouraging even. But God she was trembling with fear.

"The towels are there in case there's any blood," he'd said.

"There won't be any blood I'm not on my period," She'd replied. She was trying so, so hard to sound positive.

"I bloody know you're not on your period. Do you think I would be anywhere near you if you were?"

"Then I don't understand the towels."

"It's just in case," he'd said, with a very weird and frightening look on his face. "Now you just relax and enjoy. I'm going to give you the best orgasm you've ever had. Better than the one you had when *he* was born." He'd tossed his head to the side to motion to Andy downstairs. "Today you are going to get 'special' sex." She didn't understand what he was talking about, but whatever it was she knew for certain that it wasn't going to be 'good' and she definitely *didn't* want it.

He'd kneeled at the side of her and very gently ran his hands over her whole body. His erect penis was lying on her stomach. She should have been less worried when he was being so unusually gentle, but for some reason it just made her even more nervous, even more terrified. She'd just lay there doing nothing, but inside she was screaming, her heart beating like a drum. Then he moved to a position where he was kneeling between her legs. He'd moved forward to put his knees on either side of her and he laid her arms slowly down by her sides and pushed them in tight with his knees. Her fingers instinctively gripped onto the towels. He moved his face slowly towards hers and she could smell his rancid breath. She looked into his eyes and they were filled with sadistic menace and his mouth was twisted into a sardonic smile.

She turned her head to the side and closed her eyes tight, but she could feel him getting closer, feel, and smell his breath on her face. Then he'd suddenly gripped her by the neck with his left hand and forced her face back up towards him. But still she kept her eyes tightly shut. "Don't shut your eyes my love," he'd said softly but sarcastically, "You're going to want to see *everything.*" Then he gripped her right breast so tightly it made her scream out loud and her eyes opened in shock. But he put his hand across her mouth and said, "See, I knew that you would open your eyes. *But keep your mouth shut!*"

Then he'd sat on her stomach still using his knees to trap her arms, but he'd had to let go of her neck and as he leaned forward for a second or two, she'd thought that he was going to kiss her and that thought had made her heave. But he didn't kiss her. He'd laid his body heavily across hers but he was not inside her. Then he grabbed at both her breasts and squeezed them hard. He bit and sucked at her nipples 'till they bled. Her breasts were full of milk because Andy's feed was overdue and they were already sore before he started on them. His movements had been slow and deliberate, almost like slow motion. He disgusted her. "The *kid* gets all these," he'd said as he gripped her breasts firmly and painfully. "And the doc gets a free feel down here." He gripped her tightly between her legs as if to show where he meant. "And you love it all. You bloody well love it all," he'd hissed angrily at her. "Well now it's my turn to have some of the action that everyone else seems to be getting."

"Please don't hurt me," she'd begged him. He'd stopped what he'd been doing to her and looked at her with a puzzled look on his face.

"Ah, don't hurt you." He mocked her plea with his sarcastic reply. "Now don't be going all la-di-da prim and proper on me, pretending that you don't like being hurt. I was there when he was born remember? You went through a very painful delivery. No denying that. And then I saw how wide you opened up down here as you delivered him." He grabbed her sharply between her legs again. "Then you smiled. *You bloody smiled.* Your face was glowing, your legs were trembling and your bloody *fanny* was pulsating. And you, well you were bloody smiling. So don't let's have any pretence about *'please don't hurt me'.*"

All this was said in such a disgusting mocking manner, and he was laughing as he spoke. Tears were streaming down Sheena's face now, and she was sobbing heavily but she knew it was futile to try to explain that he was talking about something that every mother goes through. That the smile on her face was one of pure joy for her son, for *their* son, not because she'd enjoyed the pain. No one *enjoys* pain. It was because she was holding her beautiful son in her arms and she felt his beautiful warm body next to her skin. She never imagined in her wildest thoughts that Tom was thinking things like that. How could she.

Tom sat up again still straddled across her stomach and masturbated himself. When he 'came' he let it go all over her then picking up both her hands and holding on to them, he used them to rub his sperm all over her breasts. She pleaded with him, but he was ignoring her. "See if he still likes them now?" he'd said. And with that he'd moved back down to between her legs and pushed her knees up and apart so that she was now fully exposed. He was just staring at her.

"Don't look at me like that," Sheena had said trying desperately all the time to cover herself up in some way, but there was nothing available with which to cover her body up with, all she had were her hands.

The way that Tom was looking at her made her feel dirty and disgusting. She begged, she pleaded, she prayed, she cried. Anything that she thought might help she said to him. But it wasn't making any difference. All her pleas were futile. "I'm going to give you the same great orgasm that you had when the kid was born." He hadn't even used his name and Sheena was terrified.

She was praying under her breath to God for it all to stop. "Please, please God let it stop." But it didn't stop.

Then he really got started. First he tried to put his fist inside her. He'd pushed and she'd screamed. He hit her and she screamed again. "For God's sake shut up." he said. "You know you love it. You just don't want to admit it. The kid came out of here and he was much bigger than my fist. So I *know* it will fit, and I *know* you like pain." The pain she was feeling was indescribable but even as she was suffering she could hear Andy crying outside the front door. Now her tears were tears for him as well as herself.

Tom kept pushing and pushing, trying to get her vagina to open up wider, trying to satisfy some twisted urge that she had no way of understanding, and then he just stopped and got off the bed. Sheena breathed a heavy sigh of relief, thanking God quietly that it was all over. She'd reached for the towels to wipe herself with and tried to get off the bed. But he swung round quickly and pushed her violently back down and shouted at her, "**Oh no you don't.** We're far from finished. In fact, we've only just started." He paced up and down the bedroom for a few minutes, then picking up a can of hair spray from the dressing table he climbed back onto the bed. He'd moved to the side of her again. He was obviously aroused again already. Sheena was close to passing out by now and she had ceased any and all resistance. She had seen him with the spray can in his hand and she braced herself for what she now knew was to come. She'd clenched every muscle in her body with as much strength as she could muster.

Placing his left hand on her shoulder and over her throat to hold her down, he'd taken her hand and told her to masturbate him. She'd had no energy left, only silent tears and she couldn't do what he wanted. But then suddenly he'd thrust the hair spray can inside her and raped her violently with it, thrusting it inside her harder and faster and at the same time telling her to get on with it, to get on with masturbating him. But she couldn't do it. She felt all the energy going from her and she'd stopped fighting. She could hear someone shouting at her. It sounded like Tom's voice but it was so, so far away…

Then suddenly she let out such a scream and sat bolt upright on the bed. Tom was standing just looking at her. She looked down between her legs and there was a bottle lying there and she was bleeding heavily. From the position of the bottle and the state she was in it was obvious that he'd tried to insert the bottle from the base end, and that had resulted in tearing her. She must have passed out because the bottle was one from downstairs, one of the empty stout bottles that she'd drank when she was giving Andy his last feed of the night. She was also covered with more sperm. He must have done *that* himself because she knew she hadn't done it! Tom had just stood there in silence as she got off the bed but when she put her feet on the floor they wouldn't support her. Tom moved and caught her.

She'd glared at him with more hatred than she ever knew she had in her. *"Don't you dare touch me?"* She'd screamed at him.

"I'm just trying to help you," he'd said lamely. But the look on his face was one of twisted delight in his achievement, not one of sorrow.

"Don't help me! Don't touch me!" she screamed again at him.

His voice changed back to his twisted self and he said "Well, go on then, admit it, that was good wasn't it?" She just wrapped herself in the towels and with every ounce of strength that she had left she'd walked downstairs to the bathroom. She wasn't going to give him the satisfaction of helping her. In the hallway Andy was in his pram. Tom must have gone downstairs and brought him in and then gone back upstairs and continued with his disgusting plan while she was unconscious. Now she knew for sure that she'd passed out, but she didn't know for how long. She'd rushed to the bathroom to vomit.

Sheena had to hold herself together. She got into the shower and let the warm water cascade over her painful body. The water was removing his filthy body fluids that were mixed with her blood, but nothing could remove the stench of him that was permeating through every pore in her body. It was in her nostrils, it was everywhere and it was putrid. The tears were flowing faster than the water but they were silent tears.

She slowly and gently washed her now bloody body, but then she dropped to the floor of the shower with complete and thorough exhaustion, and with the water still cascading over her she held her head in her hands. Her eyes were closed, but his eyes were still in front of her closed lids, as real and as menacing as they had been just a short while ago. She didn't want to move. She wanted to scrub the smell of him off her, scrub her body till it bled even more than it did already. And she did scrub it but it made no difference.

Questions and statements began tumbling from her mouth: why had she let him do that? What had she done to make him think that she would want that? She must have done something; she must have said something, but what? She wasn't a fit mother; she wasn't a fit person; she was lower than low. How could she ever hold her head high again? Walk in the sunshine and laugh with her son; she could never do those things again. She was full of shame; utter, utter devastating shame. Then she heard Andy crying and she knew that he would be hungry, but even that couldn't stir her.

It crossed her mind that she should just leave him and walk away. Leave Andy for a *decent* woman to look after him, for she herself was surely not a 'decent' woman. Someone would take him. Her mind was racing from one thought to another and they were all bad. Then suddenly she was jerked back to reality. *"Shut that bloody kid up. What sort of a mother and wife are you? I'm trying to sleep. Shut him up woman."* And as if on auto pilot she immediately jumped out of the shower, and wrapping her gown around her and ignoring the blood that was still oozing from her painful body she went to take care of Andy. Picking him up gently and resting his head on her shoulder she rubbed his back to both soothe and quieten him. But she didn't go to her usual chair to feed him, no, she took him into the kitchen and made up a feed of formula milk whilst at the same time drinking down a full glass of liquid laxative, this was to ensure that emotion didn't get the better of her when it came to later feeds. So it was with a heavy heart that she fed Andy his formula milk knowing that with 'his' body fluid mixed with her blood, she could never again breast feed him. As she held her son close she hated herself for thinking that she could ever leave him. Somehow, some day she would get revenge and she whispered as much to her son as she held him as close as she could.

Somehow she had to deal with life as it now was and whatever happened to her, she knew one thing for sure and that was that this little angel in her arms was not going to suffer. And so now she knew. The happy times had ended forever and the 'specials' had begun.

CHAPTER 2

"Well, Sheena, pull yourself together!" she found herself saying out loud to no one at all – except perhaps Lucy, bringing herself sharply back to the reality of the day. But even just remembering that first time all those years ago was powerful enough to bring tears to her eyes but she was not going to go back to those times. That was not going to happen. Today would work out exactly as planned. She would put Tom into a good mood and all would be well.

Lucy was beginning to stir and Sheena realised that half an hour had passed without her doing any proper dusting or polishing and now Lucy needed to be fed. She smiled wickedly to herself and said to Lucy, "Well, sweetheart, the polishing and dusting will just have to wait because you're starving and I've got lots of milk for you." And then she added conspiratorially – "And don't you worry my little love, there's plenty of milk for you. He wouldn't dare! He wouldn't dare because someone else now knows his dirty little secret. No there's nothing for you to worry about Lucy darling." She hoped and prayed that he wouldn't dare go back to the 'special'.

Sheena had managed to feed Lucy herself for five months now and she had loved every minute of it, and although the 'special' had happened several times over the years it was almost two years since the last time, and she felt sure that those sessions were over now. This past five months feeding Lucy had been the most she had ever managed, as when Susie was born she only managed two weeks for much the same reason as she'd had to stop feeding Andy. He hadn't even waited the required six weeks then, so he'd still taken her completely by surprise.

But she put all that to the back of her mind and picked Lucy up and holding her up in the air she said to her, "Right! OK. I'm coming." Sheena couldn't help but smile when she was talking to Lucy she was such a good baby always smiling and gurgling and with a scary way of knowing exactly how Sheena was feeling. It was as though there was some sort of invisible bond between them and Lucy knew Sheena's every mood and responded to all her moods in an uncanny way. Lucy hadn't been a planned baby but she was certainly a wanted and much loved one, for Sheena anyway.

There was a special routine for the morning feed. It was the quietest time of the day and there was only the two of them. Sheena would put the kettle on and make a cup of tea then settle down in the armchair and relax for the twenty to thirty minutes that it took to feed Lucy – twenty to thirty glorious minutes. The tea brewed, Sheena readied herself with Lucy on her breast. Her little hands gently caressed Sheena's breast and she looked up at her mum and smiled then latched on to her breast and closed her big brown eyes and set about satiating herself as Sheena drank her tea all the while thinking to herself – *now this is heaven for sure*. Somehow Lucy feeding made Sheena thirsty! She took this quiet time to go over the events that led to her black eye and the row of the night before.

***

The trouble that ultimately caused Sheena's black eye had probably started in the middle of the previous week. Lucy was due to be Christened on the Sunday – last Sunday – and on the previous Wednesday Sheena had met up with her mother, Jeannie Williams, to go shopping for some clothes for the children. Tom, as usual, was on the night shift (he always worked nights) and Sid, Sheena's dad was also on nights last week. Sid worked three different shifts down the pit so the night shift only came around every three weeks so mother and daughter always made the most of it. Neither of the men liked them meeting up without asking permission first, but as Sheena could drive and had access to the car and the men were asleep, they tended to think – why not!

Jeannie had won some money on the bingo which Sheena's dad didn't know about and she was determined to spend some of it on new clothes for her grandchildren for the Christening. Both the children loved their new clothes and Sheena was very grateful as money, as usual, was tight. At the same time Jeannie bought herself a new outfit for the Christening which she said she was so looking forward to. This would probably be her last grandchild to get christened. Sheena had two older brothers who had two children each and had no intention of having any more, although as Sheena knew only too well with Lucy, things don't always work out the way you think they will. But the chances were that this would be her last grandchild.

Sheena loved spending time with her mum. They were more like best friends than mother and daughter and she felt that she could tell her mum anything – and mostly she did. Her mum had always been badly treated by her dad, in fact, she had grown up seeing him beat her as well as feeling his belt on her backside, or her legs, herself. Her mum had often come between Sheena and her dad to prevent Sheena from taking a beating. That usually ended with her mum getting a worse beating. Jeannie was well aware that Sheena didn't have a good sex life, or for that matter, a good married life, but if Sheena had left Tom to go back home then she would just go back to being a beaten daughter and have her mother taking beatings for her. But although she told her mother most things she couldn't bring herself to tell her about the 'specials'. She was too ashamed of them to tell her.

Sheena's mother didn't enjoy the best of health. She suffered with Angina as well as headaches and general aches and pains, but Sheena also knew that her mother often exaggerated her illnesses to make her father leave her alone. She didn't blame her mother for that, in fact if she could have done that with Tom then she would have. But on that Wednesday Jeannie was very well and happy.

Sheena's thoughts were temporarily disturbed as Lucy was signalling that she needed to be winded and moved to the other breast. Sheena did this and gave her a little kiss on her forehead as she snuggled in again to finish feeding.

With her thoughts returning again to her own problems she recalled that on the Saturday of that week, Sheena and her mum had talked on the phone, as they did most days, and Jeannie had said that she'd told Sid she was feeling ill. But she'd told Sheena that if it was mentioned she wasn't to worry because she was fine, feeling a little poorly but fine. So Sheena knew the reason why her mum had told her dad that she didn't feel well. "You will be at the Christening though, won't you Mum?" Sheena had asked.

If she'd said no then Sheena would have worried, but she'd said, "Of course I will be there, but you know how it is love." Her mum sounded a bit down and Sheena was a little bit worried, but she reassured her that she was fine and that she would be at the Christening the following day.

On the Sunday morning Sheena was busy getting the children ready for the Christening. Andy looked so grown up in his new long trousers and Susie loved her new dress. Lucy had a beautiful Christening robe on which had been saved from the other two's Christenings and Sheena herself wore a very nice dress that wasn't new but was nice. She hadn't let her mum buy anything for her because she wouldn't have been able to explain it to Tom. But Tom had a new suit. He liked to impress people; he liked pretending to be the loving family man!

Then the phone rang and it was Sheena's dad, Sid. And she remembered the conversation with her dad to be quite a worrying one. "What's the matter Dad, you should be here by now?" Sheena couldn't hide her worried tone.

"Your mum's not well. We won't be coming," he'd said.

"What's the matter with her? Put her on the phone and let me talk to her. Do you need me to come over?" The panic was rising in Sheena's voice with one question after another being fired at her dad. Her mind had been racing ahead of the conversation. This wasn't right, Mum should be here, and Sheena knew that her mother had so *wanted* to be there.

Her dad continued, "No. She's not coming to the phone, she's not well but she'll be all right. You just go ahead with the Christening."

"I can't just do that Dad, not without speaking to her put her on the phone please." Sheena's heart had been beating fast because she was so scared that he might have hit her, that they might have had a fight. He could have found out about the money she'd won and the money she'd spent. It could be anything and she needed to know what exactly was wrong.

"I said **NO!**" He'd effectively ended their conversation with that one statement. "Just save your mum some Christening cake and call over on Thursday with it, she'd like that." Sheena had remained worried all day. Tom had been angry with her for being 'distant' and fussing too much about her mother. And even Lucy had struggled when she was being fed. It hadn't been a really good day at all.

Then the following evening, yesterday, when Tom was getting ready for work, Sheena's dad rang again. That call was to be the real start of the trouble between Sheena and Tom. Sheena had been so pleased that he'd rang because she had wanted to ring her mother all day but Tom had put his foot down and said she was fussing too much, so she hadn't been able to ring her herself. "How's mum today dad?" She'd asked, trying her best to sound casual.

"That's why I'm ringing," he said. "She's not well at all and she wants to see you. Can you come over tonight?" Sheena felt her heart racing. What was she going to do? She knew Tom wouldn't let her go out at this time of night. It was five-thirty and he was going to work any minute.

"I can't come tonight dad." She'd said. Put mum on the phone and let me speak to her please" Her dad then got really angry with her.

"Well if you can't be bothered, I'll tell her that you can't be bothered, but she's not well enough to come to the phone."

Now Sheena really was panicking. "No, Dad, I'll come over. I'll come over straight away," she promised.

Tom had been listening and immediately started shouting. "No, no way. No way are you going over there tonight. I've got to go to work and you are staying put." He was livid, his face full of rage.

Sheena had pleaded with him. "I'll take you to work and drop you off and then go and see mum. I'll take the kids with me and we won't be very long, but I *need* to see her."

But Tom had been adamant. "It's probably just an excuse. I know that you and your mother lie through your teeth to both me and your dad. Your mum's probably going to have the kids while you go off gallivanting somewhere else. If I'd have gone to work five minutes ago when I should have, then I wouldn't even have known that you'd gone out, because you certainly wouldn't have told me. So no, you're not going and that's final." He went to get his coat, to get ready for work. He had been strutting and puffing out his chest, trying to scare her. Well she had been scared before and she'd known that there would be ramifications. But she'd been determined.

Sheena had braced herself and stood up to him. "I'm going to see my mother whether you say so or not." She'd tried her best to sound strong and forceful. Andy and Susie instinctively huddled in a corner. They knew what was coming and they were right. Tom shouted and threatened and raised his fist to her but she wouldn't budge. She was trembling, but she wasn't budging.

She thought of the times her mother had taken a beating for her. Well now if it had to be her turn to take a beating, then it had to be but she wasn't going to budge. To her amazement Tom didn't hit her. He'd actually backed down and agreed that she could go. Sheena had felt a sense of pride over how brave she'd been. Only now he wasn't going to work, he was going with her and then he would see for himself just how *ill* her mother was. Sheena didn't care. All she cared about was that they were going. She knew that if her dad was saying that her mother was ill, then she was really ill. Because he'd *never* believed her when she said she was ill, even if she was in fact really ill, so this must be serious. And so they all went to Sheena's parent's house.

Sheena recalled looking at her mother, then looking over at Tom and seeing him glaring at her. He was so angry. He'd missed a night's work, which also meant a night's pay that they couldn't afford to miss. And if she was honest she couldn't really blame him, and it was at this point that she'd known for sure that there would be trouble when they got home. She had previously thought that when she arrived at her mum's then Tom would understand, clam down a bit. But now she knew he wouldn't.

Jeannie was sitting in her armchair, apparently without a worry or care in the world. "Hello love," she'd said looking obviously puzzled. "What are you doing here at this time of night, and with the children as well? Bring them over here and let me see them." Sheena could remember her words as if she was sitting in front of her saying them now and she couldn't hide her astonishment that she looked so well.

Sheena recalled their conversation. "Dad said you were ill and that you wanted to see me." Her father then said that he'd make us all some tea and disappeared into the kitchen signalling Tom to come with him, as though he didn't know why they were here either. Jeannie took the chance to speak to her daughter in a conspiratorial tone while the men were out of the room. "He was pestering me on Saturday first, you know what I mean." She nudged Sheena knowingly, and Sheena nodded; she knew exactly what her mother meant. Her mother continued, "I had to say I was ill because he was determined and wouldn't be put off. He even sent for the doctor to see me. Well I had to tell the doctor that I'd had chest pains and that I wasn't feeling too well otherwise... well I couldn't say I was lying could I? The doctor said that I was a bit warm and that I had to be careful and look after myself to keep my Angina under control.

Then yesterday morning I said I was feeling better and looking forward to the Christening. Your dad brought me a cup of tea and then he started with all that again." Jeannie pulled her daughter closer to her and her voice dropped to a whisper. "He wanted 'funny stuff' sex, you know – from behind." She'd looked at Sheena and nodded her head as if to confirm what she was saying. Sheena just screwed her face up in disgust at her dad as her mother continued. "Well I'm too bloody old to be putting up with anything like that. So I had to tell him that if he did something like that, then he would probably set off my Angina again. Well, to my surprise, he looked at me and agreed! He said I was looking quite pale and that he thought he ought to fetch the doctor out again. I said not to bother but he insisted. I think he just wanted to get his own back on me and stop me from going to the Christening." Sheena had agreed that that was probably what he wanted. But she couldn't help but think that her mum was just telling her too much! It's bad enough thinking about her mum and dad having sex at all, but to think that they were going to be doing something like that – the images that brought to the forefront of Sheena's mind..........ugh! It suddenly dawned on Sheena that although both her and her mother each knew that the other had a terrible love life, if you could even put the word 'love' into the life they lived, but they had never actually gone into details before.

Sheena wondered at that moment if she should have told her mother about the 'specials'. But really, even given what her mother had just said, she still couldn't have told her that, she was far too ashamed to tell her lovely mother the horrible things that Tom did to her. Sheena also realised at that moment that her mother, herself, had no one to talk to about her worries and fears. All her mother's family were in Scotland where she herself and her brothers were born. They had moved as a family to England after the end of the war in order that her dad could find work. Her dad was English but she knew that her mother felt isolated being so far away from her family and she was also pretty sure that that was what her dad wanted – for her mother to be isolated from her family. Of course, her mother talked to her and they were exceptionally close, but some things were left unsaid out of shame or embarrassment or both, by both of them. However, Jeannie continued…

"When the doctor called I told him that I was sorry to bother him again, and your dad sounded like a stranger as he told the doc all about my pain, I just looked at him mystified, and then the doc said that my pulse was quite fast – he didn't know what your dad had wanted to do!" Her mother had laughed out loud at that, and Sheena couldn't help but laugh with her, even though she was more than a little embarrassed by what her mum was saying.

Sheena couldn't help but think that sex seemed to be all that men were concerned about. She knew that her mother feigned, or exaggerated illnesses, and she didn't blame her for that. She'd had many more pregnancies than babies in her lifetime because her father never left her alone long enough to recover from a miscarriage before starting again. And the only contraception was the word 'no', which was not in her father's vocabulary. "The doctor said that I needed some more Angina tablets and not to be afraid to take them when I have another attack." Her mother then added in a tone of complete astonishment, "that the *next* shock was when your father insisted on fetching them straight away. That he went to the Sunday chemist and here they are," she said, pointing to the bottle of tablets that was on the coffee table. "But honestly, I didn't know he was calling you and bringing you here with the kids and all. I'd have told him not to bother. I'm so sorry love. Will it be okay for you with Tom?" Sheena knew the real answer to that was going to be no, but she told her mum not to worry, that she'd deal with Tom. But Sheena was worried.

She knew that her mother had been pregnant almost every year since she was twenty years old, and that had continued until she'd had a hysterectomy in her early forties, and her mother was only a small delicate type of woman, 5ft 1in tall and about 7st 'wet' through. The downside of the hysterectomy, as far as her mother was concerned, was that it gave her dad more opportunity to abuse her and therefore it gave herself the greater need to be 'ill'. Sheena also knew that her mother had had a nervous breakdown several years ago and had to be hospitalised, and given what her mother called 'Electric Shock Treatment' so she completely understood the reasons for her mother either feigning or exaggerating illnesses, and what's more, she didn't blame her in the least for doing so.

Sheena herself wasn't averse to using whatever tactics she could in order to get out of sex with Tom. Her father had no sympathy, or time for her mother or anyone else and he was a big strong man, not one to be trifled with. He was known locally as 'Big Sid' and he was both feared and revered in equal measure in the mining community, and Sheena didn't know of anyone who'd ever stood up to him or dared to cross him. But she *was* relieved that her mother had been exaggerating and wasn't really ill.

As her mother continued relaying the events of the previous few days Sheena had been studying the different manifestations on mother's face as she recalled each fact; Shock at the concern her husband appeared to be showing for her health, guilt at having to lie to her doctor, devilment at having deceived her husband, delight at Susie's giggles as she just ran around playing, worry for her daughter, but most of all, love. Love for her daughter and her grandchildren. And Sheena's heart was itself bursting with love and pride for the mother who'd stood up to that hulk of a man she was married to when Sheena herself was a teenager. Her mother had taken many blows over the years that had been intended for her. She hugged her mum tightly. "I love you Mum," she'd said holding back the tears that were threatening to come tumbling down her cheeks.

"I love you too, my darling," her mother had replied. "But stop being so silly. I'm fine. Really I'm fine." She'd looked at her daughter's face, and Sheena knew that she couldn't hide anything if her mum looked at her like that. She knew she could see the tears welling up. "Now, we'll have none of that. You've got babies to look after, so none of that, okay."

"Okay, Mum," she'd replied. But as she'd marvelled at the amount her mother had put up with over the years in many, many different ways, she'd also wondered if she herself could ever be that strong. Was she destined for the same sort of life that her mother was living?

Then the men came back in with the tea, and Tom shot an angry glare at Sheena that sent a cold shiver down her spine. Sheena's mum made a big fuss of Susie because she felt she was losing out with all the attention Lucy had been getting at the Christening. She crossed her legs and let Susie sit on one leg and played 'ride a cock horse' with her singing out loud to her as she played. Susie loved it and was giggling again. Andy was too big to play games with his Grandma but he reluctantly gave her a kiss as they were leaving and Lucy got a little cuddle too.

"Where's your mum's christening cake?" her dad had said as they headed for the door. Sheena had given her dad a look that said; what's all this about? But he'd just smirked at her, as though he'd known that he'd caused trouble, and then he just shrugged his shoulders nonchalantly. But he'd added that she should give her mum a kiss and cuddle 'because she's really not well'. Sheena had known that that wasn't true, and what's more, she knew that her dad knew it wasn't true. She couldn't make him out but she hugged her mother and told her that she would come back on Thursday with the cake. But her mother clung on to Sheena tightly and whispered urgently to her, "Whatever happens in your life love, don't you live the life I've lived, have courage and always remember that I love you and I'll always be with you." Now it was Jeannie's turn to have tears in her eyes. Sheena was puzzled, and as her mother saw the puzzled and worried look on her daughter's face she quickly got up and said, "Come on now, those children need their beds." She was obviously changing the subject, but why? Sheena was convinced that there was more to what her mother was saying but all the same they left for the journey home.

It was 8 o'clock when they'd left her mum's house that evening, and it would be nine before she'd be able to get the children into bed that night. The journey home was horrendous. Andy had sat quiet in the back of the car, he was old enough to know when his dad was really angry, and had long since learned that the best thing he could do at times like that was to keep quiet, Susie fell asleep in the car and Lucy had been asleep in Sheena's lap. And she recalled the silence, broken every now and again with Sheena repeatedly saying sorry. Tom had said nothing but he'd been gripping the steering wheel as though he was trying to steer a tank and every now and then he just slammed a hand on the steering wheel in temper, but remained silent. That was all designed to terrorise Sheena and it worked, she'd been rightly terrified. As they'd drawn up outside their house Sheena's heart was racing. Tom just went inside without helping with the children, so Sheena simply tried her hardest to sound cheerful as she took them in and put them to bed.

Then he'd started. First it was just him shouting, but he knew she'd no answer to give him, so she just kept saying sorry. Even Sheena thought that her own voice had sounded pathetic and whimpering, but what else could she do. Tom had been determined to get her crying and when she hadn't cried in response to his shouting at her, he'd slapped her across the face then punched her. She'd reeled back but still didn't cry. She'd been just as determined not to as he was determined to make her cry. But then he'd pushed her to the floor, and with his knees holding down her arms he kept lifting her head off the floor and banging it down again. She'd begged him to stop, saying she had a headache. He'd again taken on his favourite mocking tone to her pleading – "Ah, what a shame, she's got a headache!" Then luckily Susie came into the room unable to sleep and crying for her mum. Tom let go and practically threw her towards Susie and said menacingly, "Don't think I'm finished with you yet." She'd taken Susie back up to bed and lay down beside her. She'd heard Tom getting a beer out of the fridge so she just stayed put and hoped he would have enough to drink to forget about his threat. Tom finally went to bed and when Sheena was quite sure he was asleep she went to bed herself creeping in beside him without disturbing him. She didn't really sleep because her mind was buzzing with what had happened at her mum's. She just lay there shedding silent tears at the thought of the day ahead.

****

And so that's how she found herself that morning trying to think of the best way to get Tom into a good mood when he woke up and prevent him from continuing what he had started the night before.

Sheena was just finishing off feeding Lucy and getting a nappy ready to change her. She held her close and devoured that lovely baby smell that she had, and thought to herself that no matter what she had to face that day, it was worth it to have the love of her children and to feel their love back every single day. Basically she thought to herself, *well I've got problems yes, but so does everyone else, but I've got gorgeous children too and besides that, mum wasn't seriously ill after all so not everything was bad.* Lucy smiled back at her as if in agreement.

With Lucy lying on the floor with no nappy on and giggling away the phone rang. Sheena rushed to answer it because she didn't want the phone to wake Tom up early. Her plan was to wake him later! It was her dad on the phone. "Oh, Dad, can I talk to you later? I'm just in the middle of feeding and changing Lucy," she'd said. She didn't really want to speak to him. Then she heard such a terrifying scream that didn't really sound human, it made her drop the phone and fall to the floor. For a moment she wondered where that almost inhuman noise had come from. Then still sitting on the floor she picked up the phone again and said. **"What did you just say, Dad?"**

"I said... you can get back to your precious baby. I'm only ringing you to tell you that your mum's dead..."

CHAPTER 3

Sheena really didn't know what happened next. How did she get here? She should be sitting on the floor in her kitchen, or changing Lucy's nappy but she wasn't. She was standing and staring at her mother's empty chair. She could hear noises, voices, but couldn't make them out. She was aware of other people around her but didn't know who they were. All she could see was her mother's empty chair. Her eyes were transfixed on the empty chair. But she could feel something touching her leg.

The sofa at her mother's house was also used as a bed, you just pulled the seat forward and the back dropped down and you had a double bed. Her right leg was touching that bed. She wanted to turn around to look, but she couldn't. Her head was spinning and her legs were weak, hardly supporting her. This had to be the most awful dream anyone ever had, and she just wanted to wake up. "Please, please let me wake up," she said silently to herself over and over again. She was falling, she could feel herself falling and God she wanted to fall, oh how she *wanted* to fall. Perhaps then she would wake up. But suddenly she was caught. Someone was holding her tightly and preventing her from falling. "Were they stopping me from waking up?" She wondered idly. But at the same time she liked the feeling of these strong arms around her.

"Sheena, Sheena it's me you're okay. It's just shock. Sit down a minute, love." Sheena recognised the voice; it was her older brother, Graham. Her eyes were tightly shut and her head was resting on Graham's shoulder. She knew she had to open her eyes and she also instinctively knew that as her brother had caught her, he had also turned her around. She knew that if she opened her eyes she would be looking straight at the sofa.

She sucked in a huge deep breath then let it out slowly. Then she quietly whispered into her brother's ear, "Let me go, Graham." She felt him hesitate. "It's okay. I'm okay, let me go, please I won't fall, I need to look." Graham slowly and gently let go of his sister, cupping her face in his hands as he did so and using his thumbs he gently brushed away her tears, but his left thumb hesitated over Sheena's bruised eye whilst throwing Tom a contemptuous look. "No, Graham, I banged my head." Graham raised his eyebrows at her disbelievingly, but again she said, "No, really, Graham, I banged my head. I'm fine." She could tell by his look that he didn't believe her but she had no time to go into all of that now. She steeled herself for what she was about to see, and so there she was, standing with her eyes open.

She was looking at the sofa bed now and seeing her mother lying there with her eyes open. She had covers over her that reached up to her chin, but her right arm was outside the covers and resting on her chest. She wanted to scream, to cry, to do something, but she was silent and just slumped to her knees, her head resting on the side of the bed next to her mother's head. Suddenly huge heaving sobs came from the depths of her soul and she cried out loud – "No, no Mum please, please don't let this be true. Mum, Mum, please," she begged her and looked up at her eyes they were cold, empty, but they were still her mum's eyes. Her mum was cold and

Sheena wanted to cover her up but instead she wrapped her arm across her mother and rested her head on her mother's chest in an effort to keep her warm.

With tears streaming down her face she turned around and looked at her dad, with her eyes full of pleading but no words coming from her mouth, her eyes were asking him the question, and as if she had said it out loud he answered her. "I told the doctor not to cover her up or to close her eyes. I knew that was something that you would want to do." His words were soft and comforting, which in itself was strange but she nodded, and putting her hand gently over her mother's eyes she closed them, then she lifted the blanket from her body and slowly put her arm back under the blanket and finally she covered her face. Her sobbing subsided and she was exhausted but suddenly she had to run to the bathroom to vomit.

On her knees at the toilet with her head resting on her arm her head was spinning and aching. Her heart was so heavy with pain she didn't know how she was going to survive; she didn't know if she *wanted* to survive such was her pain. But she knew that she would have to as she had children to look after, and her mother would be so angry and upset with her if she didn't put her children's needs before her own. So she stood up and stared in the mirror for a while, there were no more tears now she felt 'cried out' and so she composed herself and went back downstairs.

Tom came to her as she came back into the living room and gently guided her to her mother's chair. He brought her a mug of hot sweet tea that tasted divine. Sheena looked up at him and saw the sadness and caring in his eyes and she thought that he seemed like the Tom she'd first met, kind, thoughtful, doing kind things. Why couldn't he have stayed like that she wondered. She was so confused today as nothing was normal, especially her thoughts. But even through her confusion she knew well enough that Tom had two sides, the side that was for public viewing and the side that he kept hidden from the rest of the world. At least he thought he kept it hidden, but Sheena knew better as Graham knew and as her mother knew, it wasn't really hidden.

Still she wrapped her fingers gratefully around the mug and eagerly drank the tea. Her mother, her lovely, lovely mother was dead. Now she must take care of her dad as well as her children. She looked across at him and he seemed dazed, confused and although she knew that he hadn't made her mother happy for many years, she felt sure that he must have loved her, and she him at one time and his heart must also be aching.

Sheena also realised now that the noises she'd been hearing a while ago was in fact just chatter from the people in the room. She hadn't at first realised that anyone else was in the room because to her it only held an empty chair. But now that she looked around she could see that as well as her father sitting in his chair, Tom was sitting by the window with Lucy in her carry-cot, Graham was sitting in a chair close to her mother's head, his eyes were heavy with tears, and his wife Marie was sitting next to him holding his hand. Sheena knew that she would have to take control. She alone had to do the things that now needed to be done and so she resolved to do just that. Sheena had another brother, Iain, who was in Germany serving in the Army; she had to know if he had been contacted. This was her task now, her job and hers alone. But first she needed the answer to some questions, in fact, to lots of questions and she was determined to get those answers.

As she steadied herself and collected her thoughts ready for what was going to be the most difficult time of her life, readying herself to find out exactly what had happened and how, there were some things that she already knew for certain: one was that she herself would never be the same person again and another; that April 3rd 1979 would be forever imprinted in her brain as the day that the life she had known up until then would cease to exist.

CHAPTER 4

Sheena sat opposite her father and drawing in a deep breath she prepared herself emotionally to ask her father some difficult questions, difficult questions for both of them. "Dad, has an undertaker been called or informed that mum is here?" was her first question. Her father wasn't concentrating or perhaps even listening to her, he just stood up and going to the coffee table which was beside her mother's chair, in which Sheena was now sitting, he rushed forward almost knocking her off the chair he hastily picked up the medicine bottles that had been her mother's medication. In fact they were the very bottles that her mother had shown her the previous night, the ones that he had gone to great lengths to get for her.

"What are you doing, Dad?" she asked. "They're not important now, just sit down and let's talk."

He snapped angrily back at her, "They *are* important you stupid girl, someone might pick them up. They could be dangerous."

"No one is going to pick them up, Dad, they are not needed any longer," Sheena replied.

"I know they are not needed," he said, his voice getting louder and louder and more threatening. "That is why I'm going to get rid of them. I never want to see another bottle of tablets in this house." His tone of voice was scary as was the look on his face, which was almost maniacal. Graham intervened and caught hold of his father's arm and told him to 'ease off'. But he shrugged him off as though he was a feather, practically knocking him to the floor, and Graham was not a small guy by any means, but her father was much bigger and much more determined than him, and then he took the tablets to the kitchen and washed them down the sink. He came back much calmer and said somewhat sarcastically, "Right, now you can ask your questions." Sheena wasn't sure what she felt now, was it anger, irritation, sadness or even scared, or maybe just all of the above, whichever it was she couldn't think at that moment what the questions were that she had intended to ask. The resulting silence that seemed to have taken over the room was broken by Graham as he spoke to his sister.

"Look Sheena, we're going to have to go but I'll speak to you later on the phone and sort out what we are going to do, but you make any funeral arrangements that you need to make, and don't worry too much about the cost. I know Dad hasn't got any money and I'm pretty sure that mum wasn't insured, but we'll cover the costs of the funeral, you just let us know what's happening and when. Okay?" Sheena couldn't help but notice that he hadn't even asked their father whether he would contribute to the funeral and also that her father hadn't interrupted him either to make an offer. In fact her father appeared to be totally disinterested in anything that was happening. Then Graham added with a broad grin on his face – "But don't break the bank eh, sis?" A lighter moment was just what was needed and Sheena was surprised by the fact that she smiled when he'd said it. She hadn't thought that she would ever smile again. Then he kissed her gently on the cheek and gave her a reassuring hug before leaving.

But as soon as he'd gone her father informed her that she had to arrange a cremation, not a funeral. For one thing it was probably cheaper and for another it was what you're mother wanted he'd said. It was obvious from his tone and manner that this was not a request, but an order. She protested that her mother was a member of The Church of Scotland and that although she didn't attend church regularly she would very much consider herself to still be a member of that church and that she would want to be buried. But he pointed his finger at her, up close and threatening, and he said one word defiantly and firmly – Cremation. It was said in such a manner that Sheena was left in no doubt that any argument would have been futile.

And so Sheena duly phoned an undertaker giving him all the details and making him aware of the fact that it would be a Cremation. She also added that the Cremation was despite her mother being religious and a believer in God. The undertaker said that he completely understood what she was saying and that would be able to get to her mother's house in about half an hour to collect her mother's body and that according to his diary he could arrange the service and the Cremation for 12.00 noon on the 10th April, that was, of course, if no complications arose to delay things. Sheena also gave him her own phone number and address and explained that although the funeral cortege would leave from her mother's house, that all communication would nevertheless be through her at the address and phone number that she had given him. When she put the phone down, she thought to herself that she had sounded really calm and professional which was the last thing that she was feeling.

That was no sooner done when Lucy started to cry, and Sheena realised with some horror, that her breasts hadn't readied themselves for feeding her. They were always full and painful if her feed was late, and it was definitely late. Tom told her that he'd brought a bottle with him and that he'd feed her while she talked to her Dad. The fact that he'd offered to do that without any fuss surprised Sheena but then he shot her a furious glance that said he was actually less than happy. But nevertheless he took Lucy into the kitchen to feed her, but not without also letting out a big frustrated sigh aimed directly at Sheena, which confirmed her thoughts that he was not feeding her because he wanted to, or maybe just because he was her Dad, but merely because he was too scared to create a fuss in front of all the family, after all, it would spoil his 'good guy' image that he cultivated so carefully for anyone other than herself. However, Sheena simply ignored him, she was in no mood to deal with his 'visual' threats.

She now tried again to speak to her father. She explained carefully to him that she knew he was upset and that talking things over so soon would be difficult, but she really needed to know more about what had actually happened since she'd left their house the previous evening, as she couldn't connect in her own mind the mother that she had spoken to the previous evening, with what which had confronted her today. Her father looked less agitated now that the tablet were gone and proceeded to tell Sheena all that happened. But he had a very nonchalant manner about him. Still Sheena listened intently.

"Well you know your mother wasn't well over the weekend and that I got the doctor in to see her twice, she told you that last night, didn't she?" he'd said. Sheena nodded in agreement. "Well, she had wanted to sleep on her own on the sofa bed." They both instinctively looked across at the body of her mother still lying there, covered up now, but still lying there. At that moment, seeing her again, in her mind's eye her mother was not covered up but looking at her directly, Sheena needed all her reserve not to break down again but she was determined to find out exactly what happened – her father continued. "So I made her a cup of tea at about eleven and said goodnight and went up to my own bed. I knew from how she'd been that she needed to be on her own so I was okay with that." He sounded very matter of fact and was seemingly displaying a total lack of concern, or even feeling, for her mother but Sheena thought that he must be really distressed and hiding it well, not wanted to show any sign of weakness to his daughter.

Then they were interrupted again, this time it was by a knock at the door. It was the undertakers. Sheena stood frozen to the spot as they gently moved her mother's body, and she watched transfixed as they took her out the front door. She wanted to hit them, to scream at them to leave her mother alone, but just as before the words wouldn't come out and her hands lay limp by her sides, although her body was shaking and trembling inside, unseen by others.

She was exhausted, too exhausted to go on. She wished with all her heart at that moment that she could take her mother's place for she really didn't want to be *anywhere* if she couldn't be with her mother. But she just stood by the open door watching. How stupid and inconsequential she felt. What was she doing? What was the point of anything anymore? She wondered. She was still standing at the open door long after the hearse had gone, just standing there not knowing what to do or where to be, when her father came and slammed the door closed, cruelly snapping her out of her trance-like state.

He was aggressive again. "Sheena," he said sternly. "We're either going to talk or we're not. Which is it?" He was impatient, totally lacking of feeling for either his wife or his daughter, it was almost as if he had something better that he should be doing. Sheena's mind was racing, spinning and yet settling nowhere – is the world even real any more? What's going on? But the words that actually came out of her mouth were in the vein of telling her father that she was sorry, actually apologising to him for standing at the door too long.

Then she told her father that she was sorry but she really needed to go home. She couldn't cope any longer and that her head was banging. She'd asked him if he wanted to come back to her house with her, and she told him and that she didn't think he should be left on his own, that she could make him a meal and then they could then talk in more detail the next day. But at the moment she was just too distressed and she added that she was sure he was feeling very much the same.

Her tone had been gentle and pleading, hoping that she was doing the right thing for both her father and herself. However, the tone and the words of his reply truly shocked her. "I'm not coming to your house. What do you think I am – a child to be nursed? I'm going out for a pint later and I don't need any child of mine looking me after I've coped fine for years, and I'll cope fine now." Then he added really aggressively, "So there you have it, we talk now or we talk tomorrow, it's up to you."

Sheena couldn't take it in. She had just watched her mother's body being carried out of the house and now her father was shouting at her. Suddenly from deep inside her she shouted back at him telling *him* in no uncertain terms that in that case it would have to be tomorrow because she was in no mood to be spoken to like that. She added sarcastically that he should go out and enjoy his beer and that she would come back at ten the next morning. Her father had been taken aback for a moment and even raised his hand to her as though he was going to bring it down on her with some force.

Sheena had instinctively put her hands up to her face in a protective manner, as she had many times before when she was a child, and even when she was a young adult and it scared her, and then he laughed. He actually roared with laughter at her, and it was extremely unsettling. Sheena then stormed into the kitchen where Tom was struggling with a fractious Lucy. She just took Lucy from him and told him in no uncertain terms that they were going home. Sheena was different, her manner was different, in fact, almost everything about her at that moment was different and Tom could see it. He didn't know what had happened to her, and the look of confusion on Tom's face had not been missed by Sheena, and he meekly complied with her orders. She was even more shaken when they left, she'd never, ever spoken to her father like that, or in fact anyone else, but God she felt pleased with herself – despite the shaking and trembling that was going on unseen inside herself.

The journey home was silent except for Lucy being fractious and when they got home Sheena discovered that she no longer had any breast milk for Lucy and that Lucy wouldn't take a bottle either, so she had to be fed her milk from a cup. Sheena mourned the loss of that comfort she'd felt when she was feeding Lucy herself and she knew for sure that Lucy was unhappy with the new arrangements. Lucy was already eating some solid food from a spoon, rusks at least, so the milk wasn't such a big part of her routine these days, but it was a big part emotionally and physically for both of them and so Sheena mourned for the second time that day for something beautiful that she would never again experience.

When the children were all in bed Tom went to work. He was late going in to work but they couldn't afford for him to take another night off. There had pretty much been silence between them since arriving home, which Sheena was glad of, and although she was in great distress she didn't want him near her, she *wanted* him at work. So while she was alone she phoned the Army base where her brother was stationed to pass on the distressing news, and she was informed that her brother would be at her house the next day.

She had hoped to be able to speak to him personally, but that had apparently been impossible, he wasn't anywhere near a phone, but they assured her that he would get the message, and also that he wouldn't be alone when he was given the message, but unfortunately she would have to wait until the next day to see and speak to him. They also reassured her that he would come straight to her home as instructed and would probably arrive some time the next afternoon. Sheena looked forward so much to seeing him again, it had been a few years now since the last time they met, although they'd kept in regular contact via letters both to her and to her mother, and Sheena recalled how both her and her mother had worried during the time that he had been in Northern Ireland. Sheena was closer in age to Iain than Graham as Graham was a full seven years older than her and five years older than Iain. As a result Iain and Sheena had played together as children, and therefore grown up together. And so yes she thought, it would be good to see him again.

Sheena went to bed early that night; she couldn't really believe all that had happened in just one day. Was it really only this morning that her biggest worry in life was what sort of a mood Tom would be in when he woke up? She curled up in bed that night, but she knew that sleep wouldn't come. Then a few minutes later Susie came in to her bedroom rubbing her tired eyes. "Is Grandma really not coming back, Mum? Can I sleep with you?" The words so gently spoken threatened to open the 'flood gates' again for Sheena, but she held out her arms to her daughter and thanked God for her coming in at just that moment. It was just the touch of reality and innocent love that she needed. As mother and daughter cuddled up to each other for comfort, Sheena was temporarily transported back to when she, herself, was a child and would sneak into bed with her mother for comfort when her dad was at work. She'd loved those sweet innocent days and remembered them fondly; she hoped that when her children grew up that they would have similarly good memories, because Andy too, often crawled into bed beside her when he felt he needed an extra cuddle.

It had been very difficult telling the children about their Grandmother's death, Andy had been very quiet and Sheena sensed that he was trying to be 'grown up' about it. It would probably hit him much later she thought. As for Susie, being only four, well she didn't seem to understand it at all. She had asked if it was her fault, had she hurt her Grandma's leg when she was sitting on it. And asking her when she would be coming back from Heaven. Sheena had just hugged her tightly with no real answers to her questions, but she did promise her faithfully that it was nothing to do with her sitting on Grandma's leg and that Grandma had really enjoyed playing with her.

Now cuddling up to her daughter she told her in answer to her latest question that Grandma will always be with us in our hearts darling and we'll never forget her but no I'm so sorry, but she's not coming back. She kissed her beautiful daughter, held her tightly and gently stroked her silky soft hair as the silent tears again fell down Sheena's cheeks. She had thought that she had no more tears to shed but these ones were different, comforting somehow. And so with her arms wrapped in the embrace of her daughter, sleep did come – for a while anyway.

CHAPTER 5

Sheena had slept only for a few hours and it would be a few hours more before Tom was home and so she gently lifted the still sleeping Susie back into her own bed and got dressed and went downstairs. There was a lot to do today and there was no way that she was making herself 'available' for Tom when he came home and she knew for certain that she would never make herself so easily 'available' for him again. She knew that she would probably have to take his fists or maybe worse, but whatever was coming her way she would never again make herself 'available'. Somehow things were going to change, she had no idea how, but somehow it just had to happen.

Tom came home asking her why she was up so early and she told him that there was a lot to do and added, very much 'tongue in cheek', that she was sure that he needed his sleep so she wouldn't disturb him until as late as possible. "Well," he said sharply, before issuing his orders, "Don't make a habit of getting up before I come home. You know I like to sleep with you for a while before going off to sleep myself." He said that in a 'don't forget my needs' sort of voice stern, precise, clearly making his own needs known. Sheena knew what he meant by 'sleep with her for a while' and it was nothing to do with sleep! But whatever voice he cared to use, Sheena didn't care enough about it to comment and so he went to bed alone.

With her eldest two children at school and a really great neighbour looking after Lucy and also promising to pick up her elder two if she should be late, Sheena went to see her father. She was calmer and more determined today and she wanted, needed in fact, to know what had happened since she last saw her mother.

Her father continued his story from the previous afternoon telling her that when he woke up that morning to go to work, her mother seemed to be much worse than the previous day and so he hadn't felt that he should go to work, he was worried about her he said, so he'd stayed with her just sitting by her bed and watching her from about 5.30 in the morning. She asked him why he hadn't called the doctor out again if she'd been that ill. "I'd already called the doctor out to her twice I didn't want to bother him again in the middle of the night." His tone had changed to very brusque and even dictatorial, as though daring her to question him. He continued, "Anyway, I sat with her for hours and she was struggling with the pain in her chest and so I gave her some tablets."

"– Some?" Sheena had interjected.

"One tablet at first and another later because she still wasn't feeling any better." He was standing up now, very angry and pacing back and forth. Then he let his anger loose and started shouting at her, "Do you want to bloody well know what happened or not, or are you going to keep on interrupting me, because I'm not going to be bloody well be interrogated in my own house by anyone." Sheena apologised, although she had thought that her question was reasonable, and he continued.

"Well that's it really, she just died. I called the doctor at about 9.30 and then he came out a bit later after he'd finished in the surgery, and after I'd told him how she'd been he said that she'd obviously died of a heart attack. He also said there was nothing else I could have done, and that it would have been exactly the same if he'd been here himself so that's that. So if you've finished interrogating me…" His words and tone were that of the dictatorial father that he'd always been and when she asked, with genuine feeling for him if he was okay, his response was said with a sense of importance, arrogance even. "Right, I've got something important to say to you on that matter."

Sheena had thought for a moment that he was about to ask if he could stay with her for a while, and that he'd realised he'd been too hasty the day before, or even if *she* could stay with him for a while, but his actual words shook her almost more than the shock of her mother's death. "Let's get things straight right from the start, shall we? You're mother's dead and nothing can change that, but I'm not going to sit around feeling sorry for myself, in fact I feel free for the first time in years and I'm going to enjoy my freedom starting today."

Sheena sat there listening totally dumbfounded, but as if that sentence wasn't disgusting enough in content on its own, he then added even more hurtfully, that after the funeral was over, he never, ever again wanted to hear anyone, and he emphasised again, anyone, mention your mother's name again. He then went on, spouting even more vitriol. "And what's more, I'm going to be meeting other women as soon as I can. You kids are all grown up now and have your own lives to lead and I'm going to lead *my* own life, *mine,* do you hear me, *my own life?*" He'd said that whilst jabbing his finger on his chest as if to make his point even stronger. "You can go ahead and make the arrangements for the funeral – and by the way, don't forget that it's to be a Cremation, not an *actual* funeral, and I will be there. If you need me to sign anything important before then, then you know where to find me. But I'll stand for no interfering in what I do. *Do I make myself clear?"* What could she say in answer to that sort of statement?

What she did say was that she thought he must be in shock and not sure of what he was saying. But he moved steadily and threateningly towards her, and with his arms each resting on the arms of the chair that Sheena was sitting in, her mother's chair, his dark deep set eyes were glaring at her menacingly as he came to within an inch of her face, as at the same time, she herself tried to retreat further into the back of that very same chair. She could smell his breath he was so close, and it was a sweet, sickly sort of smell, like stale tobacco and sweat. But no, it was more than that, there was a smell permeating from all of him; his clothes, his body, his very being and it was coal. Yes she thought, definitely coal. She'd found it strange that he should still smell of coal today as she knew he was extremely fastidious over cleaning himself. He would shower at the pit head before leaving work and then strip off in the kitchen for another even hotter and more thorough wash, as well, of course, as having regular baths. Also he hadn't even been to work for two days now. Sheena reasoned that the coal must be in his pores, leaking out with his sweat. But then suddenly another realisation hit her and it awakened a memory that, although well hidden, was now a very real, live, vivid memory and it was that she hadn't been this close to her father's face since she was a child, no kisses or hugs between them for years. That fact on its own said a lot about the relationship between father and daughter.

Then suddenly he decided to make one or two things very clear to Sheena. "I told you yesterday not to treat me like a child. I'm not in bloody shock. I'm quite good actually, so bugger off and make your arrangements." Finally, with a look of sheer contempt and still glowering over her, he poked at the bruise on Sheena's face and said, "If you talk to Tom like that it's a wonder you don't have more of those, if you were my wife you certainly would. A woman should know her place. Sheena thought that she'd noticed a sinister, if not even sexual tone to his words, but surely she was just imagining that. And with that he sat down again.

Sheena allowed her body to relax, not having realised until she relaxed, just how stiff she had been holding her body. Then she looked down to the side of her mother's chair and her mother's cardigan was just lying on the floor. It must have been there all the time but she hadn't noticed it. She picked it up and with both hands held it close to her face. This was the smell she wanted and when she was finished here this was the smell that she was going to take home.

All Sheena could say to her father was that she would do as he'd asked she also informed him that Iain was coming home later that day and she asked him if he wanted to see him. His response to that was that Iain could please himself, and that he also knew where he was if he wanted to see him. Sheena was ashamed of the pitiful, childish whimpering sound of her own voice that seemed to have overtaken her when she was speaking to him and wished that she could get that temper back that she'd had the previous day because there was no denying that she was as terrified of him today as terrified as she'd been of him as a child. But she nevertheless agreed that she'd make all the arrangements and keep out of his way if that was what he wanted. "Good," he replied. "We understand each other at last." She'd driven home in a daze wearing her mother's cardigan. She simply wanted to have the smell of her mother with her at all times. And she didn't really think that she'd ever take it off, she didn't *want* to take it off.

When she'd finally arrived home she didn't really know how she'd got there. Because in her mind she was still sitting in her car outside her mother's home, she re-iterated to herself that it was her mother's home, because she couldn't, no matter what, bring herself to call it her father's home not even in her most amenable of moments. In reality she was sitting in the car outside her own home and she was heartbroken trying to cope in a world that was strange and cruel. She slumped forward resting her arms and head on the steering wheel and she tried to think what her mother would say to her now if she was here, but really deep in her heart she knew what she would say. She would want her to just do the best she could, because she always said that no one, no matter who they were or what task it was that they had to do, could do more than their best. And as far as her mother was concerned Sheena's best was more than good enough. "So just do your best kid," she would have said, no more, no less. In that moment, Sheena felt a warmth and comfort come over her and she felt her mother extremely close to her. "Yes, Mum," she'd said out loud. "I *will* do my best and it *will* be good enough." She smiled to herself, a smug satisfying smile, and now she felt ready to cope with whatever was going to come next.

CHAPTER 6

The undertaker called to see her later that day with some brochures and Sheena had to pick out a coffin for her lovely mum. It broke her heart to do that, and even more so that she had to be so careful with the cost of the funeral because it was painfully obvious that her father wasn't going to be contributing any money and Graham was the only one with any money to pay the bills and he didn't have any to throw away, so she chose the cheapest coffin possible. She reasoned to herself that it was going to be burned anyway. But she couldn't help but feel that she was letting her mother down somehow, it was heart-breaking to have to do all this as cheaply as possible. However, the undertaker was really very nice and understanding and seemed to know instinctively not to put pressure on her to spend more than she could. It was also arranged that there would be a church service first at their local church before being taken to the Crematorium which was more than twenty miles away. Sheena was so very pleased with that aspect as at least her mother would have a church send off if not a funeral. The undertaker informed her that he would let her know when all the arrangements were completed, but she could be rest assured that he would do everything that she had asked for.

Iain also arrived later that day just as Sheena returned home from picking the children up from school. She was so pleased to see him, and not only because she'd missed him, but that his timing couldn't have been better. She was just about to take Tom up a cup of tea and tell him that it was time to get up! He hugged her warmly, and then standing back with his hands still resting on her shoulders he lowered his eyes and gave her a sideways worried look, almost a pitying look that embarrassed Sheena. She pulled away from him trying to dislodge his arms from her shoulder and then tightened her mother's cardigan around her body whilst attempting to brush her hair from her eyes. It was, in effect, a bit of a pathetic attempt to 'look better' in her brother's eyes. But He pulled her in close again and wrapping his arms around her even tighter than before he apologised.

"I'm so sorry love, I was just shocked at the worn look in your eyes, not your hair, or your clothes, just that you look so terribly worried and stressed and it shows." Sheena started to sob – yet again – and she was annoyed by that because she'd only just finished deciding that she was going to be strong and cope well. "Don't cry love, don't cry. We'll sort it. We'll sort all of it together. You're not on your own and you don't have to do everything on your own. I'm here." Using his hands he wiped her tears. Then added, "Well I've had the hug, what about the smile?" he said lightly mocking her. She smiled and told him to sit down while she woke Tom up as he was on the night shift at work. Andy and Susie, impressed with Iain's Army uniform were firing questions at him and climbing all over him so he just waved her on and said, "Go, go it looks like I've got my hands full anyway. The laughter coming from all of them was good medicine.

Tom was his usual over friendly self with Iain being there, he told him that he was very welcome and that he should stay with them until the funeral. He always had another face for absolutely anyone else and Sheena was quite sure that he wouldn't want him staying the whole week, but she was equally certain that it would be her who would have to tell Iain to go at some time. With Tom, most people would be totally shocked to discover the man he was behind closed doors because he'd always had the knack of turning on the charm with everyone else.

In fact it was that same charm that had first attracted Sheena to him, but it never lasted for her beyond the first time he managed to get her knickers off. And as she was only sixteen and he was the first boy to do anything like that, he'd made her believe that she was his now and if she went with anyone else they would know that she was 'used goods' and they would just use her. He also told her then that he wanted to marry her and that if she didn't marry him then no one else would have her. He made it sound as though he was doing her a big favour. Looking back now, Sheena couldn't quite believe that she'd been so naïve, but to this day she'd never been with another man.

With Tom having left to go to work and the children in bed Sheena and Iain finally had some time to themselves to talk. Iain took a long hard look at Sheena and she could see that he was still shocked at her appearance, bruised, worn out, old and tired looking. Not exactly poster girl! But he had the good grace not to say so. He walked into the kitchen and she heard cupboard doors opening and closing then he came back in with a whisky bottle and two glasses. "You look like you could do with one," he said. Well he wasn't wrong there! She smiled at him and took his hand as he passed her the glass. "Hey," he said. "If we've got to hold hands then I'm taking it back!" She laughed with him and they sat down to talk.

She told Iain everything that had happened from the days before the Christening up until the conversation that she'd had with their father this afternoon. He listened intently and he could see how upset and distressed she was, but he told her that although there was no love lost between him and his father, in fact it was because of his father that he'd joined the army as a boy soldier of sixteen, just to get away from him, however, he still thought that Sheena must have misunderstood him or perhaps it was grief talking on his father's part for he was sure that somewhere along the line there must have been love between his mother and father, and no matter how bad a father he was, and he was a bad father. No, he wouldn't be 'looking for other women' with his wife not yet buried. He also wondered if perhaps Sheena was too worn out and too emotional to have understood what he'd said to her.

Sheena knew that she had heard her father correctly, but she didn't want to argue about it, especially not with Iain, and so she nodded and agreed that perhaps he was right. She told him that he would have to talk to him himself and then he might get a clearer understanding of what was meant. Iain agreed that he would do that the next day, but he wanted to see his mother first and so they arranged between themselves to go and see her first thing the next morning after the children were at school.

The whisky was having a relaxing effect on both of them and they spent quite a long time reminiscing about when they were children and generally catching up with each other. Sheena felt good with the whisky warming and comforting her, and then she started to top her own glass up more often and she began talking about anything and everything. About the scrapes they got into as children, her father, her mother, Tom, her upset about not being able to feed Lucy any more, in fact, anything and she was jumping from one subject to another without even letting Iain get a word in. What she really wanted, she told him was for her mind to 'shut up' for a while, but it wouldn't and as she began crying and slurring her words. Iain took the glass off her. "When did you last eat?" he asked. "Or drink alcohol for that matter," but Sheena had a silly grin on her face, shrugged her shoulders and pointed to the glass with pathetic pleading eyes, but Iain was having none of it. "Sit there and I'll make you a fabulous meal." He disappeared into the kitchen and Sheena just sat there waiting. When he came back she was almost asleep, but he made sure that she stayed awake as he announced triumphantly – "'ta-dah' your meal's ready madam." – Beans on toast!

Sheena tried to laugh and be suitably complimentary about his gesture, but all she managed was a silly drunken grin, however, she started to eat her beans on toast. But after attempting to eat just two mouthfuls of food she was off to the bathroom to bring it all back, along with thankfully, the whisky. She returned looking sheepish, but Iain just laughed at her offering her a different meal. A large glass of water and a couple of Aspirins telling her that she'd be fine in the morning! She sat with him chatting, as best she could anyway, for a while longer and slowly sobered up, at least enough be coherent and to hold a conversation but she was exhausted and so having already told him that a bed was made up for him in Andy's room they decided to call it a night.

But as they were about to go to bed, Iain had said, "Get a good night's sleep now and don't worry about mum, we will find out exactly what happened to her when they get the results of the Post Mortem." Sheena had totally forgotten to tell him that there wasn't going to be a Post Mortem so now she quickly explained that there wasn't going to be one, and that everything had been decided by the doctor himself, and he had said that she'd died of a heart attack even though he didn't see her die.

Iain could hardly believe what he was hearing. "Can't we request a Post Mortem? Why Can't we just say that we want one?" he asked. Sheena didn't know the answer to that one but she was going to do her damnedest to find out. She just couldn't understand why there wouldn't be one, it wasn't as if she was ill in hospital and expected to die, Sheena was in despair about it and angry. But Iain continued, "Anyway, I know you're thinking that Dad had something to do with mum's death but you'll be wrong, you'll see, he won't have done anything, and I'm sure that if you ask the doctor if we can have an a Post Mortem then they'll do one. Perhaps the doctor thinks we don't want one. I mean I know it all sounds a bit odd, but really it must be the truth that Dad's telling.". Then he added obviously trying to reassure Sheena. "Now, don't shoot the messenger kid, but don't you think that you could be being just a little bit melodramatic?" He mentioned the fact that she'd not long had a baby and then said, "Hormones and all that!" Sheena nodded in begrudging acceptance and said that he was probably right but she was still going to ask some questions, at least of the doctor. And so they both agreed that probably the best thing was just to find out more for now. And so they called it a night.

Between the whisky and Sheena's exhaustion she'd fallen asleep very deeply that night and was still fast asleep lying in the foetal position, still hugging her mother's cardigan, when Tom came home from work. He climbed into bed beside her and his cold body woke her up as he started to lift her nightdress and turn her over onto her back ready to 'service' his own needs, but Sheena was seething with the audacity of him, he seemed to have no awareness at all of her feelings and hurt, and she was in no mood to deal with his 'needs' and so she quickly pushed him away. "I didn't mean to wake you," Tom said apologetically. "You don't usually wake up. Was I too noisy coming in or something?" He'd sounded genuinely sorry to have woken her, but Sheena just couldn't stomach any idea of it and quickly jumped out of bed. "Hey, there's no need for that he said, get back in here I've not had any sex for two days," he said pathetically, "in fact in respect of your mother I think I've behaved pretty well, but you can't expect me to wait forever can you? Is all this fuss just because I woke you up?"

He seemed to be genuinely puzzled by Sheena's aggressive reaction because he just hadn't come up against her actually refusing sex, well not for quite a few years anyway. Sheena thought that that was partly her own fault as well for not refusing him more often, but she had tired of fighting him early on in the marriage and took the 'easy way' out. Maybe that was wrong she thought, but there really had been no way of refusing him without a long drawn out battle between them, sometimes lasting for hours and involving her being hit and it would still end up with him getting his way, but with a lot more brutality to it.

Part of her reasons to acquiesce to him was that she didn't want the children to hear what was going on, or question the resulting bruises. Tom was acting as if saying 'no' was totally alien to him, which, of course, it was. Well, she thought to herself he'd just better get used to hearing 'no' because she hadn't fully realised until that actual moment that he was never again going to get a 'yes'. How that would come about, or if she could have the strength required for that she didn't know. But she did know that today was definitely a 'no'.

Her anger at Tom was such that she felt she needed to walk away and say nothing more before she broke down with the despair of it all. Why did she ever think that he would be sensitive to her mother's death? But the sheer ridiculousness of what he was saying was too much for her. But he wasn't about to let her just 'walk away'.

And so she laughed out loud, almost hysterically, at the ludicrous things he was saying and so she told him, trying to stem her nervous laughter that he *always* woke her up. Asking him, in a demeaning and surprisingly sarcastic manner, if he was really so stupid that he thought she would stay asleep while he put his cold body on top of hers every morning before adding that she meant 'cold' in both senses of the word. She didn't know where these words were coming from but she liked them. And so she continued in the same vein saying that of course she was always awake, adding that she just lies there and lets him get on with it because it's quicker and she doesn't have to look at him, speak to him, make any required moans in the right places or worse still, kiss him. There was real hatred in her words as they were coming from the heart! Letting him 'get on with it' was for an easy life nothing else she added.

Well if she had expected him to get angry with her upon hearing what she *really* thought, then she was not disappointed. For a moment though there was a strange silence between them, with neither or them seemingly quite sure what was going to come next, and when she looked at his face it wasn't an angry expression that he was displaying at first, no, his face just had the sort of expression you might see on a child whose just been told there's no Santa Clause. But that expression was fleeting and then the anger took over, extreme anger. "You're a bloody liar!" he shouted at her. "You fucking love it, you know you do."

Then he flew at her grabbing her by both arms as she was trying to get dressed, he ripped at her clothes and threw her heavily back down on the bed. She kicked, struggled and fought as much as she could and when she managed to scratch him it brought a blow back, but to her stomach rather than her face. It was a really painful blow delivered with intent but she wasn't going to cry, not where he could see her anyway. "Let's not have all your darling family commented on your bruises eh?" he said sarcastically as he delivered the blow. And then suddenly he was inside her, going at it so hard that she screamed, but she had kept to her vow of not saying 'yes' for this had been rape, plain and simple rape, which came scarily easy to him, he quickly put his hand over her mouth. "Let's not wake the neighbours now eh!" More sarcasm! But he'd soon finished and then practically threw her out of the bed and onto the floor.

"Now make sure you wake me *before* you go for the children today. And let's get this side of our life back to normal and then there'll be no need for me to hide the bruises will there? And while we're talking 'back to normal' that means that your brother has to find somewhere else to sleep." And with that she quickly dressed and went downstairs where sitting at the kitchen table she gave way to the tears she'd managed to suppress from his view. What was she going to do she asked herself over and over again. She was in the absolute depths of despair.

Sheena decided that she had to smarten herself up and not look so much like someone who didn't care about their appearance. So she washed her hair, put on a bit of make-up and her best blouse and skirt ready for the day ahead, she didn't want Iain looking at her that morning as he had the previous night. And for Iain's part he smiled and told her she looked good, then nodded and added, "Really good." She felt better. So after Andy and Susie were at school they were about to set off for the funeral parlour when Iain told Sheena that he couldn't help but hear all that had gone on that morning. She apologised and also told him that he would have to either stay at Dad's or Graham's and she was about to invent an excuse for him having to do that when he said, "That's okay sis, I know what he's like. I knew all that 'Mr Nice Guy' last night was an act, but why do you stay with him?" She told him that she had no other choice and proceeded to explain that she had left him once just after Susie was born. She had gone to live with Graham and his wife and family, but it could only ever be temporary. She'd asked, begged and pleaded with the council to see if they could help her with accommodation which she'd believed would be straight forward considering the fact that she had two small children to care for, one of which was only a babe in arms. But rather cruelly they'd told her that as she had made herself intentionally homeless then they were not obliged to find her a place to live. The implication of what they'd said was plainly 'go back to where you belong and don't bother us' and so she did, , she'd been left with no other choice than to return home.

He then asked her if it was always like this. To which she replied, yes more or less. If I don't fight him then it's easier *and quieter* she added almost with a smirk. "It's no laughing matter, Sheena, you're going to have to do something about it or you're going to be living the exact same life as mum did." She then told him that those were the exact words her mother had said to her the last time they spoke. That was the very thing that *she* had asked her not to do. For Sheena not to live her life the way that she had.

She couldn't bring herself to tell Iain anything about the 'specials' but she did tell him that he had treated her a lot worse in the past than he'd heard that morning and that she had finally plucked up the courage to see a doctor and tell her exactly what he had been doing. He'd been the only man in her life and so she didn't know what was 'normal' and what wasn't she added. But the doctor had assured her that what he was doing would not be considered 'normal' by most people's standards, especially as it was against her will. Iain asked her to tell him what it was, saying that he 'was a grown up' and that she'd be surprised and embarrassed herself if she'd heard some of the things that he had in the Army but still she couldn't tell him.

But she did tell him that she'd made certain conditions on her returning back home, because he'd been begging her to go back, not because he loved her, she added, but because she was his possession and he wanted it back, and her main condition for going back was that he saw a psychiatrist about what he was doing and told him truthfully about it, then, and only then, would she come back to him. Tom hadn't known that she really didn't have any choice in the matter, in that she couldn't find anywhere else to live. And, she assured Iain, he *did* see a psychiatrist and he *did* tell the truth, mostly because he thought that she was making a fuss over nothing and trying to be dramatic and that what he'd been doing was perfectly normal and that anyway, he had a right to do whatever he liked as she was his wife.

Sheena had known positively that he'd told the doctor the truth, because she also spoke to the doctor about it at the same time, but they hadn't seen him together. Anyway she hastily added assuredly that he hasn't in fact done the particular thing ever since and she didn't expect that he would. But she also thought to herself that it was to her advantage that it was officially 'out there now' and when the time was right, she would be able to leave him, but not yet. She did tell Iain that things would eventually get sorted out between her and Tom and that she didn't really think that their marriage would last much longer, but also that for now she had to concentrate on her mother and the funeral. Iain said that he understood, but his expression said exactly the opposite. But, he told her, "You do whatever you need to do. And don't forget that you are not alone, you have a family besides Tom, a family that truly loves you."

Iain was shaking his head. Then he put his arms around her saying, "I don't know how to help you, love, you've got all this to put up with at home and now mum going. I really don't know how you do it." She held on to him for a while because it felt so good to have someone's arms around her that *really* cared about her. Because she was all too well aware that she would never again have her mother's arms around her, and there was no one else to give her a loving hug. Well not an adult one anyway, because Andy, well Andy liked his cuddles and she liked getting them from him, but it wasn't the same somehow. Tom *never* cuddled her, not even to console her over her mother's death. However, she told Iain not to worry and that her time would come. And she truly felt, deep down, that 'her time' was getting closer with every passing day.

Ever since that phone call from her father, Sheena had felt different, as though life was more urgent, more precious and special. She wasn't going to waste her life, she was going to heed her mother's final words to her, but she needed time and courage and then things would change, she also knew that Tom had a bit of an awakening coming. But she had to plan it carefully. After the funeral she promised herself that's when she would start her fight back.

Anyway, she quickly changed the subject with Iain and told him that they had a lot to do that day. They would go and see the undertaker first and finalise all the arrangements and then if he went over to Graham's, or to see his father, she would go and see her mother's doctor. She wasn't going to make an appointment to see him because he had been their family doctor since Sheena herself was a toddler so she was sure that he would see her at the end of his morning surgery.

CHAPTER 7

Arriving at the funeral parlour Sheena thought that everything looked really nice, homely sort of, different than she had imagined. They met the undertaker that had been to see Sheena at her home the previous day. Everything was confirmed for 12.00 on 10th April and as there was to be no post-mortem there would be no reason for a delay. Iain interrupted him there and said that they were intending to ask the doctor if they could have a Post Mortem performed on their mother, but although the undertaker was sympathetic to Iain's request, he did tell him that he had already been assured that there wasn't to be one. Iain and Sheena both nodded in agreement, although both of them thought that the undertaker would prove to be wrong.

The undertaker also informed them that everything had indeed been arranged to include church service before her body would be taken to the Crematorium, and that the family were welcome to go there as well if they wanted to, but the main service would be at the church. Sheena was really pleased that there was going to be a church service; she had hated the idea of just going to the Crematorium and leaving her there. Really she hadn't known what to expect. But her mother would have wanted at the very least a church service. In fact Sheena was still convinced that she would have wanted a burial. "Can we see her now?" Iain asked. The undertaker confirmed that she was ready, and that he would take them both through.

In the adjoining room her mother was lying in her, at the moment, 'open' coffin. Before they moved closer though, brother and sister held hands and approached slowly. Iain gasped out loud when he saw his mother, even though he couldn't completely see her, and cried such a guttural cry that it must have come from the very depths of him. "Sheena, I can't look. I can't come any closer," he said and still holding her hand he was pulling her back forcibly. Sheena herself didn't feel so scared about seeing her, after all, she had been the one to close her mother's eyes and she really, really wanted to see her again and they weren't yet near enough. She told Iain that he would regret it if he didn't see her today and that there was nothing to worry about, because she had seen her on the day that she died, and nothing could be worse than that, and also that there would be no other chance for him to see her. Besides, she reassured him, we'll be going to see her together. So they approached closer to her body together holding on to each other for support.

But as they got even nearer, Iain was visibly heaving, retching and sobbing really heavily. He had to leave her and go outside. "I'm sorry Sheena. I can't do it. I can't, I can't." He was obviously far too distressed by the idea of seeing her, and so Sheena let go of his hand while he went outside. Sheena herself was really looking forward to seeing her mother again she knew this would be the last chance ever to see her in the flesh. She looked at her mother and thought how nice she looked. Her hair was freshly coiffed; she had rouge on her cheeks and a slight hint of lipstick on. She didn't really look at all dead. Whilst she wasn't exactly smiling, she didn't look as though she was in pain, no worried frown or furrowed brow, in fact she looked quite peaceful, serene even. Sheena thought about the many, many times she'd seen her mother with at least a worried look on her face. In fact when she thought more about it her mother lived most of her life on edge, never exactly relaxed, always a little bit worried. But now she looked peaceful, in fact Sheena thought that she could perhaps just be asleep.

Maybe everyone had got it wrong she was thinking, and maybe she wasn't really dead. You hear these stories all the time she told herself. Of course, she knew those thoughts were ridiculous, but somehow the notion that it might not be real helped her to cope. She leaned over to kiss her mum, to feel her own lips on her mother's soft cheek again, half hoping for some miracle response. But she wasn't ready, she wasn't ready at all. It was all wrong. She wanted to scream, and inside she was screaming. She wanted a hole to open up and swallow her. Her grief was raw and intense and she wasn't ready. She would never be ready, not for that. Her heart was going too fast, so fast and loud that she was sure everyone could hear it. What was wrong with her? Why was all this happening to her? And then her legs buckling under her she almost collapsed.

Her mother had been truly STONE COLD, solid like a block of solid stone. She'd imagined kissing her mother's soft cheek for the last time, of getting some comfort from that last kiss, of feeling close to her again one last time. But that had truly been like kissing cold stone. Of course, she knew that dead people were cold, or course, she knew that, but she was all the same expecting to gently kiss her mother's soft cheek. She had looked so good, so alive; in fact nothing about the way she looked led her to believe anything other than she was going to be kissing her soft cheek. She hadn't really even thought about cold, but now she thought that she should have at least considered that. But even if she had thought cold, she would still have thought soft. Her thoughts were merely rambling thoughts with no sense of reality.

Because what she had in fact kissed was like a piece of SOLID STONE, it was such a shock. She was trembling, shaking, and her legs like jelly. The undertaker caught hold of her as she threatened to faint. "She's too cold. She's too cold," she screamed at him, her heart racing, and her mind panicking. "You need to warm her up. *She's too cold.*" She shouted, demanded, urgently of him to do something about it. She was dizzy, struggling, alone and so terribly, terribly distressed.

The undertaker took her back into the other room and gently sat her down. She could vaguely hear him saying something to her but she couldn't tell what it was. The next thing she knew was that Iain was sitting beside her again holding her hand. Had she just imagined kissing her mother? She wondered. Had she just played out a scenario in her mind? She looked to the undertaker for confirmation. But the look of sorrow on his face told her that she hadn't imagined it. She wished that she hadn't gone in now. She wished that her last memory of her mother had been of her closing her eyes. Now it would always be that she was STONE COLD. Sheena grabbed hold of Iain and kept saying over and over through her sobbing that she was 'too cold'. That was all she could say, no other words were coming out. All her thoughts were jumbled up and they weren't coming coherently out of her mouth.

Brother and Sister were now holding on to each other tightly, desperately, for comfort. The undertaker brought them some tea. Shaking and trembling Sheena tried to drink the hot sweet tea but nothing could warm that feeling on her lips of 'that piece of stone' that should have been her mum, that she had just kissed.

She told Iain, when she could speak again, that she was sorry for making him go through that, and that perhaps it would have been better if he'd just remembered her how she was the last time he saw her. But he said that it was something that he felt he needed to do, even though he couldn't stay and look closely at her, he had seen her and he was glad of that, because it brought everything into perspective for him, made him realise how little people valued life. But he now wished he'd had the courage to stay with Sheena for he could clearly see now that she'd had needed his help and he felt strongly that he'd let her down and for that he was sorry. He said that he thought he would try again, that he *wanted* to try again. But Sheena told him that it was not a good idea, and she certainly couldn't go in again. She didn't *want* to go in again. It all seemed so much more real to them now.

Then he said, "I'll tell you this, love, if that swine of a father of ours has had anything to do with this then he is going to pay, if not by way of a prosecution then by any means possible. You find out anything you can and together we'll do whatever it takes to get answers." Sheena was surprised by the venom in her brother's voice, because up until then she felt that she was the only one getting angry.

The undertaker had left them alone to comfort each other and to compose themselves. When he came back they thanked him and shook hands limply and left it that their next contact would be at the funeral. After they had both settled themselves they agreed that there was no time to indulge in tears, they had to find out as much as they could. And so with that, they parted company with Sheena going to see the doctor and Iain going to Graham's house.

Sheena waited patiently to see her mother's doctor, and as she suspected he was in fact more than happy to talk to her. Her very first question however, was direct and to the point. She asked him if they could have a post-mortem to confirm that her mother's death was in fact a heart attack, before following it up with, and if not, why not? That seemed to be totally the wrong question, or perhaps it was simply presented in the wrong manner, because the doctor was not happy with that request as he was immediately on the defensive sitting up higher in his chair and with a look of restrained annoyance. "Are you saying that I have made a false statement, or that I'm not capable of doing my job properly?" he'd asked. She wasn't either expecting or prepared for that type of reaction from him, and so she tried to calm the situation down as quickly as she could. Of course, she wasn't saying that she assured him, telling him that she hadn't for a minute thought that, and that was completely true, for she hadn't thought that.

But, she continued, "From what I understand, you weren't present at the moment of my mother's death so I can't fully comprehend how you can be so sure, so positive that it was a heart attack."

She went on to tell him that when her father had called him out to see her mother over the weekend prior to her death, that her mother had been exaggerating her symptoms because she didn't want to have sex with her dad – she couldn't bring herself to say that it was not 'normal' sex that her father had wanted, and that when he actually called to see her mother with her dad listening to their conversation, then she wouldn't have been able to back down and state that nothing was wrong. She tried desperately to keep her manner with the doctor friendly, but she could already tell from his demeanour that he was anything but the friendly doctor that she recalled from her childhood.

He stood up and came round from his side of his desk to sit on the edge of the desk smiling at her, his position now meant that he was towering above her, and looking at her as though she were an injured child. He then proceeded to take hold of Sheena's hand, holding it with one hand and patting it patronisingly with the other. "Look, Sheena," he said, "I'm going to make some allowances for the fact that you have not long since had a baby and that you are bound to be very hormonal at the moment, besides being distraught at your mother's – as you suppose – unexpected death. But I *am* very well qualified to say that a person has died of a heart attack. And I am experienced enough to know when someone is 'swinging the lead' and your mother was absolutely not 'swinging the lead' she was in pain over the weekend and she died of a heart attack in the early hours of Tuesday morning."

Now Sheena's hackles were rising up, her heart pounding with the anger she felt. She released her hand sharply from his hold and stood up from the chair so that with him still sitting on the edge of the desk, she was now the taller of the two, and at that moment she felt the more powerful of the two as well. She told him clearly, without allowing the nerves that were coursing through her body to show, that she wasn't a child to be patronised and that she wanted to know why he wouldn't even consider that she may be right and that surely a post-mortem would prove exactly what caused her mother's death, and according to him, by agreeing to the post-mortem, he would then be able to prove Sheena wrong.

She couldn't control the anger that was now boiling up inside her, and she had to admit that she was behaving a bit like a toddler who was stamping her feet because she couldn't get her own way, but even realising that aspect of her attitude, she still couldn't stop herself form getting more and more agitated. And so she threatened to go to the police and ask them to arrange a post-mortem if he wouldn't do it, before adding that she would greatly appreciate it if he didn't treat her in such a condescending manner again, that she was an adult and deserved her opinion to be recognised as that of a capable adult.

He stood up, obviously very angry with her, and held the door open, clearly indicating that she should leave, before stating indignantly that the conversation was over. "But," he added bristly, "you can go to the police if you want to, Sheena, if that makes you feel better then yes you can do that, but I'll tell you this: it's not the police who order a post- mortem it's the coroner who orders it, and the coroner won't order one if the doctor tells him that there are no suspicious circumstances, and that he has seen the patient more than once with heart symptoms in the days leading up to her death, and also that the description of her death from the woman's, patently obvious concerned and distressed husband, is totally compatible with that of a heart attack."

And, he added, "Furthermore, the police will treat you for what you truly are, and that is a hormonal woman who is suffering greatly from the death of her mother and who is therefore not being rational. You are, my dear – " again the condescending tone – "quite simply grieving the loss of your mother and your grief combined with the fact that you want to find another reason for her dying at the relatively young age of fifty-eight is perfectly understandable, and please don't forget that I am trying to allow for the fact of your recent childbirth and bereavement, and I am therefore keeping myself as calm as possible in the face of your patent mistrust of me. Because I can assure you that if you'd been anyone else, or even if you'd not been in the patently obvious hormonal state that you are, then I would have thrown you out of my surgery long before now." He then went on even more angrily, "But to malign me and my professionalism in such a manner is totally unacceptable and I will not stand for it. So go home, look after your children and unfortunately, attend to your mother's funeral."

Sheena was livid. She had firmly believed that it all would be simple, that all she would have to do was to ask him to order a post-mortem. Something wasn't right. The more she thought about it the more sure she was that something was wrong. She had to think this through carefully because what he had said made her consider that there could be an explanation of her father's self-assured manner. Because if the *doctor* knew that seeing his patient several times before her death and only having a description of her death from the only witness to it was enough for him to sign the death certificate, then who's to say that her *father* didn't have the same knowledge. She went home totally disillusioned and frustrated but even more determined to dig deeper into this, deep enough she hoped that would help to change the doctor's mind.

CHAPTER 8

Sheena arrived back home and realised that she was very late and she couldn't cope with any trouble from Tom. "Not today, please," she said silently under her breath. She went to her neighbour to collect her children only to find the older two sitting eating their tea and Lucy fast asleep in her pram. The neighbour said to leave them and that they'd be fine until after Tom had gone to work.

Relieved, Sheena went home and quickly made Tom a cup of tea and, putting it down hastily by the side of his bed, she said that he needed to hurry because she was late, but she would get his tea ready straight away, and she reassured him that he would have time to eat it before he went to work, but that he had to hurry. She hoped, and prayed that that would be enough to keep him from getting angry, and also the fact that he was late meant he wouldn't be insisting on sex. There was no time for her to get into bed with him – thank God she thought breathing a sigh of relief. But she knew she would have to face the 'sex' topic with him sometime because she was still determined not be readily 'available' for him. Her mother's final words still resonating in her ears, and also she needed time to think through how she would approach that without him getting aggressive.

She went into the kitchen and proceeded to peel potatoes to cook sausage and mash for him, that would be quick she reasoned. Then, she suddenly realised that the fact that the children weren't here would give him other ideas and that thought sent her slightly into panic mode, because she was well aware that he would want sex if they were alone, even if they only had a few minutes and she'd already heard him come downstairs.

She quickly changed her mind about sausage and mash and decided to cook egg and chips, reasoning that it would both be quicker and that she would have to stay in the kitchen and watch the chip fat. Yes, she thought. That should work. "Fingers crossed," she said to herself under her breath. And so she shouted out to him, "It will be egg and chips – okay?" But he didn't answer her.

However, as she was standing by the sink peeling the potatoes, Tom came up behind her and pushed his body tightly against hers, his hands were quickly slipped up under her blouse and then under her bra, with each hand cupping each breast firmly and then he was babbling on, saying that he knew she hadn't meant what she had said that morning about not liking sex, and that he wasn't annoyed with her. Sheena was sickened by both his words and his actions, but he sank even lower when he added with an air of superiority that defied description, that he *knew* she loved to fuck as much as he did, if not more, were his actual words.

Sheena froze. She was gripping tightly onto the sides of the sink, with her arms rigid and her eyes wide and transfixed, staring blankly out of the window in front of her, and seeing nothing. She was resolute in her thoughts that there was no way that what he quite clearly had on his mind was going to happen, but she struggled with the decision as to what she was going to do to prevent it. Her mind racing frantically and feeling totally panicked, she tried to think the next few minutes through as clearly and quickly as she could. If she just let him 'get on with it' then she wouldn't even have to turn around, or even stop peeling the potatoes. In fact, even her stance being stiff and rigid clearly in terror wouldn't bother him, her behaviour during sex never bothered him as long as she wasn't saying 'no.' Because she was well aware that he could easily get the access he needed from where he was, after all he'd often done it before, and she also knew well enough that he didn't require any input from her, which was the main reason why she always attempted to keep at least one of the children around when he was in, so that they were never alone for longer than could be avoided.

Still standing stock still and rigid, she frantically searched the very corners of her mind in an effort to find a way to avoid what would surely be the inevitable confrontation that awaited her if she refused him, she reasoned that it would be at most two minutes out of her life and then it would all be over. But that would mean that she had acquiesced yet again. Or she could stand her ground and refuse. Her heart was beating fast, with nervousness and panic, and he could feel the speed of her beating heart with his hands now on her bare breasts. He took the rapid beating of her heart as a sign that she was in fact *more* than keen for sex as well.

However, she tried at first to talk her way out of trouble; she tried to reason with him that he had to go to work, that there was no time for this. She was speaking matter-of-factly staccato like, but not in a pleading manner, she tried to keep it cool, as cool as she could, which was almost impossible considering how angry and incensed she was feeling inside. She tried desperately to sound interested, casual even, but too busy, too hassled. Calm but firm. But he continued even more suggestively, "But that's just it, I don't have to rush in to work, we've got plenty of time and I can feel your heart beating fast", he said as he gripped her breasts even tighter. "You know you want it, so stop playing hard to get." Sheena could feel his erect penis in her back he was that close to her.

She demanded, more aggressively now, to know why there was no rush. And all this time she was still gripping the sink, staring out of the window in front of her. "It's because your mum's dead, they said at work that I could have 'passion time' or 'passion leave' or something like that." He laughed and then with stomach churning depravity he added, "They should have said 'fucking' time, or fucking leave, shouldn't they, because that's what we're going to be doing?" His touch, his laughter, his excuse, his very breath on her neck was sickening her. Then to her horror his right hand moved quickly, deftly, first to inside her skirt and finally to inside her knickers. His fingers were searching eagerly and roughly for her vagina.

Feeling his fingers inside her was almost too much to bear and the decision making was now much more urgent, not that he was trying to arouse her, because for one thing that would have been impossible to do and for another, arousing her was not on his agenda. No, his intentions were merely that he wanted to make sure she wasn't on her 'period' because then he wouldn't want to touch her, because then he would consider *her* to be disgusting, dirty and repugnant, someone to be avoided at all costs – how she wished she were – no, the way his fingers were moving around inside her, as far as she was concerned, was on a par with him searching in her handbag for the car keys!!

He liked to grip her breasts, oh yes; he liked that all right, and did so whenever he could, at any time of the day and whatever she was doing. But he had no interest in her vagina apart from it being a receptacle for his penis, a clean receptacle, of course, so still with her back to him, her mind searching for a solution, whilst at the same time using her elbows in any way she could to try to move his hands, to try to rid herself of him, suddenly his next words proved to be the catalyst for her because he added, "They said I could come in late if I wanted to, or even take a couple of days off, *and* that they would even pay me, so the old git was useful for something wasn't she?" That was it. Her decision was now clear.

She turned sharply and suddenly on her heel, knocking him backwards and almost making him lose his footing her movement was that fast. Her blood boiling with the rage she was feeling he backed off momentarily, but was still laughing and holding his arms aloft, he said, "Hey, hey you don't need to cut my clothes off. I'll take them off for you." And with that he pulled his shirt off over his head. She hadn't realised what he'd meant until looking down at her hands she saw what he himself was looking at and referring to, she realised that she still had the vegetable knife in her hand. "Right," he said, still looking at the knife. "It's your turn now, do you want to undo my pants or shall I take yours off?" His words and his appearance almost made her giggle nervously.

This skinny, weedy, arrogant, illiterate bully who actually thought that she wanted to have sex with him looked ridiculous. He stood there grinning maniacally, his portly beer belly also now exposed, and his arms raised above his head as though her knife was a gun and he was facing a highway robber shouting 'put 'em up' at him, it took her slightly by surprise that she *didn't* burst out laughing at him. But she moved slowly and steadily towards him with the knife really close to his body and it was taking every ounce of strength and determination she could muster to not just plunge it into his stomach. In her mind's eye she could see 'beer' pouring out of it rather that blood and that image also amused her. But as she edged nearer to him with determination, the knife was now making an indent in his skin.

Then she started her own verbal onslaught. "You make me sick," she said. "You make me bloody sick. *Passion time? Passion leave?"* she repeated sarcastically.. "You mean *compassionate* leave, you moron. But while we're talking 'passion time' I'm telling you now that there'll be none of it for you any more. *Never!* Do you hear me? Never again will there be any 'passion time' for you." Her anger was rising so much that not only was her heart pounding in her chest, but she could also feel a vein in the side of her head throbbing. Tom was looking slightly scared now and walking backwards away from the knife as she herself edged forward. But then he started getting angry and tried to call her bluff by walking forward again, more into the knife.

"You're being bloody stupid. What have I done now to upset you?

"What have you done? *What have you done?"* She repeated louder, incredulous of his ignorance at what he done. "For one thing you have absolutely no empathy; you don't possess a single empathetic bone in your body. My mother's only just died for God's sake and I've spent most of today looking at her dead body lying in her coffin, and you have no empathy for that, no empathy at all, you just want sex, sex, sex and more sex. You only ever want sex and you only ever want to satisfy your own disgusting urges." She was so furious, so full of rage and she was in fact, slightly afraid that she would actually push the knife deep into his stomach. So strong was Sheena's desire to do just that, to actually stab him, that she had to try physically so very hard to stop herself before she got to the point of no return, but there would be no giving up with her fight-back now she silently promised herself. She was the one in charge at the moment and she knew from past experience that he could overpower her at any time, but it was not going to happen, not this time, not while she felt so empowered.

"Empathy," he repeated. "What the fuck is empathy? he asked. "Why the fuck do you always have to use fancy words? Why can't you just say what you mean?

"Exactly," she replied emphatically. "Exactly! That's exactly what I mean." She said all this while maintaining a very tight grip on the knife, and he looked at her as though she was from another planet. Then suddenly he made his move and lunged forward in an attempt to take the knife from her. But she didn't back away as he'd obviously expected, in fact she used the knife to prod his now bare skinny upper body, and she'd gone far enough to draw blood. That pleased her. The look of shock and surprise on his face also pleased her. It was only a small amount of blood but it was enough to unnerve him.

He yelped with the pain before shouting at her, "You bloody fucking idiot." He then added hysterically, "If you touch me with that again with that fucking knife you'll be in serious trouble, and you'll be sorry, because I'll go to the hospital and tell them that you're a crazy woman and that you tried to stab me."

"Oh, I'll be sorry will I?" she repeated, in a curt mocking tone, and looking around as she again moved nearer to him she turned her head slightly to the side eagerly searching for something, anything, and then she saw it; it was just what she wanted. She picked it up; she picked up a bottle of tomato sauce from the kitchen table with her free hand. And now mocking his pathetic attempt at getting her to stop she whined at him in the same mocking manner that he had often used on her, as though she were defending herself to any policeman who cared to confront her – "But, officer he came up behind me with this bottle, she waved the sauce bottle furiously at him, I was scared that he was going to rape me again, and I couldn't go through that, no not again, and you ask the doctor he'll tell you that he's raped me with these sort of things, and worse, many times now, and I was so scared, honestly officer. I had the knife in my hand from preparing a meal for him, officer, and I wasn't going to let him rape me again. I needed to defend myself. Honestly, officer, I didn't mean to actually kill him." Her tone was definitely more worthy of his usual sarcasm, and it was getting better all the time, she was enjoying herself now, getting a twisted sort of satisfaction out of his fear. He could see that she meant it and he was flustered, more than flustered, he was panicked!

"Okay, okay, I get it. You don't want sex tonight. You only needed to say!" was his pathetic response. "Now put that bloody knife down before you do something you'll regret." He was trying so hard to sound masterful, to sound in charge that it was almost laughable. She could see from the look of fear in his eyes that he was panicking more and more and she was enjoying the power she now felt over him and it felt good to be on the upper hand for a change. But she was far from ready to put the knife down. In fact she prodded him with it again, still not hard, but hard enough, and again he yelped as a small drop of blood escaped. Not enough to do any harm, she knew that, although she was sorely tempted to do him harm, but it was enough to scare him.

She then went on to tell him, shaking the knife nearer his face now, that not only did she not want sex tonight, but that she'd *never* wanted sex from him ever, that she hated sex and what's more she hated him and he was never going to have sex with her again. In fact he should go and see his mother if he didn't have to go to work and make some arrangements to stay there. Because if he intended to stay here for much longer then she was going to go to the neighbours, to his mother, to his doctor, to his work mates and to anyone else who would listen to her and tell them how he liked to rape her. How he beat her. How he humiliated her. Everyone would know, his children would know and he couldn't deny it because it's all on record at the doctor's. She reminded him that he admitted freely to the

94

doctor what he liked to do to her. "How do you think your mates are going to react to the way you 'celebrated' the birth of your son, and followed it up with a similar celebration for the birth of your first daughter?"

He was beaten. He knew he was beaten and that there was no argument he could put forward against that statement. He tried to say that he was sorry, that he'd already promised that he wouldn't do those things again and that he hadn't done them since he'd been told by the doctor that he shouldn't be doing things like that. But Sheena wasn't interested and was in no mood to back down. She'd gone this far and she wasn't going to stop. She still pushed forward the knife still jabbing at him.

"Okay, okay," he said furiously trying to control the situation. "I'll go to work and I'll see you in the morning when you're in a better mood and I won't have sex until you're ready. This business with your mother has had a really bad effect on you." He'd sounded puzzled, confused and he still didn't 'get' it. The arrogance of this poor excuse of a man! So she spelt it out again, only louder this time, telling him that he could stay until arrangements were made with his mother and that she had intended to wait to do this until after her own mother's funeral, to tell him to go and that it wasn't just his actions of that evening that had caused the problem.

The problem was HIM! She hated him. The words were spat out venomously, and she also informed him that the law wouldn't allow him to make his children homeless, but that he wasn't welcome here any more and she was going to divorce him and if he didn't want everyone to know his 'dirty little secrets' then he should agree with her and just go. If he came home in the morning then he was to sleep in the bed that she'd prepared for Iain, but he wasn't to come anywhere near her or to speak to her and he was to be gone completely by the time of her mother's funeral.

Still with his half naked body exposed, and dribbles of blood running down and over his 'beer belly', he grabbed his clothes and muttering something under his breath went out the door, slamming it behind him. She heard the car screech away and trembling herself now, she finally sat down. The grip on the knife now loosened, it was lying by the side of her, she closed her eyes and offered up a silent prayer to her mother thanking her for the courage she had given her, because all the way through that exchange with Tom she felt her mother's presence acutely, encouraging her to 'keep going, love, don't give up'.

CHAPTER 9

Sheena was now completely exhausted; she had lied to Tom with regard to her telling everyone about his behaviour, deliberately lied to him, and her heart had been racing ever faster as she feared he might call her bluff, terrified that he might simply say "go on then, tell them all", because the confidence that she'd been so valiantly displaying to him was false. No, she was a nervous wreck behind the façade that she'd been putting out. But somehow, at the same time she'd felt so very strong, so very superior to him. She had no doubt as to where her confidence had derived from, it was, of course, her mother's very strong presence that she'd felt so acutely all through that episode with Tom, her mother's presence that had allowed her to continue with her threats to him, allowed her to win.

But now as she sat on the sofa and the reality of how badly things could have gone wrong hit her, her legs were so weak they were like jelly. For she knew with some certainty that she could never, ever tell anyone, well certainly not anyone new, about those terrible, disgusting things he'd done to her, no, as far as she was concerned they were far horrific, and indeed embarrassing to ever repeat to others. But the important fact for her now, was that which she'd kept repeating to herself over and over again, the fact that he'd believed her, that somehow she'd managed to convince him that she meant every word of what she'd said, so now she could finally relax; now she could take stock of everything that had just passed between them. And for that, she clasped her hands together as if in prayer and said out loud, "Thank you, thank you, thank you, mum." And then she allowed herself a little wry smile as she recalled the look of horror and disbelief on Tom's face, the look that related both to her words and to the knife. She had witnessed real fear in *his* eyes for a change and that alone felt so good. However, the very use of her words to Tom regarding Susie's birth, had made her recall those terrible events surrounding her eldest daughter's birth, for they had been even more terrifying than the first time, after Andy's birth.

****

She remembered the events so clearly it was scary, she remembered how she'd been determined that he wouldn't be present for the birth of Susie, she'd been resolute in her thoughts and actions, and she'd even clearly told him herself that she didn't want him to be there, and he'd seemingly agreed without any fuss. But when she actually went into labour with Susie it had all been so very quick. She had wondered many times since Susie's birth if the damage he'd caused to her after Andy's birth, and to a lesser degree on other occasions, had somehow weakened her womb, because Susie's birth had been so rapid.

She'd arrived at the hospital apparently already in an advanced stage of labour, and as the nurse examined her she'd panicked, because she was saying that the baby was almost there. They'd put her on a gurney and actually ran down the hospital corridor with her, such was the nurse's panic, taking her straight to the delivery room. But when she arrived she'd spotted another nurse helping Tom on with a mask and gown and she'd screamed furiously at the nurse to keep him out. 'Don't let him stay' she'd said in the most forceful way she could. Tom, of course, had protested, saying that he wanted to help her, he'd sounded so sincere and caring, which Sheena knew was false, but the nurse by her disapproving look, let Sheena know that she thought she was being too hard on Tom, but Sheena had ignored the look that had been so thoughtlessly cast towards her, the nurse wasn't aware of Sheena's reasons behind her actions, and so she screamed again for him to GET OUT!

And this time the nurse had listened, and told him that he would have to go. However, all the while this was happening, Sheena was moving herself, with the help of a nurse, from the gurney to the labour bed, and while she was practically in mid-air Susie just came straight out. It had been so sudden that she had almost fallen on the floor, but thankfully she'd landed on the labour bed.

But Tom had seen it. He was still removing his mask and gown as their daughter made her unceremonious entry into the world. And Sheena had seen his look and it disgusted her. He'd stared open mouthed at her. Not at his daughter, but at Sheena, and he wasn't staring at her face! For the rapid, and dramatic birth had resulted in Sheena being 'torn', which meant, of course, that she had opened up very wide, and that was what he'd been staring at. And the look in his eyes was a look of sadistic lust. Sheena knew instinctively, in that very moment, she knew that he'd got a 'hard' on. She knew exactly what obscene thoughts were going through his mind and they had terrified her.

She recalled that his lascivious look had made her feel disgusted, dirty and totally unfeminine. She had felt dirty, disgusted and unfeminine doing the most beautiful and feminine thing possible, giving birth. He'd left the room now, but Sheena could still see his eyes, in fact she could still see them now as she was simply recalling the events. Four years later, but they were as clear now in her mind's eye now, as they had been on that day. The whole scene was so vivid in her mind; it could have been moments ago.

After a struggle inside her head to move away from 'seeing' his eyes, she went on to recall what followed, and how she eventually came to the decision to tell someone about what had been happening to her, to ask for someone's help. With Susie's birth having been so rapid it had in fact caused quite a lot of trauma to Sheena's body, and it took more work to repair it.

Sheena had also been told at the time that it would also take her longer to heal, longer to recover, than the episiotomy that she'd had after Andy's birth. It had also apparently, been quite dangerous for Susie, as such a rapid birth could have caused brain damage, but thankfully, Susie was fine. Sheena had hoped, prayed even, that her personal trauma would mean that they'd be told to wait for more than six weeks before resuming sex, but they'd only been told to see how she felt when the six weeks were up, and to see her own doctor if she was having difficulties healing, otherwise they'd said, six weeks should be enough. Sheena remembered how disappointed she'd been that they hadn't said three months!

When Sheena returned home with Susie she'd been much more tired than with Andy, because of course she now had a four-year-old to take care of as well. But Tom was in fact being brilliant. She truly believed that he'd changed, or that he'd finally accepted that he'd been wrong before, wrong in his belief that she'd loved pain.

Sheena remembered how excited and happy she'd been when he'd convinced her that he'd changed, that his only aims in life now were to show her how much he really cared about her, to try to make up for the past and to look after her. He'd been cooking meals, changing nappies, going to bed later after his night shift in order to help with Andy, and he'd even never complained if Susie woke him in the night at weekends, or even if his sleep was disturbed during the day when he'd been working all night.

Nothing had seemed to upset him, he was always in a good mood, and he was so helpful and considerate towards her. He'd even bought her flowers on one occasion, and on another occasion, chocolates, and on both of those occasions there was no particular celebration, no birthday's or anniversaries, he'd just surprised her with the gifts. In fact he seemed to truly be a changed man, so much so that Sheena felt guilty for doubting him when he'd promised that things would be different, when he'd promised to never again hurt her like he'd done before.

But he'd been lying to her then. Lying by his actions and his false kindnesses, and she had believed him. He had convinced her that he was a changed man, and it was that more than anything else which made his actions all the more horrifying. Sheena found out in the cruellest way possible just how deceitful Tom had been, she was appalled, frightened and heartbroken when his 'kindness', his 'caring', and his 'love' was exposed for the horrific sham that it was, when she discovered that he had in fact been planning an attack on her from the moment he'd seen Susie coming into the world, but Sheena hadn't seen it coming.

For Sheena, knowing all that she did about him, all his sinister depraved ways, he'd still stunned her with the way in which he'd moved to ever new depths of depravity, such depths that even Sheena could never have predicted. Those depths were reached when he'd 'celebrated' Susie's birth. As Sheena sat there recalling those events after Susie's birth she wrapped her arms around her body as if to protect herself from the horrifying memories of that time, for she could still physically feel the pain that was inflicted on her that day and it was making her tremble. She tried desperately to hold her body still and composed.

Susie had been only two weeks old when Tom came home from work a little after 6.00am one morning while Sheena was busy nursing Susie. She'd always tried to avoid feed times crossing with the times that Tom was either going or coming home from work, but on this particular morning, Susie had slept longer than normal and with Sheena being so tired herself, she hadn't woken early enough to get the feed finished in time. Despite his new demeanour and kindness towards her, she was still expecting him to be angry with her and accordingly she recalled immediately starting to apologise to him when he'd arrived home, saying that she could leave Susie's feed for now and make him some breakfast, then finish feeding her later. Having lived most of her married life on a knife edge, forever trying to predict his moods, trying not to upset him, it was difficult to totally relax, difficult to get used to the supposedly 'new' Tom.

She allowed herself to relax, however, when his actions confirmed his good mood. He'd seemed to have been in a good mood ever since Susie was born, but it had still taken Sheena by surprise. He'd told her not to worry, to carry on feeding and he'd make his own breakfast. He'd put his hands gently on to her shoulders and kissed her lightly on her forehead as he passed her to go into the kitchen. Sheena recalled clearly that she'd breathed a huge sigh of relief that morning. Then he'd further astounded her by not only making her a cup of tea, but he'd informed her that he'd put a little bit of whisky in it to help her get some much needed rest.

Sheena had been more than a little worried about drinking tea with whisky in whilst she was nursing Susie, and although she didn't have the courage to actually voice her worries, Tom had obviously picked up on the worried look on her face, and he had smiled and even winked at her saying softly, 'it's only a little whisky to help you sleep, it won't do her (nodding towards Susie), any harm' and so she'd drank it. And she did have to admit that with the added sugar it was very welcome.

When Sheena had finished feeding Susie, Tom had told her to go to bed and get some sleep. He'd insisted, and in a really nice considerate way, that she got some rest. He'd said that he would change Susie's nappy and get Andy up later. He'd told her to get at least two hours sleep without worrying. Sheena had been so relieved and happy by his attitude that she'd actually kissed him warmly and thanked him. She'd gone to bed feeling sure everything was getting so much better between them. With the warmth of the whisky along with her extreme tiredness and the happy warm feeling she had that everything was finally good between them, she'd quickly fallen into a very deep welcoming sleep.

CHAPTER 10

And then her world fell apart. For Sheena was woken violently by Tom raping her. He was thrusting hard and violently inside her, she'd screamed and fought him as hard as she could, she'd used as much strength as she'd been able to, to fight him off, and she'd been beyond panicked. Her nightdress was around her neck and her pants were off. He'd hit her hard when she'd screamed and told her viciously to shut up.

He was looking at her in a lecherous, disgusting, vile and determined manner and he was actually salivating. She was heaving now as she recalled his saliva dripping down his chin, slobbering like a teething baby, while Sheena had been in extreme agony. He'd gripped her breasts really hard and with his eyes just inches from hers he kept saying, "I can't wait any longer, you're begging for it, you know you are. You fucking love it, you fucking love it, I want my bit and I'm going to have my bit, and you're going to fucking well admit that you enjoy it, that you're longing for it." All the while he was thrusting ever harder inside her and his left hand covering her mouth to prevent her screaming. She'd had no strength left to fight him and accordingly she just dropped her arms and her resistance, she was spent. Then suddenly it was over, he'd pulled quickly away leaving his body fluids all over her. With a twisted sardonic smile on his face he'd said sarcastically, "Don't want another brat arriving now, do we?"

But at least it was over. However, as he'd moved slowly away from her, he just knelt between her legs, and pushing her knees wide apart he was staring at her, eyes agog whilst muttering almost unintelligible but clearly disgusting things to himself, and with the look on his face being beyond description.

Sheena recalled how dirty she felt and how she'd tried desperately to get him off her. But even now, four years later, she could still clearly recall how her mind had been going to silly places, how she'd been thinking that she wished he wouldn't swear so much, wished that he wasn't so coarse,, and then answering her own thoughts with 'what does that matter, concentrate on getting him off you'. But everything about the situation was surreal; she'd even considered that perhaps she'd been having a nightmare, but she was in fact actually *living* a nightmare.

However, her silly thoughts had been rushed back to reality when he'd retrieved 'items' from his bedside cabinet. That was when the sudden realisation hit her, the realisation that everything had been planned by him in advance. She'd tried to fight him, to plead for him to stop, but her voice was just a whimpering little voice, she'd hated vehemently her little whimpering voice, she'd wanted a strong dominant one, but it wasn't there, there was only a whimper.

He'd sworn at her, cursed her and he'd told her when she screamed with pain begging him to stop, that it was his intention to hurt her, and what's more he was going to continue to hurt her until she admitted that she liked it. He was trying to say that as Susie had 'ripped' her open and she had then lovingly kissed and cuddled her baby daughter, she'd obviously enjoyed the pain. Her pain at that moment was so severe that she likened it to being tortured, and to people confessing to anything to stop the pain, and she felt that the only way to get it to stop was to admit that she liked it, however disgusting that option was to her.

But then she realised that she was bleeding and knowing his horror of blood, she decided to try that first. It wasn't a rational decision, just a desperate one. So she screamed at him that she was bleeding badly and that he needed to stop before any permanent damage was done. She held her breath, she prayed silently, she pushed at him to get off her, and finally he did.

He'd jumped off her and was jumping up and down like a maniac, a totally naked maniac, and he was saying, "You've fucking spoiled it, you've fucking spoiled it." Somehow, somehow incredulous as it seemed, somehow, he was trying to make the fact that *he'd* caused so much damage to her as to make her bleed profusely her fault! He was blaming her for spoiling his fun! Sheena was lost for words. What words could she use to describe his depraved sense of 'fun'?

Sheena used her nightdress to stem the flow of blood. But Tom was quickly back to the bedside table and taking a beer bottle out of the bedside cabinet he tossed it casually to her saying, "Right, okay, I can't do it now 'cause your fucking bleeding, so you'll have to do it to yourself and I'll watch." She looked at him astounded and frightened in equal measure. She was married to a monster, a sub-human was all she could think as he was standing there holding his now very erect penis, waiting for her to start!

She was feeling a bit more able to answer back now that the weight of him was off her, and so she spat the words out to him, pleased that she'd found her stronger voice instead of the whimpering one. But she was so incensed with what he was proposing that she spat them out through gritted teeth, sarcastically, saying, "Why don't you just get a milk bottle to fuck while I'm doing this." She couldn't find a better or stronger word than 'fuck' to use, and she thought *he's got me swearing now* but if ever swearing was necessary then it was then. She'd also held the beer bottle aloft as she'd spoke.

But the response from him was like a 'light bulb' moment for him. He'd looked puzzled at first then pointing his finger in the air he'd said, "What a great idea. Wait while I go and get one." He was seriously going to do that. Sheena just couldn't believe him or his reactions, however she had then reacted quickly enough to pick up the beer bottle and throw it at him as hard as she could and it had caught him a glancing blow across the side of his head and it drew quite a bit of blood and *he* yelped in pain.

That had caused her to be terrified about his reaction for a moment, as he'd seemed to react in slow motion, but he'd just looked at the blood, just stared at it in amazement, blood which was on his hand now where he had felt his wound, and he ran from the room. Sheena made her way to the bathroom as quickly as she could, considering her pain and her obvious injury, and locked the door. She didn't know where Tom had gone, she was just glad it wasn't the bathroom, it was probably to the kitchen, but she didn't care and she wasn't going to go looking for him, and so she'd stayed there for what seemed an eternity bathing her own wounds, ignoring his shouts and bangs on the door at her to come out, until eventually when all was quiet and she was sure he was in bed asleep she felt safe enough to come out.

She knew then that she no longer had any choice in the matter; she would have to do something about it. She would have to tell someone, before one of them was murdered, for she could have easily, in that moment, have gone back upstairs and murdered him. So she bathed her wounds and put padding around the area that was bleeding, then took the children to a neighbour and went to see the doctor. It was only a small village that she lived in, so it was only a short, if painful walk to the doctor's surgery.

Sheena had sat in the doctor's waiting room terrified. She was terrified of the doctor's reaction, especially as it was a male doctor, but all the same she knew that she had to try, she had to do something or this nightmare of hers would never end. She didn't know what he could do, but the least he could do would be to tend her wounds. Then it was her turn to go in.

She had intended to speak slowly and clearly, but the doctor's gentle and concerned tone immediately reduced her to tears. He'd passed her tissues and said softly, "Come on now, Mrs Miller, tell me what's the problem, what's making you so upset?" Through her heavy sobbing she told him that it was 'her husband'. He'd tried to pre-empt the problem by asking if he had another woman. Sheena just manically shook her head. "Has he left you? Is he hurt? Please tell me the problem, Mrs Miller." He was leaning forward and gently holding her hand and giving her all the time and encouragement to speak to him that he could. So she took in a deep breath to try to stop the sobbing, and while it had eased enough to speak, it hadn't stopped. But she said: I'm bleeding, he rapes me, he uses things to rape me with and I'm scared and bleeding.

She'd held her head low, unable and too ashamed to look him in the eye. But finally she looked up through her tears, her eyes begging him for help. But at the same time the doctor let go of her hands and practically knocked his chair over, such was his eagerness to distance himself from her. "No, no, no. You can't tell me things like that." He was pacing in the surgery and not looking at her. Sheena felt ashamed, more ashamed than she had before. She'd wished that she hadn't told him. She visualised him looking at her differently every time he saw her now. She got up to leave, still heavy with tears, but full of shame and embarrassment.

The doctor didn't touch her, but stood by the door to prevent her from leaving. "Please, please, Mrs Miller, sit back down. I'm sorry for my extreme reaction but it really isn't something that you can tell to me. You need to talk to a woman. Go home and I will sort something out for you."

Sheena didn't look up, her head was bowed in shame, but she said again, "I'm bleeding."

But the doctor again told her to go home and wait; "Someone will call and see you. I promise you, someone will call today." His voice was again full of concern, but of little help.

She'd left the surgery more frightened than when she'd arrived. What would happen now, she'd wondered? If someone was to come to the house when Tom was there, well she didn't know what would happen. How she wished she hadn't gone. She truly hadn't known where to turn for help. She could never tell her mother those terrible things, they would break her heart, maybe even kill her. No she couldn't tell her mother.

When she returned home the neighbour who had her children could see that she was ill, and that she'd been crying, and so when she'd called to collect them she'd told her to go home and get some rest and that she would bring them over to her when Susie was due her next feed. Sheena recalled clearly how grateful she'd felt for what appeared to be the only kindness shown to her that day, but at the same time she knew that Susie's next feed would be from a bottle. She had nursed her darling daughter for the last time.

Sheena lay on the sofa totally distraught. She had only an hour, two at the most before Susie would need to be fed again; she needed to get some rest. She was exhausted and her mind was spinning, let alone the fact that she was also in tremendous pain. She tried desperately to close her mind to everything, to try to sleep.

She was just about asleep when there was a knock on the door. Sheena thought that it must be her neighbour bringing the children back, but it was a lady doctor, a doctor that she didn't know. However, this doctor had been told about her problem and was there to help her. She examined her wounds, which didn't require stitches; they would heal on their own, given time, she'd assured her. Sheena doubted that they would get the time they needed. The doctor, surprisingly to Sheena, proceeded to make them both a cup of tea and asked her to tell her everything. Sheena was very nervous at first, but the doctor was kind and reassuring, and so she told her *everything*.

It had felt so good to talk to someone who seemed to care, someone who wanted to listen. And it felt even better when the doctor assured her that what was happening to her was a very long way from being normal, in fact she'd said that any sexual act was abnormal if it was forced onto someone who didn't want it, but what had happened to her would be grounds for divorce. No doubt about it, she'd insisted. Sheena was more than just relieved, she was so very, very grateful for both the medical help and the emotional help. She realised that her own GP had sent this lovely doctor to her, and for that she was more grateful than her doctor would ever know.

But even so, what the doctor did next astounded Sheena, she'd told her to pack some clothes for the children and for herself, she had also contacted her brother to make arrangements for them to stay at his house for a while. She simply told him that husband and wife had had a really bad row and that Sheena needed some time away from him. Sheena felt so good, so relieved that someone cared enough to take matters in hand. As far as she was concerned, this doctor whom she had never met before, had saved her life.

Within an hour Sheena's brother, Graham, had come to collect her and her children. And during all of this, Tom had remained asleep upstairs, totally oblivious as to what had happened. She'd left a note, on the doctor's advice, simply stating that she was staying at her brother's home for a while. She was full of hope that finally she would be free of him; finally she could start a new life, preferably a life without men in it!

Sheena had stayed at Graham's home for almost three months, just meeting Tom occasionally in order for him to keep contact with the children. He'd begged her to return many times, but she was desperately looking for somewhere permanent to live. Graham had children of his own and no room for her and two more children, although he never said so. Sheena knew that he cared too much for her to tell her that there was no room for her, but she had to face reality, she couldn't stay forever. She never told her brother the real reason for her being at his house, and he'd never asked, but she suspected that he knew that it was more than just an argument, but he hadn't pushed her for any further information and she was glad of that.

But her hopes of a future without Tom were turning out to be false hopes, for there *was* no future, according to 'authorities' she had apparently intentionally made herself homeless and so there was no help out there for her. But Tom hadn't known that she had no other options, and so she made it a condition of her return that he see a psychiatrist concerning his behaviour, and that he never tried anything remotely like a 'special' again. And he did of course do that.

And so Sheena returned home, and Tom had tried many, many times to reassure her that he had changed, and to be fair, he had never again tried to either force, or coerce her into allowing him to inflict those terrible things onto her. But there was no trust, and certainly no love for him from her, she simply took the easy way out by 'letting' him have his way without any involvement from her. It prevented arguments and fights, and was, by far, her easiest way of coping. However, he was still extremely jealous and possessive, and she had to account for all her time, and explain who everyone was that she ever spoke to, and he was still far too handy with his fists from time to time.

****

But the death of her mother had made her change all that. No longer was she going to put up with him or his aggression. But would she have carried out her threat to tell everyone that she'd told him she'd tell? Well, the truthful answer to that was no.

Would she tell his mother? No. His mother was a lovely woman whom Sheena loved; she would never hurt her by giving her that type of information about her son. Would she tell her children? Most definitely not, was the answer to that one. Why would she want to load that sort of information onto her lovely children? It would be bad enough that they would have to cope with a divorce, and besides, they loved their father, so no, she would never, ever tell them, not even when they were adults. Would she tell his workmates? No, but for different reasons; Tom was not really liked by anyone, not even his workmates, but she was sure that if they became aware of his disgusting behaviour then he would go *up* in their esteem, they would probably all sit around discussing all the disgusting details. So no, she wouldn't be telling them. In fact, Sheena would never have been able to tell anyone.

Sheena recalled how she'd almost told Iain when he'd asked her about Tom's treatment of her when he'd stayed in Andy's room for the night. Iain had been so concerned about her after hearing Tom treating her so badly, and he'd also been very loving towards her, but still she couldn't tell him. She'd skirted around the issue, and hinted at things, but she couldn't *actually* tell him. As it was she'd told him more than she had ever told anyone else and it had caused her immense pain to see the look of hurt that was in her brother's eyes.

It had taken a tremendous amount of courage for her to say as much as she did to him, and she knew that her brother had 'visions' of what she'd meant by what she'd said, but she was unable to do anything about that. So if she couldn't tell someone who clearly cared for her, then there was no way that she would ever carry out her threat to tell 'all'.

But thankfully Tom didn't know that. All he knew was that she'd told someone once, the doctor, so she would tell again, and Sheena was more than happy for him to remain thinking that. The important thing for Sheena was that Tom had believed her, and so hopefully she'd seen the last of him. Surely now she could look forward to a more peaceful life, a life devoid of sex! Even just thinking about that filled her with renewed delight, and again she sent up her thanks to her mum. She'd promised her mum that she would never take a step backwards; every step from now on was going to be a forward one.

CHAPTER 11

With Tom gone wherever he'd gone, and the children now fast asleep Sheena was alone and had for the first time since her mother's death to really think through what had happened, especially in the weird times in the lead up to her death and so she analysed it in her mind very carefully, trying her best to recall every single important detail.

There was the strange behaviour in the days leading up to the Christening. There was the day of the Christening itself when her mother didn't come and her father wouldn't let Sheena speak to her. Then there was the weird phone call on the day after the Christening demanding that she came over to see her 'sick' mother, who in fact wasn't sick when she did finally see her. And her mother, herself, was acting really strangely that evening, as though there was some unsaid secret between them that Sheena just didn't get! Then there was the terrible, terrible phone call on the morning of her mother's death just coldly informing her that her mother was dead! No words of comfort – just the cold, cold information.

Then on the day of her death she couldn't comprehend why he'd just sat alone with her all morning, from 5.30am to 9.30am, apparently simply watching her die. If she'd been so ill that he didn't feel able to go to work, why did he wait until the doctor was busy in morning surgery before phoning him? Why didn't he call the doctor earlier at 7.00am or even 8.00am or any time before she died? She had never, ever before known her father to sit with her mother when she was ill. The most he would do for her would be to make her a flask of tea until someone else could see to her. But he would *always* go to work. And her mother had been seriously ill on more than one occasion when he *could* have stayed with her but chose to leave her to cope alone.

One of her worries was that she thought the strange conversation with her mother indicated that she knew what was about to happen. But Sheena couldn't accept that she would have known that. Surely if she had any genuine worries about her safety she would have asked if she could have gone home with Sheena that same night, she could always have used the excuse that she was ill, after all, that was why her father had made her call over to see her. Nothing added up.

No, no matter what she thought and what seemed unreal she couldn't 'go there' in her head. No her mother didn't know anything. Her thoughts wavered though, could she be sure? She had to answer yes to that. Because the idea that her father may have had a hand in her mother's death was bad enough, even possibly far-fetched enough, to contemplate, but to think her mother *knew* about it was really going into the realms of fantasy.

Then there was his reaction to her death. He actually seemed pleased, even thinking that, never mind saying it out loud to anyone sounded crazy. But he was, in his own words, going to be actively 'looking for another woman'. Surely someone would think that was wrong. And she hadn't imagined that. He had said those exact words to her, and in such a manner that left her in no doubt that he was serious. In fact, getting the seriousness of his statement over to her had been his main intention.

There were too many questions and not enough answers. She didn't believe for a minute that the family doctor would be involved, but she knew that her father was perfectly capable of fooling a doctor and also that the doctor would then be totally averse to admitting that he had been fooled.

Her mind was buzzing; she needed to talk all that she knew up to now through with someone who would look at it objectively, because she was very much aware that she herself *was* emotional and biased. But there was no way that she was going to accept that she was *just* hormonal! No, there was much more to it than that and so she decided that the next day she would indeed go to the police. Up until that moment the idea of going to the police had only really been a threat that she'd used with the doctor in the hope that he would reconsider a post-mortem, but she knew now that she was actually going to do it. She reasoned that they would probably think she was crazy or even 'hormonal' but it had to at least be worth a try, she just had to do something. She would also tell her brothers what she was going to do.

And so before going to bed she phoned Graham and told him of her intentions, she could tell by the exasperating sound of his voice on the phone that he thought she was being very silly, but she'd half expected that, however, he did add that if it would help her to put her worries behind her then she should go ahead. She'd been sure that she would have gone ahead anyway, but it was good that they knew what her plans were. Finally, arrangements were made for them all to meet the next afternoon and Graham told Sheena that both he and Iain were going to see their father that day as Iain hadn't yet seen him since he'd been home. Graham also hoped that the visit would provide them with some insight into whether they could either clarify or discount what Sheena herself had not only heard him say but also the manner in which he'd said it.

Sheena knew that they both thought she was reading too much into things, but she also knew that they thought it was important to her that her mind was put at rest, not that they were doubting her, just the opposite, they were trying to give her reassurance. But they both said again that she shouldn't be offended if it turned out that she was in fact just very hormonal and that everything would be fine. Although they did think the things she'd brought up about their father not calling a doctor earlier, and sitting with her rather than go to work were indeed strange. Neither of them could ever recall their father actually sitting and nursing their mother when she was sick and their memories went back a lot further that hers.

She went to bed early that night but slept fitfully. She missed her mum so very, very much more than she ever could have imagined. She picked Susie up out of her bed and put her in to her own bed that night. Susie was fast asleep and totally unaware that she'd been moved, although she did wrap her little arms around her mum in her sleep. That alone meant such a lot to Sheena.

The next morning Sheena wasn't sure that seeing the police was such a good idea, but she was prepared to be laughed at, and if she were to have any success over her post-mortem request then this is what she would have to do, and so she went to the police station early. When they asked at the police station what her business was and who she wanted to speak to, she just blurted out that she wanted to report a suspicious death and would be happy to talk to anyone in authority, she didn't have any names in mind as she didn't know any policemen. She got a strange look, which she ignored, from the officer behind the desk but was told to wait and that somebody would be with her shortly.

It was a sergeant Phil Anderson who came to talk to her and took her into a small office where he said they could talk without any interference. She looked around at the cold empty room. There was nothing more in it than the table they were sitting at and four chairs, two either side with Sergeant Anderson sitting opposite her. The only time she could recall seeing a room like that one was in films when suspects were being interrogated. She asked the Sergeant if that was what the room was used for, she whispered it actually, as if someone might hear her, and he leaned forward to bring his face close to hers and motioned with his hand for her to come closer. Intrigued she moved closer to hear his whisper. "Yes," he said, then sat back laughing at her. She laughed too, a nervous laugh but it felt like they had broken the ice.

He could see straight away that she was extremely nervous and so he told her to just take her time and explain everything to him. He assured her that there was no need to rush and that he was hers all day if necessary. He was smiling, calm and self-assured. She immediately felt confident talking to him, she was sure he wouldn't laugh at her – she hoped not anyway.

And so she found herself telling this stranger everything. Everything that had been going through her mind the previous night, all her doubts and thoughts, she told him all of it. Including how lovely Lucy had looked at her Christening! In fact she probably gave him much more information than she needed to, but he was easy to talk to and he had brought her at least two cups of tea while she talked and he listened, and then he told her what he thought about the matter, and what he could do to help.

First of all the doctor was right, he'd said, the police couldn't ask for a post-mortem if the doctor has declared that there were no suspicious circumstances. He quickly added that that didn't mean that she wasn't justified with her worries, but officially they could do nothing to investigate the death as officially no crime had been committed. Sheena was getting agitated now and felt she was wasting her time and his. But he gently took her hand, not in the condescending way that the doctor had, but in a sincere gesture of his concern. He told her that he wasn't going to dismiss her concerns because whether they were right or not, he could tell that she felt passionately that something was wrong. He also told her that he would go and speak to both the doctor and her father.

The doctor would be the most difficult as from what she'd told him he was already on the defensive, but he would try to get some more information from him, and as for her father he had spoken to enough people in his years as a police officer to know when someone was either lying to him or even being too 'cocky' when speaking to him. He assured her that the least he would be able to do was to gauge if she was in even the slightest bit correct in her thoughts. Though he did admit that sometimes even knowing that someone has done something, even such a serious something as she was worrying about, it was another matter altogether to prove it.

Sheena thought that he had been really nice and easy to talk to and she felt a lot less stupid when she was leaving than she did when she arrived. He had taken her address and phone number and he would hopefully come and see her later that evening to let her know what he had managed to discover.

Later that day and true to his word Sergeant Phil Anderson came to Sheena's home to speak to her. Tom was at home, but neither of them had spoken since the knife incident and she just brought the policeman in and went straight into the kitchen to talk to him alone without even introducing him to Tom. She had a sly little thought to herself when she went into the kitchen and that thought was that Tom would think she was speaking to the police about him. *Hope he's shaking in his boots* she thought to herself.

Sheena made the Sergeant a cup of tea and he insisted that they should be on first name terms. First of all 'Phil' told her that the doctor wouldn't budge from what he'd originally stated and he had thought that Phil was wasting the time of both of them. He also told her, as she, herself, had told him that the doctor thought that Sheena was nothing more than a hormonal woman trying to find an illogical reason for her mother's death and obviously couldn't accept that she had in fact just died of a heart attack. So that meant that without any other evidence then he couldn't take that particular matter any further.

But he did say that he'd spoken to her father and that although he didn't tell him why he was making enquiries, he'd simply told him that it was just a routine enquiry, but her father knew that it was Sheena herself who had instigated his call. He also said that he could totally understand where she was coming from, because not only was her father incredibly arrogant but there was another woman there that he didn't get introduced to and he got the firm impression that she was more than just a friend. He gave Sheena a description of the woman but she had no idea who it could have been.

Phil asked Sheena who the man was in the other room and she'd told him that it was no one of any importance – just her husband. She raised her eyebrows and shook her head as she said it. He looked puzzled. Another long story she said, but much longer than the one she'd already told him this morning. They both laughed at that and so Sheena showed Phil out. They shook hands as he left but Phil put his other hand on top of hers and looking her directly in the eyes he told her to be sure to get in touch again if anything else arose or even if she just wanted to talk about it further. As Sheena held his gaze she blushed, which embarrassed her, but there was something about the way he looked at her. She wondered if he was being overly sentimental because of her mother's death. But whatever he was doing, it hadn't got her any further with her thoughts. Perhaps she may have to accept that her mother did, in fact, just die. That thought pained her heart. She was angry and hurting and wanted to go back to the previous Monday and take her mother back to her house with her. She was lost and hurt and no one seemed to be able to help her.

CHAPTER 12

Tom had sheepishly asked what the police had wanted but she didn't answer, she totally ignored him. She didn't want to speak to him and so she didn't. She made a meal for the children and Tom glared at her, both his temper, and his frustration were showing at him not being in charge and Sheena's apparent indifference was clear and so he just stormed out again, banging the door behind him. She didn't know whether he'd gone to work or to the pub, and what's more she didn't care, but she loved the way the tables had been turned between them.

He was the one who was afraid now and that felt great. All Tom had to do now was to be gone after the funeral. Then she would contact a solicitor to get divorce proceedings under way and make legal arrangements for maintenance to be paid to her. Tom earned a good wage, although he always kept a tally of her spending, or thought he did, making sure there was enough left for him for beer and card games at work. He thought she didn't know, but she did. She was more than a bit worried about how she would manage financially after the divorce, but whatever struggles she would have to cope with, life would still be so much better without him and she was greatly relieved that things had changed and changed for good. He might have been the one who earned the money, but she was the one who managed it, the little he gave her. Yes, she would cope well without him.

She picked Lucy up to take her for her bath while Andy and Susie were eating their tea. They both loved bath time. Sheena held her arm around Lucy's back to support her as she soaped her little body, she wasn't able to support herself properly yet, but almost, and as Sheena was holding her, Lucy was kicking and splashing in the water. They played with a plastic duck and Sheena felt normal for the first time in a long time and she loved it. As she was bathing Lucy she could hear Andy and Susie playing, fighting, laughing, generally doing all the things that children always do. Then suddenly it struck her that the children were always quiet when Tom was at home. She never heard the giggles or the fighting or even the singing (Andy still liked having the radio on) when Tom was in, she hadn't previously realised that. She had thought that the children had been protected from their fights over the years but it was painfully obvious now that they were probably much more aware than she had given them credit for and that made her feel really sad.

She wrapped Lucy up in a huge towel then finally, after cuddling her lovely little body; she put her night things on and took her to get her last feed of the evening. When she went in to the living room Andy had a cup of tea made for her and a ham sandwich. It almost made her cry as he gave her a big hug telling her not to cry, that he would look after her. She felt truly blessed with her children and she was sure that Tom going would be good for all of them, maybe not in the short time while the children adjusted, but the fact that she now knew they were not immune to what had been going on, she was sure that in the long term it had to be good for them.

However, as she held Lucy for her final feed of the day she was still truly, truly disappointed that she had to give her formula milk from a baby cup. She had tried many times since that day to get her to take a bottle, she felt that she would get more comfort from sucking a teat on a bottle, but she had a mind of her own and if she couldn't have mum, then she didn't want a bottle. But the two of them still got the cuddles. She always had time for cuddles, for the children anyway!

The children were fast asleep when Graham and Iain came to see her to let her know about their visit with their father. Finally they seemed to see their father in the same way as Sheena did. They told her that he really was chasing as many women as he could, he'd even tried to 'chat up' Graham's mother-in-law, which was the main thing that Graham wanted to talk to him about, especially as his mother-in-law was an elderly widow who didn't want any attention from men and certainly not the kind of attention their father was plainly seeking, they'd also heard that he was making a nuisance of himself in local pubs. And it wasn't the grief, no, they were sure of that, no it was his sense of freedom, as though he was going to do whatever he wanted with whoever he wanted.

Sheena then filled them in about going to the police and confirmed that they had said much the same thing to her. But the police also thought something was very unnatural about their father, but if he kept to his story then there would be nothing they could do. Then Sheena suddenly remembered about the bottles of tablets that her father had dramatically removed from the coffee table emptying them out. She said that the police officer, Phil, had said that she should get in touch with him if anything else occurred to her so she would ring him and tell him about the tablets. It still didn't mean that they could do anything further, but she thought that she should at least tell him.

They were both pleased to see that Sheena seemed to be a bit better herself, but she didn't tell them that the reason for that was because she had almost stabbed her husband, they *would* think then that she was hormonal. Come to think of it, that could have been a further excuse on her side if she had actually stabbed him. That thought amused her.

Iain then continued regarding the visit to their father saying that when they had been at their father's house, mother's house, Sheena interjected, "Okay, okay," they agreed. They told Sheena that there was a woman in the house when they called and he was playing her love songs. "Love songs," Repeated Graham bitterly. "When did he ever play mum love songs? It was sickening. He was playing 'If I Said You Had a Beautiful Body' to her and she was lapping it up. They were sitting together on the sofa hands all over each other and kissing like silly teenagers, drinking what looked like sherry together," he added. "When we asked who she was he said that she was his girlfriend and if they didn't like it they knew what they could do."

They still couldn't really get their heads around the idea that he had done something deliberate to cause their mother's death, but thought that maybe he had withheld her Angina tablets when she was having an attack, that in itself was bad enough, but to think that he actively 'did' something was just too much. Although they did now agree that Sheena had been right about his general attitude.

Sheena hadn't heard any of what they'd been saying beyond the bit about her father and some woman sitting on the sofa kissing, cuddling and drinking. For the colour had completely drained from her face, for what she saw in her mind's eye was the grotesque, repulsive, obscene caricature sight of her father sitting atop her dead mother's body with some woman. She couldn't see the woman in her mind's eye, just a female with no features. But she didn't need to see her features to despise both of them. She could clearly 'see' the two of them laughing together and totally ignoring her mother's open eyes looking up at them with a pained expression etched across her face due to the weight that was bearing down on her. It disgusted her, it was beyond description, what she was 'seeing' was beyond the comprehension of any normal human being and it was causing her great distress.

As her brain swirled around she became light-headed and fell forward like a rag doll unable to remain upright, and both Graham and Iain, who had still been talking to her, quickly caught hold of her before she fell completely and noticing her tear filled distressed eyes they realised what had actually happened to her and the distressing state their sister was in. They had been so shocked themselves by their father's attitude that they had momentarily forgotten the toll all this was taking on their sister.

They tried to hold on to her and managed to stop her falling completely, but her body was limp. They brought her a little of the whisky that was left from her session with Iain and they sat either side of her until she had calmed enough to be able to support herself. And when she could finally speak, it wasn't to decry her father's behaviour; no, all she kept saying as she looked wide-eyed from one brother to the other was 'the sofa' not 'the sofa'.

When she was more settled she asked what else had happened so then they also realised that she hadn't been listening properly so they relayed their conversation to her again. Finally, she was convinced that they also thought that there were too many suspicious things surrounding her mother's death and for Sheena, the very fact that they actually thought that she might have good reason to doubt the details of her mother's death and that she wasn't just 'hormonal' was a reassuring feeling. They all then agreed that they didn't know what more they could do to find out exactly what had happened but they were going to do their best. They were all hoping that maybe Sergeant Anderson would prove to be of some help.

After Graham and Iain had left, Sheena was extremely tired, she had no idea, where Tom was, and cared even less, as she looked forward to finally putting her head on the pillow after a particularly distressing day. So her heart sunk as she heard his key in the door. He wanted to speak to her telling her that it was important. Hoping that he was going to say that he was leaving she sat down to listen. But what he said was almost unbelievable.

He started off with, "I want to let you know that I forgive you for the way you behaved today. I am prepared to put it down to the fact that you are not your normal self after the death of your mother." His words were coming out slow and stilted, but wide-eyed she listened on. "I want to tell you that I love you and that I know you love me. So I'm prepared to give you another chance. What do you say?" She was quiet for a while in order to contemplate a suitably humiliating answer to his question. He forgave her did he? Hmmm... She wanted to know what his thoughts were on the fact that he'd hit her. In response he said that he was sorry for that. So undeterred, she thought that she would push that a bit further. So she quietly enquired if he also wanted *her* to forgive him for hitting her. "Yes," he replied enthusiastically. "I want us to start again, get back to how things used to be when they worked so well. When all this business with your mother is finished we need to be able to get back to normal."

Still remaining hypocritically calm, she decided again to push him a little bit more. So she told him that *maybe* she would forgive him hitting her if he promised never to do it again – she lied, but he apparently believed her. However, his reply was even more shocking. "You can't ask me to *never* hit you again. I *have* to be able to hit you if you need it." *Hmmm…* She thought again, her anger rising but still somehow managing to display an air of false timidity; it was time to put him straight.

She informed him in a surprisingly very calm and controlled manner that as far as she was concerned, nothing had changed since their fight earlier that day. She added much more venomously now that she hated him, loathed him in fact and that if he didn't move out soon then she would carry out her very real threat to tell everyone about his 'dirty little secret.' She stood up to go to bed ignoring him, but he caught hold of her arm and began pleading pathetically with her. "But I love you. Look," he said, "you can see how much I love you, here's the proof." And suddenly grabbing hold of her hand he placed it firmly on his penis in order for her to feel his erection as if somehow that were to prove his love. She felt sickened but suddenly she had a wicked idea.

She rubbed her hand gently over his penis – through his trousers – and said mockingly, "Oh yes so you do!" As she was rubbing him she was also slowly pushing him backwards and he was getting more and more excited, grinning manically at her.

"You see," he said with much more excitement than he would have had if he'd known in advance what her true intentions were. "You see how much I love you?" She nodded in mock agreement and as she was 'caressing' his penis his right hand moved forward as though he was about to grab hold of her breast. But speaking slowly, softly and steadily to him she gently, seemingly playfully, moved his arm out of the way. "No," she'd said mockingly teasing him; "let me 'please' you for a change." She told him to put his hands behind his back, which, grinning that maniacal grin of his, he did, and she slowly edged forward whilst he moved backwards. When he was finally up against the wall she put her left arm against his neck, but gently at first, and used her full weight to push him firmly against the wall. She informed him that she was about to give him the best orgasm he'd ever had. His eyes lit up seemingly unaware of the significance of her statement, for those were the exact words that he had used on her before he started his 'special' sessions. Pressing slightly more firmly on his neck and using her body to keep him still, whilst smiling sarcastically at him, she undid his trouser belt and then his zip until his pants fell to the floor.

She looked into his eyes and the delight in his eyes bore testament to what she believed, and that was that, he couldn't see the hate, sarcasm and vitriol in hers. So she slowly put her hand inside his underpants and onto his bare penis and testicles cupping them in her hand but still gently – for the moment. He was breathing heavily and shouting out ridiculously, "Yes, oh yes. Oh I knew you loved me." Then using all her limited strength she pushed as hard as she could on both his neck and his body until he was firmly trapped, then she gripped his genitals as hard as she could, digging her finger nails into his flesh and twisting until he screamed. He screamed, he yelled, he cursed, he swore and he cried. Sheena felt so triumphant when she saw tears streaming down his face!

Her hold had in fact only lasted a few seconds as he'd managed to kick out at her knocking her to the floor and thereby freeing himself, cursing her as he did so, and she was forced then to release her grip. He dropped to his knees and the tears, *real tears* tumbled down his face as he nursed his injured genitals.. Then, sitting on the floor where he had knocked her, she told him calmly, much more calmly than she actually felt, "*Well that is how much I love you.* Now get out and don't come back unless you want more of the same." She then added loudly and defiantly. "Don't come to my mother's funeral and don't make any more contact with me unless it is through solicitors. I will let you know when you can see the children. Now give me your keys and go." She spat all the words at him with all the venom and hatred that she had left in her. She had to leave him in no doubt that there would never be any way back for him, because after all that had happened he was still delusional enough to believe that she loved him. She had to make it clear that he must never again try to 'prove' his love. He left still with tears in his eyes for his damaged genitals and walking none too steadily. And so after thoroughly scrubbing her hands to remove every last trace of him she went to bed happy.

CHAPTER 13

The day before the funeral, Sheena spoke with Graham on the phone telling him that Tom had moved out and taken the car with him so she had no means of transport now. She didn't want to go into a lot of detail so simply told him that it had been coming for some time. He didn't sound surprised but was concerned that Tom going at just this moment in time might be too much for her to cope with. She told him not to worry about that because she felt it actually made coping with the following day would be easier now because she had one less worry to trouble her. She told Graham that all the arrangements had been confirmed by the undertaker and that they should all meet up at her mother's house, she emphasised 'mother's' at about 11.00 the following morning, as the funeral cortege would be leaving from their mother's at 11.30. She also said how worried she was that they would never find out exactly how their mother died, because in little less than twenty-four hours there would be no way to prove anything. Graham then added rather sceptically, "That's if there's anything to prove of course." Sheena was livid. She had been so sure that he had been thinking along the same lines as her. His thinking appeared to be though, that while everything doesn't exactly 'add up' and his father was one of the worst men he knew, he still couldn't accept that was *that* bad that he would deliberately kill their mother.

Sheena was taken aback. Not only because he thought she was wrong, but also because that was the first time the word 'kill' had been mentioned. But he argued with her that although she hadn't used that word herself, it was what she had been thinking. She was getting upset and was about to cut the call short when catching the change in her voice, Graham told her that he just wasn't sure either way and that he respected her opinion, but if they were never going to be able to prove it, then he thought that maybe she should try to convince herself that she was wrong or she would be tormented all her life with the 'what ifs'. Which, he said is what he was trying to do. That made sense and she settled a bit, but she told him that she was going to have one last word with Sergeant Anderson to see if anything more could possibly be done before the funeral. Graham thought that was a good idea, but asked her to promise him that she would then finally accept that their mother's death was just 'unusual' if the police couldn't prove otherwise. "For the sake of your sanity and for the sanity of your children," he added. Out loud and spoken, she agreed with him. But inside and silent she knew different, she knew her father had at best, not prevented her mother from dying and at worst, directly caused her death.

She called Phil and they met unofficially for coffee and they talked for hours. She looked at him and thought how easy he was to talk to, how conversation flowed between them in a way that it never had between her and Tom. But there was still nothing he could do to help her. "I will have one last go at your father and see if I can trick him into telling me something that might incriminate him," he told her. But he also added that she shouldn't get her hopes up as her father was extremely cunning and knew that they had absolutely nothing to go on.

He told her that he would also try talking to the doctor again and that he would come to see her later that evening to let her know what had happened. Sheena knew that there was no hope really and that he was really doing everything he could. He was a really nice person who was trying really hard to help her, but deep down she knew that he wasn't going to get anywhere.

Phil called to see her that evening as promised and she was a little taken aback, but pleasantly, when he kissed her cheek on greeting her. She put her hand to her face where he had kissed her, it was a soft, tender, but warm kiss which barely touched her skin, just brushed it really, but she realised with a start that she had never been kissed like that by a man before. How did she get to be a married woman and mother of three children and never experience a tender kiss? she wondered.

Her look of amazement and wonder obviously wasn't lost on Phil. "I'm sorry, was that out of order?" he said with a puzzled expression on his face. "It sort of felt natural to me; I mean we are friends, aren't we? And surely that's how friends greet each other?" He was panicking now and rambling. She laughed lightly and told him no, that it wasn't 'out of order' but asked if it was a kiss that was bringing good news with it. Unfortunately he shook his head. He told her that the doctor was tired of him asking the same questions over and over again because as he said he was only going to be giving the same answers over and over again.

"As for your father, well he's a cool customer. I would stake my reputation on the fact that he had a more than just a hand in your mother's death, I would go so far as to say he planned it all along." This news left Sheena totally distraught and confused; it was only hours now before the cremation and then any evidence that might otherwise be found would be gone. She had never really considered 'planned' before and that idea brought with it her other thoughts that maybe her mother knew what was going to happen. This was too much. But Phil continued, "I even brought him into the station for questioning, hoping that it might unnerve him being there, being questioned in a police station, but it didn't and my Inspector was not pleased that I had done that without approval."

Sheena thanked him for what he had done. No one could have done more she assured him, before adding, with her heart saddened, that it looks as though he's just going to get away with it. She got up in readiness to open the door for him to leave and she was thinking that this would probably be the last time she would see him when he asked if he could see her after the funeral. Not in any official capacity... His words trailed off, unsure of her reaction. She told him that she didn't think that was a good idea. Her children needed stability and reassurance with losing their grandmother and then their father not being here. She added that she was not ready for anything like that. In fact, she didn't really think she'd ever be ready for anything like that but she didn't add that. She was quite sure that all men were nice in the beginning when they were trying to attract a woman, but that they quickly changed afterwards and she couldn't really see how those opinions would change no matter how much she may think that she liked him.

He looked deflated, and to be honest she, herself, felt deflated, but she really was far too scared of men to get involved again. She didn't like sex, in fact the very thought of it terrified her, and she knew all too well that sex was *so* important to men. So when he asked if she was sure, with a sort of hurt puppy dog look in his eyes, she just smiled and said that she was. But she thanked him for all that he had done and again he kissed her on the cheek as he was leaving, and again it was nice! She did agree however, to accept his home phone number from him in case anything more came to light that he could help with. He stressed that he meant she should call even if it was only for him to listen to her worries. "Sometimes talking worries through lessens them," he said.

She thanked him and closed the door behind him. And leaning her back against it she wished that it could have been different. She was sure he was sincere in liking her, but she didn't know why, she let out a heavy sigh and tried to put him to the back of her mind for it was going to be a very stressful day that lay ahead for her and she was truly dreading it. She didn't think that she would be able to sleep that night but she would have to try. The thought that she would never find out for sure how or why her mother died would haunt her forever, whether she was asleep or awake.

She went to bed and she talked to her mother asking her, as though she was in the room with her, pleading with her to let her know what had happened to her. She just needed a sign. But, of course, nothing came. She took her mother's cardigan from under her pillow and devoured the smell of her. She felt incredibly close to her and warm and comfortable. She slept for a while, but again only fitfully.

CHAPTER 14

Sheena arrived at her mother's house at 11.00am as arranged and the first person to greet her was Iain, he looked resplendent in his dress uniform and she told him so. He asked cautiously, looking around, where Tom was and Sheena held her head high and said with an air of finality that he'd gone. Iain smiled at her and nodded his approval and he put his arms around her protectively. But as she embraced him, what she saw over his shoulder instantly stopped in her tracks. For straight ahead of her was her 'mother' her back was to her but there was no mistaking that it *was* he mother. Her hair was the same, her build was the same, and her height was the same. She *was* the same. Why is no one saying anything she wondered? Iain had sensed a change in her body, she had suddenly started to hold herself stiff and as he released her he looked round to see what she was staring at.

What she could see was Graham's face as he was talking to her mother, his speech was obviously animated as he was smiling and gesticulating with his arms. Why was it only her that thought everything was unusual? She wanted to move forward, but she couldn't. She wanted her 'mother' to turn around and speak to her, but she just continued talking to Graham. She couldn't move, she wanted to rush forward, but she couldn't move. She could feel her eyes well up with tears.   She had prepared herself she thought, for everything today; she had steeled herself against what she had thought was anything and everything possible, but not this. Her mind racing and her feet felt like lead weights on the floor she just stood there bolted to the spot, panicking. She looked around the room, her father was talking to no one, and Sheena looked urgently to see if her father's 'woman' was there, but she couldn't see anyone that she didn't know. Perhaps she's in the kitchen she thought idly to herself, but she didn't care enough to go and look, all she wanted to do was to go to her 'mother'.

However, when Iain realised what Sheena's was looking at with her head frantically searching the room for answers he quickly put her worries to rest, and just as Iain was going to tell Sheena who she was seeing, Graham looked up and noticed that she was staring at them. He called over to her and to her immense relief her 'mother' turned around. It wasn't her mother at all it was her mother's younger sister, their Aunt Joyce.

Sheena hadn't realised that she had been holding her breath until she let it go. Graham explained to her that he had been in contact with their mother's family in Scotland and out of the many relatives living in Scotland only their Aunt Joyce could come, money as always was tight, but their Aunt Joyce had been closer to their mum than any of their other relatives and had been determined to find the money, determined to come to say goodbye. Sheena had met her Aunt Joyce many times when she herself was just a child. She used to go with her mother on the overnight bus to Scotland for holidays. The boys had always stayed home with their dad. There was no room for all of them to stay at their Aunt's house and it was always good for her mother to spend time with her family, although it only happened about once a year, or maybe even less. But as soon as Aunt Joyce began speaking to her and embraced her she realised her mistake and felt rather silly.

Graham quickly told Sheena that he had called the family because he knew that she had made all the other arrangements, which neatly got Sheena out of trouble for having forgotten to do that. He had also organised some food for everyone after the funeral. Sheena hadn't given a thought to *anything* for 'after the funeral'. All she had been able to think about was 'the' funeral.

Aunt Joyce wanted a quiet word with Sheena. She had an anxious look on her face, like that of a woman who wanted answers, and wanted them now! "I don't know what you think Sheena, but all this is not right. Your mother would have wanted to be buried for one thing, and although we didn't get the chance to be together often, we wrote to each other regularly so I know your mother wasn't happy, in fact she was down-right miserable at times, but she certainly wasn't ill, well not that ill anyway! What exactly happened?" She didn't wait for an answer, she just continued. Sheena waited to be able to get a word in! "Whatever has happened I can tell you now, for certain that your father has had a hand in this." She quickly tried to quell what she was expecting to be Sheena's protestations, raising her arms as if to brush aside supposed protestations, and so she was surprised when Sheena told her that she thought the same thing. But Sheena also told her that there was nothing to be done about it, because there was no proof that it was anything other than a natural death. She explained how much she had tried to find out otherwise but all her questioning and enquiring had got her nowhere.

Aunt Joyce's reply was blunt and to the point. "Your father's a Bastard and always has been a Bastard." She was irate and agitated, and Scottish irate agitated at that! Which despite the terror going on inside Sheena's body made her smile; she thought how much her mother would have agreed with her, as of course did Sheena. It was also uncanny that the two sisters looked, thought, and even acted so much alike. Sheena liked her Aunt Joyce.

Then a more sombre mood overtook Sheena as the funeral cars arrived outside the house. Sheena looked at the coffin and found it impossible to think of her mother inside there. The image in her head was the one in the funeral parlour and she didn't want to dwell on that. Everyone must have gotten into the cars and been driven to the church, but Sheena didn't really know what had actually happened or how they got there, because one minute she was looking out of the window staring at the coffin and the next thing she knew was that she was standing in the church sat the end of a pew. Her brothers were standing beside her. The pallbearers moved the coffin past her and placed it on a stand up near the front of the church. Sheena couldn't take her eyes off it. There was a lot of noise, a lot of people making noise but she didn't know who was making the noise or why. People just kept on talking. She remembered thinking; why don't they just shut up? But she was quite sure that she didn't actually say that.

Sheena's eyes and mind were completely on the coffin, nothing else. Her mother was in there, was all she could think over and over again. Her mother was in there. She wondered if she was still cold or if they had wrapped her up. She could 'see' her eyes and they were smiling at her. They weren't the eyes that were stone cold in the coffin though; they were the eyes that held contact with her own when she saw her the night before she died. Nice eyes, loving eyes, *warm* eyes.

They must have warmed her up she thought, feeling quite relieved with that thought. And so she just stood there while all sorts of people were making noises! Then all of a sudden, the coffin started to move, and big red curtains were drawing across to hide it. NO! NO! NO! A voice inside her head was shouting at her. She could see her mother and she didn't want to go. Sheena felt her own body float towards her to stop her from moving. "They're going to burn me," her mother was saying. "Sheena, don't let them burn me, please?" She was begging her to save her. Sheena floated nearer, her legs not moving; just her body floating, she was going to save her mother and she going to stop the curtains from closing. "I won't let them burn you mum," she shouted out loud as she floated nearer and nearer to stopping to the coffin.

Suddenly and firmly, Sheena was pulled sharply back to her seat. And she went down with a thud. Graham had hold of her and she was really, really annoyed with him. She was shaking and trembling as she tried her hardest to pull free but he wouldn't let her go. He had her head buried in his chest and she struggled to free herself. She was breathing rapidly and frantically, but she was so tired, so worn out that slowly but surely she slowed her breathing down and her body became more relaxed. When Graham was sure that Sheena was more settled he tenderly cupped her tear stained face in his 'big brother' hands and gently lifted her face until they were eye to eye.

Sheena could see the pain etched on her brother's face. She could see his grave concern for her, his little sister. She wanted to tell him not to worry, that she was okay, but she just lowered her tear stained eyes, she couldn't get the words out, she didn't want to talk, not to anyone, she just wanted to be left alone with her grief, such was her despair. But Graham *was* worried for his sister, for he'd realised, probably for the first time, that this had all been too much for her. She was too vulnerable, too emotional, they had all piled too much responsibility on to her, and he felt especially guilty for that and now he worried for her sanity. Sheena turned her head, still cupped in her brother's tender hands, towards the coffin and she saw that the curtains were closed. Her mother was gone.

Her eyes rose up again and they pleaded with Graham for an explanation. She whispered softly, despairingly, to him that she'd been so close to stopping them from burning her. She begged him to explain to her why he'd stopped her, why he'd prevented her from saving their mother, but even as she was saying that, her mind was telling her that she was being ridiculous, of course her mother couldn't have called out to her, perhaps she was losing her mind, and at that moment it certainly felt as if she was. But she *had* heard something, she was positive that she *had* heard something, someone was shouting and she now wanted to know who it was and what they'd said, she was getting frantic. But Graham just held her tight, hushing her, telling her that everything was okay. But it wasn't okay, she had nothing now, she was gone; her lovely mother was now gone forever.

Iain had moved around so that one brother was now either side of her and he put his arm protectively around her, they were trying to calm her, trying to get her to sit upright and concentrate while they explained what had happened. But she didn't want to sit up, she didn't want to move, but she did want, and did need, someone to hold her. Her mother couldn't hold her, not any more, but she needed desperately to be held.

Graham just held her, rocking her back and forth like an ailing child, waiting for her to be calm enough to talk to. When she was finally more settled he eased his gentle hold of her and held her hand, then step by step he explained that she hadn't been anywhere near the coffin or the curtains, in fact she hadn't moved from her seat at all and that it wasn't until she screamed out and was *about* to go towards the coffin that he had stopped her.

She was now totally confused and her eyes were darting from one brother to another asking questions that she seemed unable to voice. Graham shook his head and told her as kindly as he could, that the only person shouting anything was in fact

141

her, that she had been the one shouting out for them 'not to burn her'. Sheena though was convinced that he was wrong. If the sound of her mother calling out was only going on inside her head, then surely the sound of someone shouting 'not to burn her' was also only inside her head. Surely she hadn't actually been so silly, behaved so badly. She was so terribly, terribly distressed. However, when she studied the tormented look on her brother's face, she knew for certain that he was telling her the truth.

He continued his explanation, "You interrupted the service and everyone was very worried about you." He tried to get her to understand what he was saying without her breaking down again so he reminded her that it was only a week ago that she was a nursing mother and now she'd become a grieving daughter. "It's all been too much for you. We've all put too much on you. But," he told her confidently, "somehow though, through all your own troubles you managed to organise all of this." He spread his arm out, indicating that she'd organised everything in the church they were sitting in. "And I don't know how you managed to get that lovely coffin, and it really was beautiful. I find it hard to believe that you got one so good for the price you told me, but obviously you did, so you can be rest assured, and pleased with yourself that you've done mum proud. She really would be so proud of you."

He then implored her to go a little easier on herself adding that they also needed to go a lot easier on her. He tried to explain about his worries as tentatively as he could. "I know you don't like anyone mentioning 'hormones' to you, but you have to realise the dramatic change in your life over this last week and the fact is that your hormones will have played a big part in that."

Sheena couldn't really fathom any of what Graham had been saying to her. She was sure, so sure that she'd been almost on top of the coffin. Could she really have imagined that? Perhaps she was going a little bit mad she thought idly to herself. Still, she'd managed a teary smile when he'd told her that her mum would be proud of her, she so hoped she would be, however, she was quite sure that the comment about 'the lovely coffin' had been said very much 'tongue-in-cheek' because although she hadn't noticed the actual coffin herself, she had seen photographs of it and it had been the cheapest, plainest one she could get. But she was now truly exhausted and so she happily allowed Graham and Iain together to support her as they left the church with her mind still struggling to take in all of what Graham had said.

She turned back suddenly when she remembered that the coffin was in fact gone and she wanted to know where it had gone, but they told her to relax, and that it was finally all over now. But Sheena didn't want it to be 'all over', and she didn't want to 'relax'. What a stupid thing to say to her, why would she want to relax? The thought passed through her mind that perhaps it was her brothers who were going mad. She still wanted desperately to go to the Crematorium but they both insisted that it was best if she didn't. She was furious that they should be deciding what was 'best for her', as far as she was concerned, what was 'best for her' was to be near her beloved mother, to just be close to her until the end of her journey.

But she knew deep down that they were concerned for her, and that fact was emphasised when they held her closely and lovingly, as they told her that she had to try to just remember her mother for the good times they'd shared together, the love they had for each other. They were trying their damnedest to lighten the whole mood with Graham laughing lightly as he said, "We knew you were mum's favourite and to be honest, we liked that, because mum needed you, a daughter, as much as you needed her, and you know that she wouldn't want you to be this upset, she would want you to think of your children. Then as though to lighten what was a really dark time he laughed and pointed to Iain saying, "Mind you, this one, he said pointing to his brother, was jealous when you were both vying for her attention as children, but he grew out of it. You did grow out of it, didn't you Iain?" he said with a mock look of concern and doubt on his face, and then he affectionately wrapped his arm around his brother's shoulder as he spoke, and Sheena felt comfort from the warmth of the camaraderie that was between them all.

Deep, deep down Sheena knew that what they were saying to her they were saying for the best of reasons, but she hurt too, too much. The pain was so raw in her heart that she couldn't even think of her children. She felt like a child herself who desperately needed her mother.

Graham and Iain took Sheena to the pub where they had arranged for some tea and sandwiches to be served in a room away from the bar. Feeling calmer and promising herself that she was going to be strong, she looked around the room and realised that a lot of her mother's friends and neighbours were there and she was pleased that so many people had come to say goodbye to her mum. A lot of people spoke to her and said how sorry they were, and talked to her about how nice a person her mum was. She knew they were trying to be kind but she really didn't want to talk to anyone. She found a corner away from everyone else and sat down with a cup of tea. With her head bowed she just sat there alone with her thoughts, she was exhausted and wanted to get home and go to bed. She didn't want to smile to well-meaning people and make small talk.

It's all too late now she thought. If her father had had anything to do with her mother's death, then it's too late. She had gone now totally, no more chance to get any evidence, she would have to accept that she did all she could and let it go. She would never know what happened to her. That thought broke her heart. And silently she whispered 'sorry' to her mother. How would life go on now? What would she do and how would she ever cope? Who would there be to give her a hug? Who could she laugh and joke with? She had so many, many questions but absolutely no answers. She sat quietly in a corner of the room to contemplate things for herself.

CHAPTER 15

Her silent contemplation was suddenly and dramatically over when she was suddenly gripped tightly by her forearm, so tightly in fact that it hurt. Someone was dragging her off the chair and into another, room. Her feet hardly touched the floor so hard was he pulling her. She looked up and it was her father. He pushed her down hard onto another chair, she looked around desperately for help, but the room was empty, they were the only people in there. Without letting go of her arm, he used his free arm to pull another chair up close to her, so close that his face was just inches away from hers, his breath hitting her face. "What sort of a spectacle was that?" He shouted angrily at her still holding her arm so tightly that she wanted to scream with the pain of it, but perhaps it was the shock, or just the fact that she didn't want to plead with him to release her, she didn't even want to talk to him that she said nothing, just stared at him in amazement. "Eh! Come on tell me then. What sort of a fool do you think you have just made of yourself?"

She couldn't think what he was talking about. She couldn't think what she had done to cause him to be so angry. But she replied sheepishly that she was sorry. "You're a bloody grown woman for God's sake. Whatever possessed you?" She still didn't know what he meant, but he'd made her feel like she was ten years old again, and so like a whimpering child she said she was sorry for whatever it was that she'd done to upset him so much. I'm talking about your bloody stupid outburst in the church, telling everyone 'not to burn her'. I've never heard anything so ridiculous in all my life, 'not to burn her', he repeated shaking his head.

She then realised that what Graham had told her must have been true. She hadn't realised that everyone in the church had heard her, including she supposed, the vicar. She felt hugely embarrassed and was again about to apologise, beg his forgiveness even, when suddenly she really did feel the presence of her mother around her. There was no doubting it this time either, because she could feel it really strongly. She could hear her mother encouraging her to 'stand up to him' not to let him bully her. She knew that she was hearing her inside her head not out loud, but she *was* hearing her, in fact she could actually smell her, that undoubted perfumed smell that only her mother had, it was on her cardigan that she took to bed at night and it was in her nostrils now. It boosted her confidence enormously.

She snatched her arm out of his hold and held her head high; she'd moved her arm so suddenly that it had taken him, for a moment, by surprise allowing her to free herself from his grip. She told him that she was ashamed of nothing, before quickly adding that no, she didn't mean that because she was in fact ashamed of something. He'd been about to shout back at her but changed his mind when she had again said sorry. But she continued by saying that it was *him* she was ashamed of. She spat those words out so hard that the actual spit from her mouth went over his face. He used his sleeve to wipe his face, but still she continued saying that he was a lousy father and that he'd been a lousy husband before adding that she knew that he'd killed her mother. There she had said it and she had said it out loud and she was so glad that she had said it. His face was going purple with rage and then suddenly he exploded with laughter...

"Now we're getting to the bottom of it. Now you're admitting what's been on your mind. But you didn't have the bottle to face me and ask me yourself did you? No you had to send your little policeman around to try to scare me. Well I've scared off much bigger things than him and it would have taken more than him to 'make me talk'." He laughed again that deep, guttural belly laugh that so disgusted her. Isn't that what they say in the films? Leave him to me 'I'll make him talk.' You're pathetic Sheena. You're a grown woman, but really you're just a child. You don't even have as much fight in you as your mother had."

He'd stood up and turned away from her with those words, ringing in her ears, ready to leave, but those words cut her to the quick. She was getting stronger and braver by the minute and so now she stood up and *she* pulled at his arm to turn him around to ask him the question directly, before adding pointedly that she didn't think he was man enough to tell her the truth. She was standing tall and proud, with a sense of bravado that she'd had no idea she possessed, as she threw the words angrily at him.

Had he killed her mother? She wanted, demanded to know what he'd done. There followed a long silence between them. He was staring hard at her, seemingly deep in thought, it was as though he was wondering whether or not to tell her. She hoped, no she prayed, that he was going to say calmly and honestly that no, he didn't kill her. That he'd sat and nursed her all morning, that he'd cared for her and that he'd done everything he could to help her. Her heart was thumping loud in her chest, but still she felt strong. She felt secure. She had her mother helping her.

"Okay", he said, "you want the truth, you get the truth. But you have to hear *all* the truth. Are you capable of hearing all the truth Sheena?" He had turned his head slightly to the side with a look of intrigue on his face, daring her, challenging her to say no, But Sheena told him that there was nothing he could say to her that she hadn't already imagined. Nothing could be worse than not knowing, of just imagining what had happened she said in a now falsely confident voice.

"All right then." He said. His dark evil looking eyes were staring hard at her, as though he was now daring her to hurry him, to ask him to 'go on then' but she wasn't going to do that, she wasn't going to give him the satisfaction of that. He had to just tell her. He brought his eyes right up close to hers and with a smirk on his face he said "Yes, Yes he hissed defiantly. I killed your mother and there is nothing you or anyone else can do about it. Do you want to know how I killed her? Do you? His voice rising all the time with each word, is that what you need to know Sheena, is it?" She put her hand up to her mouth, gasped and staggered backwards, she really hadn't wanted to hear that, and he was getting such a thrill out of telling her. Such a sickening thrill that she could see it in his eyes and now she didn't want to hear any more. Yet she couldn't turn away either, no, she *needed* to hear more.

Again he laughed at her. He caught her as she was staggering backwards. "Oh no you don't." he said as he pulled her back upright. "I said you had to hear it *all* and you *will* hear it all." She said that she needed to sit back down, and in fact she nearly fell back down, such was the shock of what he'd just said. She also wanted Graham or Iain to come and listen to what he had to say. After all she'd argued, as confidently as she could under the circumstances, they would want to know as well. But he wasn't going to have that, it was *her* he wanted to shock and so he replied "No, this is just going to be between you and me. He was definitely getting a thrill out of her plight. He was bragging, he was bursting to tell someone how clever he'd been, that he'd committed murder and got away with it. She detested that twisted look of self-satisfaction on his face.

It'll be our little secret," he continued. "And if you tell anyone else then I will simply tell them that you are deranged, and there were plenty of witnesses at your mother's funeral to confirm that. Even the doctor thought you were slightly 'loopy' but he put it down to your hormones." He noticed the surprised look on Sheena's face when he mentioned the doctor. "Oh yes, I know all about your trips to the doctor." He said. "Nothing happens around here that I don't get to hear about." Sheena knew that was true. Big Sid, she thought Big Sid, the man that no one crossed, or kept anything from, apparently not even the doctor.

She asked him nervously if the doctor knew that he'd killed her, in effect asking if he was somehow involved in the 'cover up'. Her whole body was now seething with a mixture of anger and incredulity. "Of course he doesn't know, he sneered, but he was easy to fool, oh so easy to fool. If I'd realised how easy it all was, I'd probably have done it years ago, he boasted, I just had to keep telling the doctor how 'grateful' I was and how 'wonderful' and caring *he* was, and then he was ready to believe anything. And I really worked hard on him in the days before your mother died. I put in a lot of hard work actually. I could have won an Oscar for my acting talent!" He'd said that as if he was so terribly, terribly proud of himself. And of course he was.

Sheena still wasn't going to give him the satisfaction of asking for the gory details and when she caught a glimpse of the look he gave her, she knew that he'd realised that. But such was his arrogance that he couldn't wait to tell her all.

"I was sixty last month," he said. That statement perplexed Sheena; she couldn't think how that had anything to do with anything. However, she replied that she knew that, that they

150

had all taken him out for a meal to celebrate his birthday. She wanted to know what that had to do with anything. "Yes," he replied, you all took pity on the 'old man'. Well I didn't want your pity, or a bloody meal. I wanted sex and your mother was always saying no. She was always *too ill*." He emphasised sarcastically. Well after that meal I told her straight. I told her that things were either going to change or she would know all about it. I told her that she had to agree to regular sex, and sex anyway I wanted it, he added salaciously, and I left her in no doubt about what I would do if she refused me even once. It was your mother who was the author of her own downfall; she only had to agree to do what she'd agreed to do when she married me."

Sheena knew he was a bad father and husband, in fact totally bad person, same as he'd always been, but could he really do that. She had another question that she needed an answer to; she wanted to know now if her mother knew that the night before her murder was to be her last, she desperately wanted to know but that was one question that she truly was too scared to ask. Her father however, saw the question in her eyes and he goaded her. "Go on then ask the question. I can see you're dying – pardon the pun – he added disgustingly, to ask. "So ask. I've said that I'll be honest with you and I will." So she asked the question he was waiting for and he laughed triumphantly.

He paused, smiled a black, twisted, sardonic smile and said slowly yet confidently, "Yes she knew. Although to be fair she didn't realise that it would be *that* night until you turned up. And when she did finally realised that I'd especially called you over, well yes, she'd figured out what my plan was so she knew. You should be pleased really." She hated that he was getting so much pleasure out of telling her this, out of her own distress he was getting pleasure. He was almost salivating as he continued triumphantly. "I made sure that you two were alone together on the last night of her life. I made sure that I took Tom into the kitchen to leave you both alone. I also left her eyes open for you to close. I did all that to make her last night special. I did it that way so that she could say goodbye to you. So I'm not totally heartless am I?" The sarcasm in those words was horrendous, for there hadn't yet been any words invented that could provide her with an answer to that one!

Her mind was reeling. He was actually thinking, he actually believed, that he'd done a good thing in letting mother and daughter be alone together for the last time. How she wished she had that knife with her now that she had almost used on Tom for she would surely use it on her father. She now knew for certain that those final words and that final hug from her darling mother had indeed carried a lot of importance. She'd been saying goodbye to her, begging her not to live the life that she herself had lived.

Her heart was weeping, can a heart weep she thought to herself? For an answer she had to say yes, for surely her heart must be weeping blood if not tears, because it was breaking, breaking up into little pieces. She wanted to go. She wanted to run away. She wanted to kill, but mostly she wanted to wake up from this terrible nightmare. But she was rooted to the spot. She was saying a silent prayer to herself that either Graham or Iain would come looking for her. She must have been gone for some time now. Why didn't they come looking for her? She needed help. She needed help now more than she had ever done in her life. But no one came.

Again as she looked at her father, no as she looked at this sub-human being, for he could no longer have the title of 'father', for there was no way that she would ever refer to this 'being' in front of her as father, she could see that all this talk, all this relaying of what he had done, of trying to hurt her, was really thrilling him. She knew in that instant that not only had he done what he said he'd done, he'd actually enjoyed it. And his thrill had only been enhanced by Phil going to see him. She was done, her body slumped forward on the table and she buried her head in her outstretched arms. But he sat so close to her that he lifted her head and again took a firm, painful grip on both her arms in order to so make her sit up, making her look directly at him and listen to his disgusting account of her mother's death.

"I'm not finished yet." He said obviously angry that she'd almost collapsed and might possibly not stay to hear the rest. "I told you that if you wanted to know *anything* then you had to know *everything*." He wasn't about to let her leave.

He then tried to sound serious. Attempted to add gravitas to his words! Sheena could only shake her head in disbelief. "You're a woman Sheena, you have a husband and children, you know what sex is about and about how important it is." He looked at her like he'd looked at her previously when she'd been asking him what had happened on the day that her mother died and astonished as she was, there was no doubting that he was leering at her, his look was sexual and that made her feel really uncomfortable, dirty even. "I bet your Tom wants it every way possible, you know what I mean." He actually winked at her. "Yes" he said, "Your Tom told me that very night in the kitchen how much you enjoyed sex, and I didn't have to push for that information, no, he was proud of it, rightly proud if you ask me, but I have to say I was a little bit surprised, but looking at you now, well I can see what he was getting at." Sheena felt sick; she didn't want the picture in her head of *him* and Tom talking about Tom having sex with her, and both of them getting sick enjoyment out of it.

But still he wouldn't let her go; still he was determined to continue. "She was supposed to die quicker" he said and he looked genuinely surprised by that. "It took a lot longer than I thought. I told her to take her Angina pills. I gave her plenty but she wouldn't take them all, she'd apparently decided that she didn't want to go, that she wasn't ready, so she only took three or four. Even so I still expected her to die much more quickly than she did, but when she wouldn't take them all, well I decided at that point that *I* wasn't ready for her to go yet, that I wasn't going to make it easy for her. She wouldn't take them, she fought me. She could fight if she wanted to you know. Kicking, biting, scratching, anything and everything she could do.

Anyway I had sex with her then, just what you might call 'normal' sex, but I suppose some people would say that I raped her because she didn't want to do it, but personally I don't believe you can rape your wife, do you? I mean she's yours isn't she?" Sheena looked at him incredulously, convinced that she must be truly going mad. She had just imagined her mother talking to her in the church, so surely she must be imagining this. There really couldn't be any other explanation.

She had to dig deep to muster the courage to speak. And so she asked him why he didn't just divorce her, why he'd had to do what he was saying he'd done. Inside she was screaming those words at him, but outside, out loud, they came out as pathetic little whimpering words. He replied calmly that he'd considered that, but had come to the conclusion that all that would take too long and besides he would have to find somewhere else to live and he liked living where he was, and it would have cost him money, and he wasn't about to give her any of his money. Then he then added rather sickly "Besides, I get a lot of sympathy from the women now. I can now tell them, with all honesty, he added with nauseating bad taste, that my wife died suddenly and so then they feel sorry for me, and for the most part sorry enough to have sex with me, but of course I can't push it too far, they're not married to me after all so I have to go a bit steady, still there have been plenty who have wanted to console me up to now and it's only been a week. So look out world here I come! It's even better than I thought it would be."

He still insisted on telling her all of it, she didn't want to hear any more but he still had her in his tight grip and wouldn't let her move and so he continued. "Anyway she took more of the tablets after that. Then I wanted sex in different ways, you know what I mean Sheena don't you? Every way possible, every orifice was used." He actually nudged her knowingly and sickeningly! Sheena couldn't escape his hold, but she closed her eyes tight in an attempt to shut him out, but still he went on.

"Well she said no again, so again I just had to take it, again without her consent. And so it went on he said, in fact it went on for some time, like I said, she could fight if she wanted to, but eventually she gave in. It was a case of some tablets, some sex, some Angina tablets then some sleeping tablets, with *lots* of sex in-between, good sex, and really rough sex. " His face was so sickeningly contorted as he was telling her that he didn't actually look human, but then she wondered if he actually *was* human. Then he brought his face far too close to hers, before adding almost triumphantly. "But it took a long time! She took a big handful of tablets in the end. She could have done that in the beginning couldn't she? Sheena hoped that that question was purely rhetorical and that he didn't actually expect an answer. However, he didn't wait for an answer, he just continued.

"And of course by getting the doctor out to her so often and being such a 'concerned' husband I knew that there wouldn't be a Post Mortem. I'd actually told the doctor that I was so worried that she might die, and therefore if I was all alone with her the police might think I'd not given her any medication and that they might think I'd neglected her. I wasn't going to say 'they might think that I'd murdered her,' that might have made him suspicious, but he assured me that because he was seeing her on a regular basis anyone who needed to know would be told by him how much of a caring husband I was! I told you Sheena, I was a great actor, very convincing!"

He finally released his hold on her and so she stood up, she staggered to stand at first her legs were that wobbly, but then she kicked out in anger and disgust at him, she missed, so she kicked out again hitting him this time, but when she raised her foot to kick him again he just grabbed at her ankle with his hand, and his grip was firm and painful, and it hadn't taken much of his enormous strength to stop her, so she rushed back into the other room holding her hands over her ears, she could hear no more. She was trying, unsuccessfully to block out the sound of his voice, but nothing could block out the pictures in her mind of her poor mother lying beneath this monster of a man and trying to fight him off.

This slightly built woman was up against a monster that was not only determined, but also far too strong for her. She'd have had absolutely no chance of defeating him. The pictures were too vivid and as she ran back into the other room to find her brothers, but still he shouted after her "And now I'm going to start to live. After all I'm only sixty, lots of sex left in me yet! His voice was getting further away but she could still hear him laughing, that deep disgusting belly laugh.

CHAPTER 16

She was forced to run to the bathroom to vomit, she couldn't believe what she'd just heard. Surely no one could get pleasure, not only out of doing what he'd said he'd done, but to get such sickening pleasure out of relaying it all to her. She felt as though she was going to faint, but she had to find Graham and Iain, she just had to tell them what had just happened, maybe they would tell her that she was going mad, she pondered, for she would rather be going mad than for what 'that man' had just told her to be reality.

She found Graham and Iain talking quietly together, she was hyperventilating badly which caused them both to panic when they saw her, and her indisputable distress caused them a great deal of worry and the had to ask her if she needed an ambulance to be called, she was as white as a sheet they'd said, but she shook her head, waving her arms frantically, she was doing anything and everything, bar talking, for she couldn't yet talk, to make sure that they didn't call an ambulance she just needed a little time to calm down enough to speak. Someone brought her some water to drink and she took little sips until she was able to tell them slowly and clearly that their father had just admitted to killing their mother. That he'd just told her that he'd planned it all and that he had killed her. And more than that her mother had known the night before she died what he was going to do.

Graham and Iain took her to one side so that no one else could hear what she was saying, because they were convinced that she must be delirious, that she must have imagined it. But at the same time they could also see from her demeanour that something really serious must have happened. They listened intently to her as she repeated most of what he'd said, she mentioned the tablets, the fact that he'd conned the doctor, and that he'd planned it since his sixtieth birthday and that he wanted a life of his own with plenty of different women involved. But she just couldn't bring herself to tell them about the sex part of it, besides the fact that she didn't think that she could repeat it to them, there was no need for them to hear all of that, nothing could be done, it was all just too horrendous. She wished for all she was worth that she herself could 'un-hear' it wipe it from her memory.

She was also angry with them for not coming to look for her but they said she'd only been gone about fifteen to twenty minutes and that they'd thought she was just getting some fresh air, having some time alone with her thoughts. They felt dreadful that she could have been through such an ordeal. Fifteen or twenty minutes Sheena thought to herself, surely it must have been more like an hour or more.

Their anger was so vivid in their faces that Sheena feared that they would do something stupid, but her fear abated slightly when they said that they should all go to the police and tell them exactly what he'd said. But shaking her head, Sheena told them that it wouldn't be any good, he'd already told her what the answer would be if she did that, if any of them did that. And he was of course right, it would be her word against his and his word would be that she was a hysterical, hormonal woman given to outbreaks of hysteria.

She also added despairingly that too many people would probably agree with him, people whose words would carry some weight, especially the doctor and possibly the vicar. Also there was the indisputable fact that there was no evidence. Her mother was gone, cremated. The tablet bottles were gone, destroyed. Of course now they realised why he'd been in such a hurry to destroy the remains of the tablets the day her mother died. He wanted to make sure that there was no physical evidence left behind. They had to face facts, if they couldn't get the police, or the doctor, or whoever, to organise the absolutely vital Post Mortem before the cremation, then they had absolutely no chance whatsoever of proving anything now.

She was about to ask them if they in fact believed her, for she needed them to believe her, she needed someone to believe her, but again that look of anger and distress on both their faces gave her the answer to that particular question. Then they said the very thing she didn't want to hear, the thing that had crossed her mind right at the outset, right when she began telling them what at happened, and that was that they would sort it themselves, they would take the law into their own hands if necessary and deal with him, they insisted. They were so fired up and angry and that anger was made worse when their father walked in and looked disdainfully at the three of them, daring them to challenge him. Sheena took hold of each of her brother's arms as they were about to get up, they looked at her face, at her distress and they knew that the words her look alone was saying to them were the correct ones.

Ignoring the visual taunts of their father's twisted amoral face, they instead had a discussion regarding what they *could* do. Sheena told them that having listened to her father, who she demanded was no longer to be referred to as father but as Big Sid, telling them that as far as she was concerned he'd forfeited his right to be called 'father'. She was painfully aware of the fact that he would gain another victory if they tried to take the law into their own hands. Even if they were to be successful he would still have managed to ruin their lives even further and then their lovely, lovely mother would never be at peace. They hated it, but they all knew that what she was saying was right. They also doubted that no matter how strong their hatred of him was, and it was about as strong as it could be, whether they would be able to actually 'make him pay' which was the 'polite' way of describing what they all knew were the actions which they were contemplating. They all held on to each other for some time for support, but their grief and frustrations were palpable. Sheena told them that she would speak to Phil again and tell him all that had happened and maybe he would have a legal way of getting justice for their mother.

Graham and Iain both feeling equally distressed took Sheena home. They wanted her to bring the children and come to stay with them. She said that they were already overcrowded with Iain being there, but despite saying that they would make room for them all somehow, Sheena, looking at them both could see their pain, and clearly see that they wanted to do the best thing for her, the right thing for her, they didn't think that she should be alone. But Sheena wanted her children close to her; she needed her children close to her.

They could clearly see the pain etched on Sheena's face and were well aware that she was emotionally fragile, too fragile to be left alone, and if she didn't want, or wasn't able to come to them, then Iain decided that he would stay the night with her, both to help her with the children, but mostly to ensure that she wasn't alone, while Graham went back home. None of them knew what, if anything, they could possibly do next. Or even, if in fact they could do anything at all.

Sheena was glad that Iain was staying because she desperately needed someone to talk to. She wanted to talk about her mother, not her mother's death, but about the mother she loved and missed and she knew that Iain would understand that need in her, and that he would just listen. So she collected the children from her neighbour and between the two of them the children were bathed and made ready for bed. Iain managed a story for Susie, but Andy just wanted to hear about the Army and what it was like to be a soldier. Sheena bathed and caressed her lovely baby Lucy, her mind wandering while she was doing so and she couldn't help but think about Lucy being held in her mother's arms the night before she died and of Susie playing 'ride-a-cock-horse' on her mother's leg. Sheena remembered feeling angry that her mother *wasn't* ill that night. How could she possibly have thought that? She wondered. But in her heart she knew that she wasn't angry with her mother for *not* being ill, she'd been angry with her father, no Big Sid, for worrying her the way he manipulated her visit, and also with Tom for what she'd known would be coming her way later. Sheena put Susie in her own bed to sleep; they would be comfort for each other later.

Sheena and Iain had some supper together and they talked. Or more to the point Sheena talked and Iain listened. She recalled that when she was growing up she was very much a daddy's girl, but her mother didn't object to that as she'd been proud to finally give her husband a much longed for daughter. She'd had many miscarriages but when Sheena was born she felt that their family was complete. And Sheena had been a happy child, probably totally unaware of what was going on in the background of her parent's lives, and so she was happy.

But Sheena was only about Adam's age when she started hearing the rows, no she thought, that was wrong, she *had* heard rows before, but it was at that age when she actually first saw her father strike her mother. Sheena quickly learned to hate him, and life changed then forever. But whatever she did, and whatever teenage tantrums she'd had, her mother was always on her side. She was ashamed to say it now, but she was a selfish teenager who compounded her father's anger with her behaviour and that in turn caused her mother to be struck more often.

She was struggling to speak through her tears and feelings of despair, whilst Iain sat next to her and held her with a comforting arm around her shoulder. She told Iain that she knew that especially as a teenager, she had caused her mum so much heartache that she couldn't bear it, her deep heart-breaking sobs would only allow her words to come out one syllable at a time as her tears were in danger of overcoming her completely. Iain implored her not to put herself through this. He reminded her how happy her mother was in her company, how she adored her grandchildren and how much she loved and was so very, very proud of her. "You were her soul mate sweetheart." He told her gently. "Whenever I spoke to her she was always talking about you. She loved you and you know that's true." Then suddenly, against his will, his tears also flowed.

Sitting upright he tried to lighten the mood, wiping his tears defiantly in front of her he said light-heartedly, "Now look what you've made me do. I've only just finished telling Andy how strong and brave soldiers are." And so in spite of herself she had to smile, he was good medicine she thought to herself. And in her heart of hearts she knew that Iain was right. After her 'horrible' 'teens were over, mother and daughter had indeed become the best of friends and she remembered how proud her mother had been when she saw Sheena in her wedding dress, but she'd never liked Tom, she didn't think he was good enough for her. Well she thought to herself, she was right there. But Tom was gone and her mother was gone and she knew that she would never have either a mother or a husband again. But it was the former fact that devastated her so much. Suddenly and brightly, trying so hard to sound 'normal' she told Iain that their mum would be glad that she'd finally got rid of Tom as she'd never liked him. They finally managed to laugh together, and so after a really long distressing day they went to bed. Sheena wrapped herself round Susie's lovely warm body with her mother's cardigan under her pillow. Tomorrow she would contact Phil to see if he could help them in any way.

The next morning brought the time for Iain to go. He told her that he had things to do before he went back to the Army. Sheena looked at him with a very worried look. But he knew what she was thinking and told her not to worry and that he'd agreed with what had been said on the matter of dealing with Big Sid' and although they would have loved to 'arrange' something, somehow, well that would be bringing themselves *almost* down to his level. No, he said, somehow, in some way, in the future he will slip up and justice will be done at some time. We may have to wait, possibly years, but it will happen he assured her. No, the things he had to do were merely to do with the Army as his compassionate leave was over and he was due back the next day. She told him that she would let him know if Phil was able to come up with anything to help them and she'd added with a smile on her face, that he was glad he'd said 'almost' when talking about Big Sid, because as she'd said before, no one could actually get as low as him. They agreed to keep in close contact and Iain embraced his sister before leaving.

CHAPTER 17

Sheena phoned Phil and asked him to call and see her. When he called he again greeted her with the same slight kiss on her cheek, barely brushing her skin with his lips, but he'd smiled as he did so. He knew that Sheena liked that and also that it embarrassed her and Sheena knew the same thing, but still he did it. She was puzzled, no; more than puzzled by the way he was with her as it was certainly something that she'd never experienced before.

She made them both a cup of tea and Sheena put the cups onto the coffee table and they and they sat down to talk. But Sheena got up again and paced up and down the living room, contemplating what to say to him. She knew that if she wanted police help then she would have to give him *all* the details. She wondered if she could do that, tell a man who effectively was a stranger, but somehow had become a friend, the most intimate of details. She struggled with her inner self. But she also knew that if she wanted official police help, which is definitely what she wanted, then she would have to tell him everything.

As if to help her with her dilemma Phil told her to just take her time, tell it like it is, and pretend I'm not here if it helps. She stopped pacing and looked directly at him while convincing herself that she could do this. She nodded to him. She was ready to tell him. She had to tell him everything no matter what. And so she paced again up and down the living room, drew in a deep breath, and while staring at the carpet she gave him all the details of what had happened the previous day, she left nothing out, including the mention of the tablets which 'Big Sid' had forced her mother to take, effectively giving her an overdose, and she also told him the most difficult part, which was all the terrible, terrible sexual details.

Then she stopped and looked at him, he looked horrified, but he said quietly that she should sit down and drink her tea, maybe even put a bit of Brandy in it if she had some, but in answer to that she just shook her head, before she could sit down she said there was something else she wanted to add. She then told him that she knew it all sounded too much, too far-fetched and that everyone thinks that she's 'lost the plot' so to speak, but what she was telling him was the truth.

She talked about the fact that up until a week ago she'd been a nursing mother and she admitted that that would make her overly emotional and hormonal. Yes, she admitted that all of that was true. But, she added firmly, this was not hormones, this was all fact and she showed him her arms which were badly marked and already discoloured with the severe bruising.

She'd stopped pacing to tell him about her own emotional turmoil, but she'd remained standing, standing in front of him while speaking as clearly and precisely as she could while still trying to contain her very difficult emotions. Trying desperately to calm herself and stay in some way professional, she told him that she really needed to know if there was anything that he could do to help, in an official capacity.

She'd tried so very hard to tell him all of this without being reduced to tears, but unfortunately she was unable to hold them back. Perhaps it was the severe look of horror on his face as she was speaking; perhaps it was the genuine look of concern that got to her, whatever it was she couldn't hold them back. Just when she thought that she was all cried out, the 'taps' were turned on again. Her last words were said through ever increasing tears and so she finally sat down and with her head in her hands and her eyes closed she tried to hide her embarrassment from Phil.

Suddenly she froze and the tears stopped, but she still had her head in her hands and her eyes closed as her brain started to work overtime, with her heart beating rapidly. What had she done? What signs had she given out? What should she do now? How does she alter signals that she didn't even know she'd given out? She didn't know what, but she knew that she had to do something and do it quickly.

The reason for her extreme anxiety was that Phil had moved from his seat, while her head was in her hands, to sit next to her and he'd put his arm comfortingly around her shoulder. Sheena knew that if women let men get to stage one, then they expected to get to stage ten. And if he managed that and she complained, then it would be said that it was her fault, and that she'd 'led him on' somehow. She'd been talking to him as a policeman, not as a man, and as far as she was concerned, talking about the sexual acts that had happened to her mother was not a sexual signal to him. And so she quickly turned around and pushed his arm roughly away, so roughly that it shocked him.

He quickly stood up and she could see the genuine pain in his eyes, she'd hurt him by her rebuff of him, by her pushing him away, but the hurt in his eyes was there for only a fleeting moment for the look of concern which he was now showing was much, much stronger. He quickly apologised if he had given her the wrong impression by his act of concern, but he wanted to reassure her that there was nothing sinister intended, that he genuinely felt her pain and wanted to offer some form of comfort to her, nothing more than that, he insisted.

Now he started to talk while Sheena listened. First of all he told her that he in no way doubted any word of anything that she had just told him. But, he added, that officially there was still nothing that could be done. It would still be her word against 'Big Sid's', Sheena, more relaxed now, couldn't help but smile at that remark, as he himself had been smiling at her when he said it. He added that there was no physical evidence at all. The doctor was convinced that it was a natural death, and even though they both knew that 'Big Sid' had conned the doctor, getting him to admit that would not only be very difficult, it would also be futile as there was no longer any 'body' to examine. He did, however, add that he would speak to his inspector giving him all the details and maybe he would bring him in for questioning, but he very much doubted it. For his part he would go again and talk to the doctor giving him this new information and see if it changed his opinion in any way.

Phil then asked Sheena if she would get more comfort for her pain if Tom were there to help and comfort her. Sheena had no problem with that answer and she told him firmly and positively that the last person she would want to comfort or indeed help her in any way with anything was Tom. She told him that Tom was gone for good and was not coming back. She added that getting rid of Tom had in fact been one of the bravest things she'd ever done and her only regret was that she hadn't done it sooner. She noticed that Phil couldn't hide his pleasure with that revelation!

However, as to his evaluation of the legal situation Sheena was crestfallen. She'd pinned so much hope on Phil being able to do something, anything to help her. But listening to him she knew that she had to be realistic. As for bringing 'Big Sid' in for questioning, well she knew that he would in fact get a kick out of that. She also felt shamefaced in her actions towards Phil who was obviously just trying to genuinely comfort her in her grief, but she had never experienced any other man than

Tom, and he never put his arms anywhere near her if he didn't expect sex. She couldn't quite say the words needed to apologise to him, but she hoped that her look of contrition would get the message across.

Phil then sat down again next to her and this time he pointedly held her hand in both of his. He looked her steadfastly in the eye and said that he could see by her reaction, her assessment of Tom and her general demeanour that she herself must have suffered badly at the hands of men and that as he'd said before he wasn't able to do anything officially for her, but he was sure that she knew he liked her. She smiled at him feeling truly embarrassed. He added that as he couldn't be a 'policeman' for her he would like to take her out for a meal that evening. He added hastily, that it would just be as friends, for he truly felt that they were friends, it would not be a date and not a commitment to anything else. He hoped that she'd agree and believe his intentions.

Now Sheena was more than just embarrassed and she could feel her face blushing. But she looked earnestly at him and repeated, somewhat shyly, – just friends – he nodded. Sheena smiled as she noted the nervous look in his eyes as he waited for her answer, and in return he could see the hesitation in hers, so again he assured her 'Just a meal' and so she told him that a meal would be very nice and that she would look forward to it. So feeling pleased and full of confidence he went on to tell her that he would pick he up about 7.30 and during the evening he could report back to her with what his inspector had said and what the result of his conversation with the doctor had discovered.

As he was leaving and feeling more confident now he smiled and gave her that little kiss on her cheek that she liked so much. But still he turned back again, and with a look of mock terror on his face he said, "Oh, unless you think that Tom will beat me up for feeding you?" Sheena blushed and shooed him off smiling as he left. One thing that Sheena knew for sure was that Tom would never beat any man up, no matter what the provocation; Tom was like 'Big Sid' in that way, in that he only beat up women!

As she closed the door behind him she leaned back against it and considered what she had just agreed to. She had badly misjudged him and she regretted that, she realised that somehow she would have to learn the difference between someone being a friend who felt your pain and someone who only ever had one thing on their mind. In the past she had only ever known the latter, but she was confident now that she had met the former and the thought of that sent a little quiver of excitement through her body.

As the time neared for Phil to be arriving, Sheena became more and more nervous. She didn't know what to wear, should she wear her very best dress or should she keep it casual. She wanted to do both. In the end she settled for casual. She wasn't sure if she was nervous of meeting Phil, nervous about what he had to say, or nervous as to whether she would have anything to make 'small talk' over. But however the evening was going to turn out she made sure that she had enough money to pay her own way. She couldn't think that she'd ever been taken out for a meal before, not if it hadn't been for some special celebration anyway, Tom had never just taken her out for a meal, not even when they were courting, and that fact only added to her nerves.

And then there was a knock at the door. She had made sure that the children were safely tucked up in bed and her neighbour, who was babysitting for her, kept telling her to relax, which only made things worse! She opened the door and Phil was standing there looking incredibly smart. She looked directly at him, drinking in the sight that was before her, and she suddenly realised that she'd never seen him in anything other than his police uniform and now here he was standing before her, taller than she'd noticed before, wearing casual trousers and open-necked shirt with his shirt sleeves folded back to just below his elbows exposing his very manly arms. Her heart skipped a beat as she thought idly to herself that there was a tall, dark, incredibly handsome, very manly man with piercing blue eyes standing at *her* door, and he was there to see *her*, then she looked down at her own clothes, not smart or dressy and so now she felt dowdy and even more nervous.

But he looked her up and down admiringly and gave her a definite wink of approval, and such a look that again, like a silly schoolgirl, she blushed then he took her gently by the hand and noting her nervousness, told her to relax, that she looked great. They went to a local pub to eat, she was grateful for that because she had been dreading going to a restaurant, this was much more informal and relaxed.

However, he didn't have any good news for her. He had been to see her mother's doctor again presenting him with the situation as it was, but calling it a hypothetical situation in which he could be manipulated by a husband such as 'Big Sid'. Sheena still couldn't help but smile when he called him that and she was so grateful to him for respecting her wishes in that way. Anyway the doctor did admit that if the situation had been as he'd described then yes, he could have been manipulated, but as things stood, it was all merely academic, because as he'd said there was no body and no evidence, just one person's word against another's, and one of those people was very hormonal! It was in fact just as Phil had predicted earlier.

He did say though that his inspector trusted Phil's intuition and agreed with him that foul play had probably happened, but again without any evidence then they could do nothing. Neither Phil nor his inspector had ever heard of anyone being brought to trial with such flimsy evidence. And with her mother now having been cremated then there never *would* be any evidence; there could never now be a post-mortem. He hated to admit it, but he said that if her father…'Big Sid' had in fact murdered her mother then he would get away with it. In her heart Sheena had known that that would be the outcome but she was still really pleased that Phil had tried so hard to help her. She told him that she would tell her brothers that they had to 'let it go'.

They then talked for hours about all sorts of other things. They laughed out loud together at she didn't know what, but they laughed and talked and she felt very much at her ease. She couldn't remember when she had last laughed so much, or so easily. It made a big change from all the tears she'd shed over the last week, and Sheena found him so easy to talk to. She found herself telling him things that she had never told anyone else, but she didn't talk about Tom, especially not about what the main thing was she'd hated about him. She really didn't want that subject to come up in any sort of connotation. But she did reaffirm to him that Tom was not only gone, but gone for good. She didn't mention the knife either, but she did add conspiratorially that she'd scared the life out of him and that he wouldn't dare come back. He'd looked at her clearly puzzled by that remark, but she in return just smiled smugly.

When he took her home her heart was pounding. She didn't want him to kiss her, but at the same time she didn't want him *not* to kiss her. In the event he kissed her that beautiful soft, tender kiss on her cheek, his arm just resting lightly on her shoulder. And inside she glowed. After the kiss he took hold of her hand and told her that he was sure she knew that there was a connection between them, a special connection, and that he loved the feeling that connection gave him. He added that it had taken him by surprise as it had happened so quickly, but he felt as though he'd known her forever. She looked panicked and worried and the look was not lost on him. "Don't worry so much, Sheena," he said gently, and so she tried to relax a little. He continued, "I'm not going to push things with you, we'll always go at your pace, but I think that if you'd care to admit it, that you like me too," he said while smiling at her such a smile that again she blushed. She felt like a silly schoolgirl, because all she could do was to nod in agreement, because her stomach was doing somersaults!

He again told her how disappointed and upset he was that he'd been unable to help her over the death of her mother, but that he thought her brothers were right when they'd said that justice will 'out' one day, in one way or another. But he reminded her again that as he was no longer officially a policeman to her now, helping her with a 'case', he sincerely hoped that he would be able to see her again. Sheena looked at this very manly, man with deep, piercing blue eyes full of concern looking at her, but she was too, too scared to say yes to that.

She was no good with men; she knew that she was no good with them. They wanted sex and she *hated* sex and although she really, really liked Phil she couldn't face up to what she would have to do in the end. She didn't want to do it, not ever, not even with Phil. But she was also too scared to say 'no' because she didn't want to stop seeing him. She was so very, very confused. She hadn't expected anything like this to be a problem that she would *ever* have to face.

It seemed as though he could sense her confusion and that he could see right into the very *heart* of her, because he said quickly, "Look, Sheena you don't need to say either yes or no. We can both just agree to be friends, as we said, friends who kiss on the cheek and embrace each other now and then," he said with a very mischievous smile, before adding hopefully, "and perhaps even go out for a drink together. What do you think about that?" She nodded and moved forward boldly, so boldly that *she then kissed him* on the cheek. They both laughed out loud at that and for Sheena it took all the tension of the situation away. She was really pleased with their

172

decision. But she was well aware that her nerves had only been abated for a while. One day, she knew for sure that if she kept on seeing him, then he would want sex. As far as she was concerned, all men wanted sex. Her worries were still there lurking beneath the surface and she would have to face them sometime.

She went to bed that night with a whole new mixture of emotions. She thought about how strong and good-looking Phil was and wondered, not for the first time that evening, what it was he wanted from her, because he surely should be with one of these good-looking confident women who liked sex! She liked him, there was no doubting that she liked him, just a simple touch from him made her body react in a way that it never had before, there was everything about him *to* like, good looks, charm, concern, consideration, the list was endless and then, of course, the sweetest of lips, but what could he see in her? However, she slept well that night, better in fact than she had for some time.

CHAPTER 18

The following morning, after taking the Andy and Susie to school Sheena returned home still feeling drained over all the recent events, but she resolved that she just had to finally accept that nothing more could be done regarding her mother's death. She had spoken to both Iain and Graham the previous evening and they'd all agreed that they had to stop torturing themselves over something with which they had no control. They consoled themselves with the fact that they had indeed explored every avenue available to them to gain a conviction, indeed they'd explored them as much as was humanly possible, and although they shockingly now knew how their mother had died, they'd regrettably been unable to alter anything.

For Sheena herself, she knew that it was inevitable that she would never fully recover from the shock of the previous week, but if she were to remain sane then she reluctantly had to come to terms with the finality of it all. Graham and Iain had both been right in their conclusions that her mother would not want for either her children, or her grandchildren to suffer any more than was necessary and normal over her totally avoidable death.

Sheena recalled how 'Big Sid' had cruelly informed her the day after her mother's death that he never wanted to hear her mother's name mentioned again. Well he would have no need to worry on that score, for he would never hear any of his families voices again, whether they were mentioning her mother or more mundanely the weather. She would never either see or speak to him again. He'd revelled; gloried even, in relaying to her in particular, all the horrifying details of her mother's death, and for that as much as for her murder he would never be forgiven.

Her thoughts then turned to Phil and a comforting smile spread across her face as she thought about him. Still she worried as to whether they could possibly remain 'just friends'. She had never heard of a man and woman being just friends, but she'd vowed to take this wonderful new relationship with him one day at a time. Just thinking about him had a stirring effect on her, and his touch, oh my God, she grinned to herself, with her eyes fluttering as fast as her heart, the slightest touch of him sent feelings through her body that threatened to stir her emotions in her in a way that she had truly never experienced before.

However, she hoped and prayed that she would simply be able to enjoy his touch, maybe even a kiss, and a proper kiss at some time, but the inescapable truth was that the day would come when the friendship ended, for Phil would want more, and 'more' was something she just couldn't give. She wished with her very being that she *could* give more of herself to him because if she could give more to anyone, then it would be to Phil. But the indisputable fact was that she couldn't do that. She wondered idly if her touch meant anything like the same thing to him, but she quickly dismissed that thought. Men were basically mechanical she mused, they had one main intention in life, and that was sex, and sex would *never* be her intention, main or otherwise.

She was just sitting deep in thought, staring out of the window at nothing of any importance, just quietly daydreaming, when there was a knock at the door, a knock that she'd been expecting, for it was Iain. He was on his way to the station to return to his barracks when he'd realised that he'd left part of his dress uniform behind and he'd told her already that he would be calling in on her.

On arriving he looked intently at her and he was pleased to see his sister looking more positive and he told her so, but he also commented, with a look of pleasant curiosity, that she seemed different somehow, that she seemed to have a bit of a 'glow' about her. Something was definitely different about her and his playful asking her if her 'glow' had anything to do with Phil. He felt that he'd 'hit the nail on the head' when Sheena blushed and squirmed in her chair but she laughed off his comments and told him, truthfully, that she had just been daydreaming. His demeanour then took on a more serious tone when he told her to 'be careful' and to give herself time to just enjoy life before getting involved with anyone else. She told him again truthfully, that although she liked Phil there was nothing 'going on' and there wouldn't be. Tom was gone and she didn't want another man in her life, but Phil was just a friend. He didn't comment on her description of Phil, but his look of censure warned her that Phil better be just a friend and not someone who was bent on hurting his little sister.

Getting more relaxed, Iain informed Sheena that he had some time to spare before his train was due to leave so they shared a cup of tea together and resolved to talk about anything other than 'Big Sid' or their mother's murder, they freely called it murder now, for that was indeed what it was. Other than that they merely repeated what has been said by them all many times before, and that was that one day, God willing, he would get his comeuppance. And so they talked about anything and everything else. Iain even said that he was looking forward to the welcoming 'normality' of Army life.

Then just as Iain stood up to leave there was another knock at the door. Sheena looked at Iain perplexed, she certainly wasn't expecting anyone else to call that day. Iain sat down again whilst she opened the front door. To the surprise of both of them it was the undertaker who'd called to see her previously when she'd picked out her mother's coffin. She panicked at the thought that he'd called for his money because so far she hadn't actually received an invoice, although she did in fact know the total cost, but Graham hadn't given her any money yet, and she certainly didn't have that amount of her own to give him.

The undertaker looked very nervous and unsure of himself; he asked if he could sit down as he had some really distressing news for them. Sheena and Iain just glanced from one to the other wondering what on earth he could mean. Her mind was working overtime trying to predict what this man wanted, what the problem was, then Sheena recalled Graham commenting on what a lovely coffin it was that she'd organised for her mother, and so she expected him to tell them that they would have to pay more money.

She stood looking at this little man in amazement, astonished that he would even contemplate doing something like that; surely if he supplied the wrong coffin it would be his own error not hers. But the undertaker then took the lead in the conversation by saying calmly but firmly that he felt it would be a good idea if they all sat down.

He coughed to clear his throat and sat forward in the armchair with his book on his knee, and he immediately started apologising profusely. "I can assure you both that for the many years that I have been an undertaker nothing like this had ever happened before." Sheena was getting a bit irate and impatient now for she was sure that he wanted to increase their bill, and so she told him directly that if they had to pay more, then he would have to give them a complete breakdown of the additional costs. She was in no mood to be swindled by this man, and certainly not after all they had been through. But he insisted that he wasn't trying to swindle them, in fact there was to be no charge at all for the funeral, because the fault, besides being extremely serious was all his. They were now both at a total loss as to what he was referring to.

Seeing their anger and obvious distrust he implored them to please let him finish. So Sheena sat down again and waited for him to continue. "Your mother's funeral, Jeannie Williams, was booked for 12.00 noon on 10th April." They nodded in unison. "But we had a booking for a Jean Williams for 10.00am for today 12th April." Again they nodded, looking thoroughly perplexed, while the undertaker continued. "Well, unfortunately somehow, the two women and the two dates and times were mixed up. Jean Williams was due to be buried today, so their family are even more understandably irate, because their error cannot be corrected." Iain had grabbed hold of Sheena's hand and Sheena's heart was pounding in her chest. Was he about to say what both of them were thinking, hoping, and surely praying that he was going to say?

And they begged him furiously to tell just them what had happened. And so he said it. "Your mother is unfortunately still in our funeral parlour, but he added very rapidly, we will do everything we can to arrange a new date for you all as fast as is humanly possible, perhaps even for the day after tomorrow, and as I said there will, of course, be no cost whatsoever and if any relatives need to make new arrangements we will of course cover all of their costs. I really don't know how to apologise further. I hope you will believe me when I say that it has never happened before and that we as a company are fully aware of the distress this news must be causing you." Sighing heavily he leaned back in his chair and spent the next few moments quietly looking from one to the other of them waiting for what he believed would be their inevitable angry outburst.

Sheena and Iain just looked at each other and then at this man sitting there begging their forgiveness. The huge grins on both their faces rather scared this nervous little man sitting before them. And then in complete unison they said, "Do you mean, are you trying to say that our mother hasn't been cremated?" He shuffled uncomfortably on his seat and nodded in the affirmative before saying over and over again that he was so very, very sorry. Sheena stood up and taking his hand she shook it furiously saying thank you, thank you, thank you over and over again.

But Sheena's elation quickly abated as she realised that there was an important question that she *needed* to ask him, it wasn't a question that she wanted to ask, but she knew that it couldn't be avoided, that she would *have* to ask it. Iain was looking at her perplexed, wondering why she had suddenly appeared disappointed, disappointed with what was in fact incredible news. Sheena gestured towards Iain to sit down again which he did.

So taking a deep breath she asked that very vital question: Are you absolutely sure? Have you actually looked inside the coffin? She then asked the undertaker very clearly in order that there could be no mistakes, "Is there any chance, any possibility that it could simply be that the wrong bodies that were put into the wrong coffins?" She glanced at Iain and his face had gone white. Neither of them wanted to hear the answer to that particular question, but the undertaker again leaned forward in his seat and said yes they were sure, they were positive, and that there was absolutely no doubt.

He went on to tell them that that question had been the first thing the family of Jean Williams had asked, even though your mother's name was on the coffin. And accordingly they'd opened up the coffin whilst they were there; they needed the proof as much as Sheena and Iain did. And the proof was there, the coffin, she was told was the one Sheena had initially picked out and the body inside was absolutely that of their mother.

Both Sheena and Iain breathed a sigh of relief and Sheena told the undertaker to leave their mother where she was and that he wasn't to make any other arrangements at all, none at all, she said emphatically. "I will totally understand if you wish to use another undertaker, and I will personally make all the arrangements for the transfer of her body," he said sheepishly.

But they told him that they couldn't thank him enough because their mother hadn't ever wanted to be cremated and now she could be buried. They didn't think it would be appropriate to mention to him the fact that they should now be able to prove that their mother had been murdered. They accepted gratefully that they wouldn't have to pay for the funeral and also the fact that relatives would be compensated financially in order to be at the new funeral. They also told him that they wouldn't be using another firm and that they bore no ill will at all against him, they'd said it was an easy mistake to make. But they added firmly and positively that he wasn't to make any new arrangements until they told him to. And, they added, that of course they would like to send their personal condolences to the family of Jean Williams who had obviously been cremated two days ago.

They were, however, both curious as to how the mistake had been discovered, to which the undertaker replied hesitantly, and somewhat shamefully, that the family knew as soon as they saw the coffin in which they thought their mother lay, was not in fact up to the standard of the one which they had ordered, and after noticing that and bringing it to their attention, they all then thought that the Christian name had been engraved wrongly, which of course it wasn't, because it was the wrong woman. He was babbling even more nervously by this time, so they just thanked him again and said that they would be in touch. And with that he left, bemused by their strange behaviour, but pleased that he wasn't going to be sued.

Iain and Sheena were truly delighted; they couldn't contain their excitement at this unexpected but thrilling news. Iain however, still had to go back to barracks, he would explain this new situation to his commanding officer and hopefully return back home in a few days, if there was some positive news he added hurriedly. Sheena told him not to worry as she had a good friend in Phil and he would know exactly what to do. Her body though was trembling. She offered up a silent prayer. They had to get it right now, and *he* had to pay, nothing more could be allowed to go wrong.

Sheena embraced Iain and told him that it had taken all her reserve not to jump up and kiss the undertaker. He nodded, grinning like a Cheshire cat himself. Sheena telephoned Graham with the good news and it was agreed that she would see what the legal implications were now. They were all so very hopeful. Surely now something could be done. Sheena would contact Phil without delay.

Phil came to see her almost immediately after receiving her frantic telephone call. He looked extremely worried for her and was anxious to discover what the problem was. Pointing to the sofa she told him that he would need to sit down for this, but then she noticed his tormented look and realised that she needed to reassure him, and quickly. She smiled, put her hand gently on his arm and told him that it was essentially good news; at least she hoped it was. He breathed a sigh of relief and said, "Right let's hear it then."

And so she explained what had just happened with the undertaker and asked him excitedly if they could now order a postmortem on her mother. Could they now prove what 'Big Sid' had done, taking into account his confession and the fact that the doctor admitted that he might have been fooled?

Phil's whole demeanour told Sheena how excited he was for her. He said he was also pleased that a murderer might at last get his due punishment. Sheena picked up quickly on the word 'might' she didn't want to hear 'might'. But he had to remind her that there was still a long way to go before he could be charged, firstly though he had to let her know that he, himself could no longer be involved with the case. To say Sheena was disappointed was an understatement and it showed, she glowered at him as her immediate thoughts were along the lines of, that all the time he was being 'friendly' towards her, he did in fact have other intentions in mind, and those intentions were that he knew all along that there would never be a police case. She was crestfallen with the idea that he didn't want to personally help her and she said so in a very curt manner.

Sheena had stood up and was pacing angrily now, but Phil took hold of her and asked her to let him explain. She was prepared to let him explain but she was also convinced that she wouldn't like his explanation. However, he told her that because they had now become friendly, which he quickly added was still the case and that he was still more than pleased about that, but because of their friendship he would be considered to be too closely involved to be neutral, and if there was to be a chance of a conviction then he didn't want to hinder it by breaking the rules. He did tell her though that he would speak to his Inspector and tell him how things had now changed and then his Inspector would take over.

Sheena wanted to know what he thought their chances were of actually getting a conviction. To answer that he said that his Inspector would speak to the funeral parlour manager, then to the doctor and then they would bring her father in for questioning, noticing the look of mock disdain on Sheena's face he immediately changed 'father' to 'Big Sid'. He also said that his Inspector would want a detailed statement from her, and that he would want that before actually seeing anyone else involved, so that would be his first move in the matter. Phil then took all the details regarding the funeral parlour with him and as he was getting up to leave he told her that his Inspector was a nice guy and that he'd already been made aware of the situation up to now and he would contact her later, possibly later today, for her statement.

Sheena stood next to him looking at him nervously, she apologised for her initial reaction and she hesitantly asked him what his opinion was with regard to a conviction. He looked at her long and hard, then smiling he leaned in to her and whispered in her ear that he thought the chances were more than very good. He was about to give her a kiss on the cheek as he was leaving when in her excitement Sheena threw her arms around him, holding on to him tightly.

When she finally let go of him they looked at each other intently for a moment or two, their faces only inches apart. Sheena gazed at those lovely tender lips that had only as yet brushed her cheek, and she thought dreamily about how much she would love to kiss him full on those soft, tender lips. And not for the first time, she wondered where her sanity went when she was faced with Phil. Then slowly her eyes moved up to meet his, and if there had been doubt in her mind before it was gone now, because even she, with her limited experience of men, could tell that he was longing to kiss her.

Slowly with one finger he gently and lovingly brushed a loose strand of hair from her face, his hand resting on her cheek for a moment longer than strictly necessary. Such was her desire for him at that moment that her warm eyes were moist with tears and her lips wet with expectancy and then it happened. He kissed her full on the lips, and she kissed him back. It was a warm, tender, soft kiss. Not a hungry, hard demanding kiss, but a long lingering soft one, so long that her lips tingled as her heart beat ever faster.

When their lips finally parted there was no need for words between them. That kiss had spoken more words than either of them ever could have. Phil left quietly, smiling and walking away with what could only be described as a 'spring in his step' and then Sheena closed the door and cried. But this time her tears were tears of wonder, tears of pure happiness. She had never in all her life been kissed like that or felt like that for another human being. She'd loved her mother immensely and of course, she loved her children, but possibly the closest she'd ever been to feeling like that was when Adam was laid across her chest seconds after being born and she'd tenderly kissed his brow. She had, of course, had similar feelings when each of her children were born, because there was nothing quite like that initial rush of love that a mother felt when her new born child was placed across her chest, but the first time that happens, well that is special. And now she knew that Phil was special, his kiss was *very* special.

CHAPTER 19

Much later that same afternoon, Inspector Jeremy Loughton called personally to see her. He had brought with him a female police officer to take notes on his behalf, but she was also there in case Sheena felt too embarrassed to talk through these extremely harrowing details with a strange man. Sheena appreciated the lengths he had gone to in order to make sure that she was as comfortable as possible. She was feeling nervous and embarrassed, of that there was no doubt. She felt nervous because she wanted to get everything right, without exaggerating, without leaving anything out, but whilst still remaining as clear as possible, and the embarrassment she was feeling resulted from the fact that she was aware of the reason he was in her home, and that, of course, was because Phil couldn't continue with the investigation on his own due to his close friendship with her.

She needn't have worried though, because as Phil had assured her, Inspector Loughton had indeed proved to be very easy to talk to. Sheena had led them both to the kitchen table, in order that it would be easier for notes to be taken, and speaking directly to Inspector Loughton, she told him everything, leaving nothing out. She told him about her father's strange behaviour in the days leading up to her mother's death, about the fact that no matter how ill her mother had been throughout her life, none of her children could ever recall him sitting with her and nursing her. She told him about the medicine bottles and finally about his confession to her. And she left nothing out concerning that confession, much as it was breaking her heart to relive the details again, she nevertheless included all the sex details as well as about all the tablets he'd told her that he'd forced her to take.

Sheena thought that she would have been too nervous to tell a stranger all those sexual details about her lovely mum, but in the event her confidence rose with every new detail she gave them. In her mind, every detail was one more fact to ensure that *he* went to prison for the rest of his life. She wanted to make absolutely sure that there would now not only be a post-mortem but that her father would be put in jail, hopefully for the rest of his life. (She felt that she had to say 'her father' to the Inspector to keep things professional.) But in her own mind, he was, and always would be 'Big Sid'.

All the while that she'd been giving these details to Inspector Loughton the female police officer had been writing them all down. When she'd finished talking she gave a big sigh of relief and sat back in her chair, waiting, expecting them to say something to the effect that they now had everything they needed and that they would now go and arrest her father. She was keen to know when her father would be arrested. But her hopes were severely dashed when the Inspector told her that it probably wouldn't be for a day or two. And he also reminded her that 'arrested' didn't mean charged. There was a long way to go he'd said before he could get to the stage of charging him. He informed her that he needed to talk to the doctor first and hopefully he would re-iterate what he had previously said to Sergeant Anderson.

His intention was to avoid rising her hopes too far while still reassuring her that everything possible would now be done. However, he felt compelled to add that if the doctor intended to stick to his opinion of Death by Natural Causes, then he would have to prepare a report to put before he coroner and then the coroner would decide if he believed that a post-mortem would, in the interests of justice be required.

Sheena was terribly shocked and distressed by what she saw as the police not really believing her, and she felt strongly that they were thinking – we'll just placate this emotional, hormonal woman – and she wasn't going to stand for it. She stood up so fast that her chair fell to the floor and she almost ripped off her cardigan in her effort to display her truthfulness, she wanted to display the now purple bruises on her arms that her father had caused. She ordered them to 'look at these' if you don't believe me. She insisted that she wasn't hormonal, or if she was, then being hormonal didn't create such bruises, she added sarcastically. She banged her fist on the table; such was her anger as she told them that every word that she'd said had been the absolute truth, truth without the slightest exaggeration. Her heart was thumping so hard in her chest that she was visibly clutching it due to the pain it was causing her, and her anger was palpable.

The female police officer gently sat Sheena back down and moved to make them all a cup of tea. Sheena put her head in her hands and was totally unable to stop the tears from cascading yet again down her face. She'd felt so good and so positive just a few hours previously, now it seemed as if the whole world was intent on being cruel to her. She wondered now if her tears would ever cease, would life ever be good to her for more than just a few moments. She despaired of the answer.

Inspector Loughton had himself been distressed to see the state of this young lady in front of him. The last thing that he'd wanted to do was to upset her and so now he tried to reassure her. He explained gently that he *did* absolutely believe her, that he absolutely thought she was right in her belief that her father had murdered her mother, what he had been trying unsuccessfully to get across to her was that the wheels of justice turned very slowly in the legal world. However, he again reassured her, he would do everything he could to get a conviction. The fact is, he quietly explained, one route is quicker than another. "For example", he continued. "If the doctor were to admit that he could have made a mistake and personally request a post-mortem, then that would be the quicker route. If, however, he kept to his original cause of death a being Death by Natural Causes, then that would be the longer route." But, he said with some authority, offering her his heartfelt assurance, "If I'm as good at my job as I know I am, then in the end your father will end up in prison."

The policewoman interjected when Inspector Loughton was busy complimenting himself, with, "He is, you know." And she'd smiled at Sheena whilst saying that.

Sheena tried to smile back but her head was banging and she was completely and emotionally drained. She lifted her head and looking directly into the eyes of this Inspector, she asked as slowly and as calmly as she could if he believed her, if he believed some, or all that she'd told him. He put his hand lightly onto her arm and moved his head to be closer to hers and he told her that he categorically and totally believed her. She nodded and broke into a half smile. Her eyes were searching his for authenticity and she clearly saw it.

They got up to leave but promised her that either himself or Phil would keep her up to date with everything that was happening and the female officer gave her a phone number that she could call if she had any questions, any at all she'd reassured her. Inspector Loughton added that the first thing he would be doing would be to get the undertaker to bring her mother's body to the county morgue in readiness for what he was sure would be the long awaited for post-mortem. But in any case it would at least make sure that everyone knew where the body was. His next move would be to talk to the doctor and he would be doing that first thing in the morning. Sheena attempted to apologise for her behaviour, although actually getting any words out was still difficult for her. But in the event the Inspector wasn't about to let her apologise and as she looked into his eyes she just nodded, consoled by the fact that his face told her that his words were genuine.

Phil called later that evening to see Sheena. He sat beside her and put a consoling arm around her to offer some vestige of comfort, for her part Sheena just rested her head gently on his shoulder. There was complete silence between them because there was no need for words.

After some time Phil prepared a meal for Sheena, but she ate very little. He eventually led her up to her bedroom and gently undressed her, enough to make her comfortable, but not so much as to deny her any dignity. Sheena was spent, so she offered up no resistance and allowed herself to be 'looked after' by Phil; she needed so much to be 'looked after'. However, as he was removing her cardigan he gasped at the severe bruising on her arms and it pained him so to see that. He also recalled that the first time he met her an ugly bruise on her face was still clearly distinguishable and he so wanted at that moment to enfold her in his arms and protect her forever from any more harm. But he knew that for now he was unable do that, one day though, he silently promised himself.

Sheena quickly and quietly moved into the foetal position on her bed, and Phil gently placed the bed covers over her. He stood quietly for a while contemplating this amazing woman that in such a short period of time he had come to love, and yes, he thought, love was not too strong a term for his feelings, he just prayed that one day she would feel able to fully reciprocate them, he knew well enough that she cared for him, but love, well she'd suffered a lot of hurt in her short life and so he was sure that love returned would take much longer for her.

As he gazed at this woman gently sleeping now in front of him, he realised that she was like a woman possessed, the type of woman who would move heaven and earth, find hidden untold amounts of strength, that she wasn't even aware she possessed, to fight for her children, except that for Sheena those roles were now reversed, for she was the child moving heaven and earth and finding that very same hidden, untold amounts of strength to fight for her mother. And he knew that nothing and no-one would stop her from fighting, and hopefully winning that battle.

Sheena didn't wake the following morning until 10.00am and then she woke with a start as she realised that it was way past the time for the children to go to school. She rushed downstairs, wondering at the same time why she was only half undressed, to find Phil sitting happily with Lucy on his lap. Her eyes searched the scene before her, unable to come up with any logical explanation. Phil smiled at her clearly amused by her wonderment.

"Adam and Susie are both at school, Lucy has had her breakfast and has been changed and now just wants to play," he said with such a huge grin on his face that Sheena could do nothing but smile. With a more than puzzled look on her face she asked – how? Phil had to admit that he'd had help from Adam. Adam, he said, had informed him as to what they all wanted for breakfast and although Phil had finally managed to change Lucy, Adam had been giving him all the instructions and now they've both gone to school with your neighbour," he added triumphantly.

Sheena looked at the blanket still lying on the sofa, and then she looked at Lucy sitting with Phil happily giggling away. She had been married to Tom for ten years and known him for twelve, since she herself had been only sixteen years old, and he'd never done anything close to what Phil had done for her during the previous night and then today. She was so overcome with emotion that her eyes started to well up and tears were again threatening to roll down her cheeks. But Phil could see what was happening to her and he gently put Lucy into her play pen and put his arms around Sheena and just held her. He whispered softly to her, "Don't say anything, sweetheart, I'll always be here for you. We'll always be here for each other." And Sheena's heart swelled with pride because she knew that he was right.

But reluctantly releasing her from his hold, he reminded her that there was still a long way to go before 'Big Sid' is finally locked up and that he was going to find out what was happening and what was being done next. But as he was on his way out Inspector Loughton rang to tell Sheena that he'd spoken to her mother's doctor and he wasn't inclined to change the cause of death which he'd written on the death certificate. However, they were going to arrest her father later that day and bring him in for questioning, he said that he was hopeful that her father would now confess all once he'd been told that his wife had not in fact been cremated. He felt sure that by doing that her father would be caught 'off guard' because he didn't as yet know that the wrong body had been cremated. He told her again not to get despondent about this little setback, as he'd expected that it may happen, and he was also personally preparing a report to send to the coroner in an effort to bypass the doctor.

Sheena was obviously upset by the news but she had an idea of her own that she didn't want to share with anyone yet, so she was still very much hopeful of the right outcome. Phil was pleased to see her taking that news so well and even more so when she smiled and said that she wished that she could see 'Big Sid's' face when he was told that her mother's body was still in the mortuary. Phil told her that he would go into work and let her know later exactly what his reaction was, because although he couldn't take part in the interview, he would be able to see and hear it from another room.

After Phil had left, Sheena decided to put her own plan into action and having taken Lucy to her neighbour, to whom she was extremely grateful, she went herself to see her mother's doctor. She waited calmly while the doctor completed his surgery and then, in a much more conciliatory tone than before she went to speak to him.

She greeted the doctor warmly and apologised profusely for her inexcusable behaviour the last time they met. The doctor had appeared irate and annoyed with her at first, with this same subject coming up yet again but his anger was quickly assuaged by Sheena's tone. She told him that when she had last spoken to him she was angry without cause and that if he wanted her to just leave then she would, but she implored him to please 'hear her out'.

The doctor now being much more relaxed she told him of the events leading up to her mother's death and about the fact that her mother had so much respect for him that there would be no way that she would have wanted to admit to him that he'd been called out on false pretences, especially she quickly added, that they weren't entirely false because her mother was indeed feeling ill, but rather than actually having chest pains, she was simply afraid that she could feel an attack coming on. Sheena added that she herself had the utmost respect for him as he'd been her doctor too for most of her life and she had absolute total faith in him.

Sheena could see the doctor now swelling with pride, his chest literally puffing out such was his arrogance, and so she continued. She told him word for word what her father had told her on the day of what should have been her mother's funeral, but she added somewhat dismissively that she knew that he'd *probably* just been bragging, saying the word 'bragging' slower and with slightly more emphasis, because, she added while leaning forward conspiratorially, that he'd also bragged that he, her mother's doctor was easily fooled. Well, she'd exclaimed emphatically, that part of his confession was so ridiculous that it just *begged* to be ignored, because she said, clearly playing up to his arrogance, she knew him to absolutely be a man of principle, of integrity, and a man who would quickly see through the very wicked machinations of a man like her father.

The doctor was warming to her more and more so to finally illicit as much sympathy as possible she'd asked him if he would mind advising her as to what she could either put on her arms to relieve the pain of them, or perhaps recommend a medication that she could ask her own doctor to prescribe for her, before adding with a pained expression, that she was finding it difficult to hold her young baby. She felt quite sure that the mention of her baby would pull at his heart strings. And she was right, for when he saw her arms he was truly shocked. He gently rubbed them over the bruising whilst examining her, and Sheena grimaced with overly pronounced pain, saying 'ouch' meaningfully each time he touched her, clearly indicating to him that the pain was too much for her to bear being touched.

He was extremely sympathetic and immediately recommended that she saw her own GP as soon as possible in order for him to prescribe the appropriate relief that she quite clearly needed. Sheena then shook his hand warmly and thanked him so very much for his time and patience and again apologised for being so rude the previous time they had spoken.

Sheena left the doctor's surgery feeling very satisfied with herself, she muttered under her breath that 'Big Sid' had been right about one thing, the doctor was *very* easy to cajole, flatter, and manipulate. She hadn't mentioned the post-mortem to him once, and that was deliberate, for she felt sure that *not* mentioning it would work in her favour. Her main aim had been to put to the back of his mind that her mother had lied to him regarding how ill she was when he last saw her, and to bring to the forefront of his mind the fact that her father had found him easy to fool, to manipulate, and the fact that he ridiculed him to Sheena. She had used her feminine wiles on him, feminine wiles that she was only just beginning to realise she had, she smiled to herself wickedly.

When she'd arrived home later that day she prayed that her intervention regarding her mother's doctor would have had the desired effect. She tried to carry on with mundane household duties in a wasted effort to distract her mind.

But hours had gone by and nothing had happened, she chided herself severely for her arrogance in believing that her subtlety, her interference would somehow make a difference, that she would succeed where others had failed, and she had all but convinced herself of that when there was a knock at her door. It was Phil with Inspector Loughton, she looked rapidly from one to the other, desperately trying to read the news from their faces, it looked to be good because Phil was smiling and looked happy, but the Inspector just looked very official, she was so nervous now that she'd convinced herself that Phil was just smiling to make the bad news more bearable. Oh God, it was tearing her apart not knowing.

Phil could see her nervousness and so he sat next to her holding her hand. He gripped her hand tightly and Sheena searched his face desperately, was that grip for good news or bad? She didn't know, but the Inspector sat down and she waited for him to speak, her heart pounding furiously.

CHAPTER 20

The Inspector started to relay to Sheena the events of the day. "As I already mentioned earlier today your mother's doctor refused to amend his cause of death from Death by Natural Causes, to one of Suspicious Death. However, as I told you we were not prepared to give up on the case just because of that one setback." Phil looked at the Inspector in such a beseeching manner, imploring him to ease the pain that was so patently obvious in Sheena's demeanour. She was trembling and shaking and he needed him to quickly get to the point before Sheena collapsed, because he was seriously worried for her mental health as more and more pressure was being piled onto her.

Inspector Loughton nodded his agreement to Phil as he then got to the central point of his information. Accordingly he then informed Sheena, "We have some news for you, Sheena, but I'm afraid that it's not the news that you were hoping for." Phil interjected simply by putting his hand on his Inspector's arm with his facial expression clearly requesting that he himself be allowed to break this very important news to Sheena, and Inspector Loughton duly nodded his approval to Phil. So Phil turned round to face Sheena directly and now taking both her hands in his he gently and carefully informed her of the news she had been so anxiously waiting for, unfortunately it wasn't the news she wanted to hear.

"Your father, sorry 'Big Sid', Phil said, while the inspector gave Phil a puzzled look, which Phil duly ignored, as he was well aware of some information that his Inspector clearly wasn't, and that was now this murderer's new title. "'Big Sid'" he continued, "I'm so sorry to have to say, had pleaded not guilty to the murder of your mother." His Inspector was totally in the dark as to the fact that Sheena herself had removed the title of father from this man who had acted so dreadfully, but he didn't ask for an explanation, it wasn't necessary. What was necessary was clearly for this young woman to be comforted.

Sheena had stood up sharply and was on the point of collapse, it was all too much for her and Phil rushed to catch her before she fell completely, "Are you all right Sheena?" Phil asked clearly and sharply, whilst gently tapping her face, trying desperately to bring her mind quickly back into order, to bring her back to him, and finally she nodded her head frantically. Then composing herself as best she could, in order to at least 'appear' normal, she quietly asked them to explain to her everything that had happened. She needed to know what had gone wrong, she'd been so sure that he would now admit his guilt.

The inspector then took over and he gently informed her that they had arrested her father earlier that day and he was basically laughing at them, because he was under the false impression that they had arrested him only because of her information regarding his confession, that they had no proof, no justification to detain him.

However, when they then informed him of the fact that his wife hadn't in fact been cremated at all, but was still lying in the mortuary awaiting burial, he went as white as a sheet, but the fear that had momentarily been showing on his face quickly disappeared as he composed himself, because he was still of the opinion that we'd be unable to do a post-mortem on her. "And to be frank, Sheena," the Inspector added, "we were at that point getting more and more worried about our ability to bring him to justice, especially in the face of your mother's doctor's refusal to change his Cause of Death statement. But we weren't at all ready to give up at that point.

Whilst we were interrogating him," the Inspector continued, "we were interrupted by a telephone call from your mother's doctor, and the call was to the effect that he had changed his mind on Cause of Death from Death by Natural Causes, to Suspicious Death. Obviously we were thrilled by this new state of affairs as it made our whole investigation so much easier. I no longer had to apply for a post-mortem because when it is requested by the deceased's doctor, it is merely a formality for the coroner, and I have to say that at that time I fully expected that your father, when faced with this new information would change his plea to guilty."

But, he continued, "I found your father to be truly a very arrogant man who thinks he is much cleverer than anyone else, and so he was still under the impression that we won't be able to prove that he was responsible for the murder, he obviously still thinks that it's your word against his, which, of course, it isn't now." Sheena was looking increasingly confused and worried, and Phil was worried for Sheena's mental health, he hoped that she would cope with this setback, and for him, he knew that he would do all he could to help her cope.

Inspector Loughton did his best to quell her worries by saying, "Please don't worry, Sheena, when we get the results of the post-mortem it will prove that he is guilty, all the evidence will be there, trust me, he added firmly. And in the meantime we have in fact charged him with murder and he will be detained in prison until the trial. And for what it's worth, I also told your father that I believed, and fully supported all the details which you had given to me in your statement to be true, and that in due course, they would indeed be proved to be true.

I then made your father aware of the fact that a guilty plea at an early stage could possibly go in his favour when it came to sentencing, but as I have already stated, he is an arrogant man who believes that he can outwit the law and so he has maintained his *not guilty* plea. Finally I can let you know that the post-mortem will in fact go ahead in the next few days and your father will go to court for trial at a later date."

Then dropping the official tone he had been using, he smiled warmly at her and told her that she should feel very proud of the tenacity which she displayed, in the face of such adversity, and that of her resolute refusal to be beaten, because, he added, without you and your desperate search for the truth, your father would almost certainly have escaped justice. It is not the type of clear cut case of murder that we would generally investigate. Then sitting back and relaxing now he looked towards Sheena for her response.

Sheena having recovered slightly from the shock of his news told him that she was pleased and relieved that her father was now at least locked up, and that she was sure they would do all that they could to obtain a conviction. She thanked both of them warmly for what they had done for her and her family. Then remembering her visit to her mother's doctor that morning, she asked Inspector Loughton, seemingly casually, when it was that the doctor had phoned. He told her that it was quite amazing really, and totally unexpected because he'd been so adamant earlier in the day, however, he added, in answer to your question it was at precisely 3.15 this afternoon.

He added that he knew the precise time because that was the time the interview with your father had been suspended for me to take the call. Sheena allowed herself a little smile. Of course she would never know for sure, but that would have been about two hours after she had left his surgery, and that along with the Inspector's assertion that the doctor had previously been adamant about not co-operating, not changing the cause of death, allowed her to think that her visit had indeed made some difference. How good it felt for her to have been able to use 'Big Sid's very own, *admitted* tactics of dealing with the doctor in exactly the same way in order to get him at least charged and detained. She had effectively turned the tables on him.

The Inspector then got up to leave and informed her that she could relax now, he'd smiled knowingly at Phil before adding that there was nothing more for her to do now apart from wait for the results from the post-mortem, and then ultimately the trial. And he added finally that he was very confident that any sentence he got would be a very long one.

With the Inspector gone, Phil embraced Sheena warmly, but she was now over excited and was repeating to herself and to Phil over and over again – he's in prison, he's finally in prison. She told Phil that even though it was late now she was going to ring her brothers and give them the good news. But she suddenly realised that at some point in the near future they would also have to hear some very terrible news as well. They would have to listen to the details of *how* 'Big Sid' had murdered their mother, for the horrific details would surely be laid bare at the post-mortem, and again at his trial.

She hadn't said to either Phil or the Inspector that she was still worried, it hadn't seemed appropriate when they had done so much and seemed so confident, but she was still scared that he had pleaded not guilty because he knew that they wouldn't be able to prove positively otherwise, 'beyond a shadow of a doubt' as the saying goes. She was terrified that he would still win in the end, still get away with it, but she tried as hard as she could to put those worries to the back of her mind.

Phil was so very pleased for her, he knew possibly more than most just how much all of this had actually taken out of her. He knew her brothers were also concerned for her health and well-being, but she'd been very adept at keeping things from them, especially the harrowing details of her mother's murder, she had borne those alone. He told her to ring her brothers, taking as long as she needed whilst he prepared her some food.

It had taken Sheena some time and a lot of emotional effort to tell both her brothers everything that had occurred, and prepared them for what was yet to come, and so she sat down next to Phil exhausted, emotionally and physically. She attempted to eat the food that Phil had so lovingly prepared for her but she didn't want food. He eyes brimming with tears she put the food down and held on to Phil for comfort.

With her own eyes still brimming with tears, she looked into the piercing blue eyes of this lovely man and she wanted him, needed him, to hold her. Phil had no hesitation in wrapping her in his arms, he kissed her tears away, he kissed her neck, and he nuzzled in closer to her as she did with him. She loved the feeling of his sweet tender lips on her skin and for a moment they pulled slightly apart whilst gazing into one and others eyes then Phil kissed her full on the lips, it was a gentle, soft, tender kiss at first and Sheena responded eagerly.

The mere touch of his hands, on her body, his lips, on her mouth and the feeling of his love were now allowing her mind to drift into a cloud of sheer happiness, she was giddy with excitement coursing through her veins, her troubles for now, pushed away, deep into the recesses of her mind. And oh, she adored the strange feelings that were going on in her body as he kissed her, feelings that were totally alien to her. Their kisses became more urgent, more passionate. They were hungry for each other, totally absorbed in one another. They fell to the floor and Phil's arms enveloped Sheena's body, her mind was heady with excitement.

His fingers brushed gently through her hair, his hands caressed her body. She was happy, truly happy. His hands slipped under her blouse and onto her bare back. Oh, the gorgeous feeling of his hands on her bare skin, he deftly unfastened her bra and his hand came around to cup her breast. Her body reacted to his touch that in a way that it had never reacted before, she felt her body force her breasts even closer to him, her nipples pert and reacting to his touch, and now she wanted to feel his skin, feel his body with her own hands. Her hands rushed up inside his shirt, his body was hot and sweaty, and she clawed at his back as he kissed her harder now and much more hungrily. She responded with every sense, every fibre of her very being, her response was automatic, uncontrollable. She was struggling to understand what was happening to her, but she couldn't stop, she didn't want to stop, she wanted this feeling to go on forever.

His tongue now searched out hers as their kisses became more passionate than she had ever in her life experienced. His tongue tasted sweet, his mouth tasted sweet and his lips were like electricity charging her body, forcing it into life. She felt the pulsations in her loins and a deep, deep longing to be even closer to him. Everything was happening so fast and everything was pure ecstasy. Their bodies were completely intertwined and his hand reached to stroke her leg and then her upper thigh. She could feel his penis pressing against her pubic bone, she wanted him so much. But the feeling of his hard penis against her body had suddenly jolted her back to reality, suddenly she was panicking, her body wanted to go on, her heart wanted to go on, but her fears, her very real fears meant that she had to stop.

She stopped abruptly and pushed him away, firmly pushed him away shouting loudly now no, no, she couldn't, "Please stop, Phil, please stop," she begged him for she knew that she shouldn't be doing this. It was a mistake, a huge, huge mistake and she was so, so sorry. She had been carried away with the moment, she had been lost in ecstasy, but she couldn't take that next step, she wouldn't take that next step. She apologised to Phil over and over again.

She stood up and adjusted her clothing which by this time was in severe dis-array. Phil was worried that somehow he'd hurt her, he himself looked emotionally hurt and confused for a moment before realising that of course, this was not the right time, this was not what she wanted. And if he was honest, it was not what he wanted either. It had been animal instinct that had taken over him, his love and his need for her.

But he didn't want to move to the next stage of their relationship whilst she was obviously in such distress with the traumatic events of the day. He wanted to wait until she was absolutely sure that she was ready. But he knew one thing for sure now and it was that he loved this woman, she was special to him. He would never have believed that he could have fallen in love so quickly and so deeply, but he had and he was enjoying it. There was no hurry, he told himself. She had been through too much; she needed time to be sure. But he was so very sure, he was sure of his love for her and also now of her love for him. He was dancing on air inside, such was his happiness.

And so Phil apologised to Sheena, put his arms around her and kissed her gently on her cheek. He told her that she had nothing to apologise for, nothing at all he added fervently. He then moved her slightly away in order that he could look directly into her eyes and he cupped her face gently in his big soft hands and told her, assured her, that there was no hurry; he insisted that it was his fault that things had gone so far, and that he completely understood her reticence. Although he then tried his hardest to make her smile by saying in a whimsical manner, "You made me feel really good though." She did smile but it was a weak smile. She still looked terribly worried.

So he sat her down and told her much more seriously that she'd been through so much recently, and especially today. "It was wrong of me to let things go that far, and I'm truly sorry. Please forgive me, Sheena, I would never do anything to hurt you, you know that don't you?" She nodded, because she did know that, and it wasn't his fault entirely. She had wanted him in a way she'd never felt before, in fact it was in such a way that she never even thought existed. She had been unable to control her reactions, and that scared her. Phil added quietly and sincerely, "What you really need right now though is some rest, some time to process in your mind all that had happened today." Not what had happened with him, but what had happened everywhere else in her life, what had happened with 'Big Sid'.

He'd smiled warmly with the mention of 'Big Sid' and she appeared to be more relaxed, more reassured, and so he decided to help her to settle herself, to calm down so he made her a cup of tea with a drop of whisky in it to help her to sleep and begged her to eat just a little if she could. He also asked her if he could stay the night, pointing to the sofa as he spoke, in order for her to fully rest her body. He added that he would gladly organise the children in the morning so that she could sleep longer. He looked at her lovingly, his eyes pleading with her to say yes. And eventually she smiled and nodded before mouthing to him silently, sorry, again.

When Sheena was struggling to sleep that night, she was confused and worried and her thoughts and worries were with Phil and what had just almost happened, as much, if not more than the serious news that she had also received that day. She loved him; in fact she was delirious in her love for him. And she trusted him, she trusted him completely, absolutely. If she'd had any doubt about him in that way, then she would never have allowed him to sleep on the sofa, but she had absolutely no doubt at all he would remain on the sofa, that he wouldn't come to her bedroom without being invited.

She had never, ever felt that way, with that level of confidence, for any other man, and Tom certainly had never engineered that sort of reaction from her, not even in the early, although not even then heady, days of their relationship. No, this was something new altogether. She was also sure, well almost sure, that Phil felt the same way and therein lay her problem – sex. Phil, she knew, would inevitably want sex at some point whilst at the same time she also knew that she wouldn't, or more pointedly, couldn't give him sex.

She fully realised that she would have to make that clear to him, because no matter how much she wanted him, needed him, and loved him, it wouldn't be right for her to 'lead him on'. She was also well aware that telling him of her decision would be a huge risk as it would probably mean that they would no longer see each other, but she had to tell him, and sooner rather than later. She was utterly convinced that once they'd had sex he would turn into a brute, a brute in the way that all men are brutes when it comes to sex, then all his charm and kisses would be saved for the times when he wanted sex again. No, she couldn't, she wouldn't do that.

CHAPTER 21

The following days passed in a whirl of activity for Sheena. She had the funeral to re-arrange, and it would definitely be a burial this time, there were family members to contact, and, of course, she had to prepare herself emotionally for the funeral. The inquest apparently wouldn't now happen until after the trial but at least the coroner had given permission for the funeral to take place and she'd now been given a date which would be the following week. All the relatives in Scotland had been contacted with the new date, and they were told that they had no need to worry about the costs of travelling to the funeral as they were being paid by the undertaker.

Sheena had met the undertaker again on several occasions to finalise all the details and he was still so very, very sorry about the mix up so she told him that for them it had been a good mix up. She felt that now 'Big Sid' was going to prison, and going to prison because of his mistake, that he should know how much that mistake had in fact helped them. She didn't know about the other family and she didn't ask.

Aunt Joyce was not at all surprised when Sheena told her that 'Big Sid', she still couldn't call him her father, not even to Aunt Joyce, was going to trial accused of murdering her mother. In reply Aunt Joyce merely said that he was a Bastard, always had been a Bastard and always would be. *Not a woman to mince her words* thought Sheena, smiling secretly to herself, smiling at the clarity of her Aunt Joyce's description of her father, and of course, she was right as well. Sheena loved to talk to her Aunt Joyce as her Scottish accent sounded so much like her mother's, only a lot broader, of course, nevertheless it reminded her very much of her mother's voice. She would look forward to seeing her again.

Iain was coming home on special extended leave from the Army due to the exceptional circumstances of their mother's death and along with Graham they would of course be going to the trial which they were told was going to be held shortly. She still hadn't told either of them the horrific details of their mother's actual murder, for she knew that they would be laid bare at the trial, she also couldn't bring herself any longer to say those things out loud. But she had hinted at them by telling them that there would be some very hard to hear details of the post-mortem came out during the trial, and although they had asked her what she'd meant by that, she'd told them honestly, that there were things that were too hard for her to say. They seemed to understand and accept that explanation from her.

Phil had stayed with her each evening after work, sleeping on the sofa, ever since the other incident. They were still incredibly close and it didn't seem as though her rebuttal of him had harmed their relationship. However, she hadn't yet had a chance to explain her reasons and he hadn't pushed her, but they were going out together for a quiet meal and a drink later that day and she intended to try to explain things to him then.

When he picked her up that night she marvelled, and not for the first time, at how good he always looked. He seemed to have the ability to look as though he'd managed to get changed in two minutes flat, just throwing on casual clothes, but still looked so great. Her heart still skipped a beat each time she saw him, but her heart was breaking tonight as she felt sure that when she'd told him that sex would always be 'off the table', that he would end their relationship. She had considered waiting until after the funeral to tell him, but decided that making him wait until then would not only be terribly cruel, it would also be terribly selfish of her, because she'd just be using him for support, and in her mind that was almost as bad as a man using a woman for sex.

Whenever they were out their conversations always flowed easily. Because as was beginning to be the norm with them, they never seemed stuck for topics of conversation, and that wasn't because so much was happening to Sheena right now, it was because they talked about anything and everything, mundane things that 'normal' people presumably talk about. When they were out together it always felt like it was time for enjoyment, time for much needed laughter, not time for dwelling on the bad things in her life.

Sheena so much enjoyed their nights out, she was so proud to link his arm as they walked together, or to hold his hand. He had such a knack of making her feel like she was the most important person in the room. Such closeness and ease between them meant so very much to her.

And when they sat closely together either eating, drinking or maybe just chatting easily, there were times when their knees were so close that they touched somehow secretly, and on those occasions it felt as though Phil was pushing his knee, almost imperceptibly ever closer to hers, and those touches, those seemingly innocent touches were like electricity to her. She never moved away from them, and Phil appeared outwardly to be unaware of them, but she knew that he *was* very well aware of them, and knowing that thrilled her even more. At times like that the reaction of her body, of her inner self was uncontrollable; it was as though her body was alien to her, reacting in its own way, but she loved it.

And so it was with a heavy heart that Sheena told him that night that she needed to talk seriously to him, that there were things that she needed to say, but he'd stopped her. He took hold of her hand across the table and told her that he knew she had things to talk about, but he wanted both of them to just enjoy their evening as usual, they could talk later. So happily, Sheena agreed to wait.

When they arrived home though Phil wanted to talk first, he wanted to plead with her not to end their relationship, for he was sure that that was what she was about to tell him, he again apologised for what had 'almost' happened previously, but he asked her to consider the 'bigger picture', to consider how well they fitted together. He told her that he couldn't bear it if she chose not to see him any longer because he loved her and couldn't now imagine life without her.

Sheena was totally taken aback by that. That had been the last thing that she'd expected to hear, and it made what she had to say so much harder. But she looked deep into his tear-filled eyes as she herself began to weep. They held each other tight for some time and when Sheena felt composed enough she told him that she still had to talk to him. There were things he needed to know and that when he'd heard them, well then it would be him that would be ending their relationship. But she kissed him on his sweet tender lips, possibly she thought, for the last time, and told him that she loved him too.

Sheena then told him that she would never, ever be able to have sex with him. She told him that sex to her was disgusting and she knew that she couldn't do it. He tried to interrupt her but she wouldn't let him. She told him that she had never, ever liked sex; in fact it was more than that, because she loathed the very idea of it. She also told him that it was the thought that sex was about to be the conclusion the other evening that had made her stop. It hadn't been, as he'd supposed, the trauma of her mother's murder, because she freely admitted that his touch and his kisses had truly driven her wild, so wild that for a short sweet time she had forgotten about the murder because it was him, her need for him, and only him that had been on her mind that night.

She also added that if she were never in another man's arms again it wouldn't matter to her, because what she had felt that night had been something completely new to her and it had scared her. It had scared her because it had excited her so much. But, she told him, men change when sex has happened, they become different; everything becomes different, and she couldn't bear that to happen to them. She added finally that she completely understood that their relationship would now end, but she wanted him to know how happy he had made her at the most dreadful time of her life. She loved him, she said again before the tears took over once more.

Phil hugged her tightly and rocking her body to and fro he was also fighting back tears and he was saying, "Oh, Sheena, Sheena you've got it all so wrong. I love you darling, I love you, and if you're not going to force me out then I'm staying where I am. I'm staying in this relationship. I'm staying with you. Please don't say that you don't want me. Please don't say that."

They held each other saying nothing for a while. Then with Sheena's head resting on his shoulder and their arms around each other, Sheena protested, "But the sex, Phil, what about the sex?" She insisted again that she couldn't do it; truly she said again, she couldn't do it trying desperately to convince him of her seriousness.

Easing her slightly forward, Phil kissed her tears, her cheeks, her lips. They were tender soft kisses to assuage her tears, not demanding sexual ones. And she was so thoroughly confused. When they had both settled and the tears had eased he asked her to listen to him now, as there were things that he also needed to say. Sheena was nervous now but he gazed lovingly into her eyes and told her that he'd known almost from the start that she'd been treated really badly in her life, especially by the men in her life. He told her that the very fact that she had never mentioned Tom to him had on its own said a lot. He knew that Tom had treated her dreadfully and cruelly and that her father, 'Big Sid, he smiled when he called him that, had not only very obviously treated her mother badly, but he'd treated *her* badly too. That, he said was plain to anyone who cared to spend some time getting to know her.

He paused for a while, his mind searching for the right words to explain what he needed to say. He drew in his breath deeply, and decided that the best way was simply to say it as it was, and hope that she understood him. "I never want you to tell me what Tom has done to you," he said, "because already the pictures in my mind are bad enough, and I'm sure that even those pictures don't come anywhere close to what has actually happened to you. But you have to understand that it would be too horrific for me to hear what he's done to you."

He finished off by saying that he realised that she might think that selfish of him, but he hoped that she'd understand that he just couldn't bear to think about anyone being so cruel to her. He tried to ease the tension of his words, to lighten the strained atmosphere that was in danger of engulfing them, by adding, "Because if you tell me those awful things, then you'll be attending court again, because it will be me on trial for murder!"

Sheena tried to say something to ease his worries, but he stopped her, he needed to finish. "And as for sex," he continued, "I don't *ever* want you to do anything for me, or anyone else for that matter, that you don't want to do. But I have to tell you that your impression of men is completely wrong. We are *not* all the same; some of us are capable of love, real, genuine love. And when you love someone the way that I love you, you respect their wishes; you don't force things onto them that they don't want. I would never want you to do anything you didn't want to do, and if that meant no sex ever, then it would be no sex ever. The only thing you have to do is to keep on loving me the way you do now."

Sheena hugged him and kissed him rapidly and furiously. She couldn't believe what she was hearing. She kept telling him over and over again that she loved him. Then she said that if he changed his mind he only had to tell her and she would understand. He laughed at that remark and smiling cheekily he winked at her, saying, "Well the same thing goes for you. If you change your mind, you be sure to let me know."

She laughed out loud at him and hugged him again. But she couldn't help but wonder how he'd known so much about Tom, because she'd always avoided speaking about him, apart from telling him that he was no longer in her life, she'd never said anything else about him. But she was nevertheless glad that he'd worked things out for himself, because Tom was not a subject she wished to talk about to anyone. The only thing she wanted from Tom was a divorce.

"Right," said Phil suddenly, while grinning broadly at Sheena. "Now that we've got that out of the way and no one's throwing anyone out, let's have a drink to celebrate!" Feeling warm, comfortable and now totally at ease Sheena reminded him that he hadn't yet told her what he'd seen when 'Big Sid' was interviewed at the Police Station. He told her that it had been an amazing thing to watch. "He had been taken into the interview room, you remember the room," he said and she nodded enthralled and desperate for all the details. "Well, when he first came in he was all cocky and sure of himself, totally arrogant and treating Inspector Loughton with contempt. Inspector Loughton was not amused and kept asking him about his wife's death and 'Big Sid' just sat back on his chair, tipping it back so that it was only on two legs."

Sheena snuggled in closer to hear more, and she couldn't help but laugh as she watched Phil's facial expressions and his gesticulations, while he mimicked 'Big Sid's reactions to his interrogation. "Inspector Loughton was playing with him, waiting for him to slip up, and when he didn't he said to him – you do realise that your wife wasn't in fact cremated on Tuesday don't you? Well," Phil said, "you should have seen his face change, it went as white as a sheet, he dropped his chair down hard on the floor and banged on the table saying that he was being ridiculous, that he'd been at the funeral and saw her body go to the Crematorium. 'Big Sid' told Inspector Loughton that he couldn't fool him into saying something that wasn't true. He'd added that even if they thought that he'd murdered his wife they would never be able to prove it. He was more or less telling the inspector that he'd gotten away with murder. Then the phone call came.

When he was then informed that there was in fact going to be a post-mortem, he at first thought that they were bluffing, but when the duty solicitor informed him that it wasn't a joke, that they did have his wife's body he became a broken man, no," Phil corrected himself. "He became a broken bully, a broken murderer. The duty solicitor told him that it would now be in his best interests if he admitted his guilt, but he added sadly, as you've heard from Inspector Loughton, he was too arrogant to even listen to his own solicitor's advice. But he'll come off worst, you mark my words," he added smiling at her.

Sheena was amazed; enthralled, and she wished that she could have been there to see that. She would have loved to see him broken. Phil told her that she would see him at his trial, but she would never have to speak to him, just give her evidence in the same way as she had given her statement. "There will be all the medical evidence to back you up so there's nothing to worry about, and he'll go to jail for a very long time."

"In fact," he added, "when you see him at the trial, you'll see the broken man that I saw when he was told his wife's body was still in the mortuary, prison will break him, you'll see." Sheena hoped and prayed that he was right, but she knew 'Big Sid' well and she knew that he could be cunning and manipulative. The only thing she could do now was pray, she thought to herself, but her fears were assuaged a little by the fact that her mother's doctor had changed his mind. She was though determined to do everything she could to remain positive, she was not going to be beaten, and she would get justice for her mother somehow.

As Phil got up to leave, Sheena again asked him if he'd meant what he'd said earlier, regarding the no sex issue. "I meant every word of it," Phil replied clearly and precisely.

"And we can still hold each other and kiss and love each other?" she asked.

Phil replied with that wicked sense of humour that she loved so much saying, "I hope so!" So Sheena then tentatively asked him if he wanted to stay the night. Phil agreed immediately and said that he would sleep on the bed in Adam's room as it's a lot better than the sofa, but Sheena said boldly, whilst blushing, that she'd like him to sleep in her bed. For an answer he merely wrapped his arms around her and kissed her again. And so for the first time they actually slept together without actually 'sleeping together'. Sheena, although she had asked Phil to stay, was nevertheless incredibly nervous. But she needn't have worried as everything seemed to fall into place quite naturally. Whilst neither of them was completely naked, they were naked enough for Sheena to be able to feel the bare skin of Phil's manly body next to hers, and she couldn't help but smile secretly to herself when she noticed that Phil certainly didn't have a 'weedy' chest like

Tom had, and he *definitely* didn't have a beer belly. Then as Phil put his arm around her, gently cupping her right breast in his right hand, which she was very pleased about, they both slept incredibly well.

CHAPTER 22

Iain had arrived home from the Army and was staying again with Graham. Sheena decided that she needed to go over to Graham's house to see them both. There was a great deal of things for them to talk about, not least of which was the up-coming post-mortem report. She had worried endlessly about the fact that neither of her brothers knew the real details of their mother's death.

Their mother's death had been truly horrific and she hadn't previously thought herself capable of telling them the details, those soul destroying heart-breaking details. And she still didn't feel that she personally could tell them, because these were the only other two people in the world who'd loved her mother as much as she did, and they deserved to have some advance information of those details before they heard it from strangers. Because once they'd heard those them then, as she knew only too well, those details would remain in their minds forever. And so she decided to tell them as much as she could bear to.

When Sheena arrived at Graham's house there was a lot of pleasantries and laughter between them all which helped them all to relax. They had both told her that they were amazed at the fact that 'Big Sid' had pleaded not guilty despite the fact that he knew a post-mortem would now be carried out, they were convinced that he would be found guilty and they didn't even know all the facts, and that astounded Sheena, she wished that she had half as much confidence as they did. They were eager to know exactly what had happened, and more importantly what had made the doctor had change his mind, which obviously meant that the job of the police to convince the coroner to order a post-mortem had now, of course, been made much easier.

She went on to tell them about Phil being able to 'look in' on 'Big Sid' being questioned and there were howls of laughter as she herself now recreated, as best she could using the same sort of facial expressions and gesticulations, his blatant arrogance, his demeanour and finally his false bravado as he refused to plead guilty. Then getting more serious she told them that the results of the post-mortem would probably be out in the next few days and that they would then hopefully, officially be told the cause of death, then shortly after that they would be given a date for the trial, apparently it wouldn't be too long before a trial was able to take place.

She went on to ask them if they would be going to the whole trial, or perhaps just attend for the verdict, half hoping they might that they were only going to attend for the verdict, or perhaps even not attend at all, and then she wouldn't have to tell them anything, but of course, they said that they would be there all the way through, they wanted to see his face as he realised that he was going to be going to jail for hopefully, the rest of his life.

Iain then said to Sheena that although they were, of course, going to go, they, Graham and Iain, had talked about it between themselves, and to them it seemed pretty clear cut. They said that the only explanation could be that he'd fed her too many pills, and that that would make it poisoning. But they couldn't really understand why 'Big Sid' didn't try to get out of the murder conviction by saying that she'd committed suicide, or that he'd thought that maybe she'd had a heart attack because of the amount of pills she'd taken. Graham interjected with, "Well he's obviously not as clever as he thought he was then, because that would have been a pretty obvious defence."

They asked Sheena if he'd had a solicitor present when he was being interviewed. The reason for them asking that was because they were trying to pre-empt what any hiccups in his pending conviction might be, what might stop him from being found guilty. "After all," they added, "no one could disprove suicide because the rest of the tablets are gone, and if his solicitor has anything about him then he would advise him to say that she'd committed suicide." Sheena confirmed that he did indeed have a solicitor present, but there was no way, she added, that he could say suicide because there would be too much 'other' evidence.

They wanted to know what she meant by that. Their suspicions were immediately aroused as they realised to their horror, that Sheena knew more about this than they did, more than she was in fact saying, and so they challenged her. "What are you not telling us, Sheena?" they demanded, almost in unison. So she reluctantly told them that 'Big Sid' had told her all the horrific details, more than that, she added, he'd actually enjoyed telling her them. Although before they asked for any detailed information, she quickly clarified that with the fact that she still couldn't bring herself to tell them absolutely everything he'd said. Not even now that they'd asked. No, she replied before adding that she could only   tell them the barest of details, and that was that he had repeatedly raped her until she'd agreed to swallow the pills that would ultimately kill her.

Iain stood up and started pacing up and down, such was his frustration, and he was shouting at her. "You knew this. All this time you knew this and you didn't think to tell us?" Iain was so angry with her, and it hurt her deeply. But then she surprised herself by immediately shouting back at him that she hadn't told them because she *couldn't* tell him. That she didn't want them to remember their mother that way if they didn't have to.

She tried to reason with him by saying that she hadn't thought that it would ever come out, because she didn't think, as they also didn't think, that it would ever get to court. But Iain was getting more and more angry with her now, demanding to know just who she thinks she is to decide what they could and couldn't be told.

"What the bloody hell makes you think that you alone are the only one that can cope with bad news? Just tell me that;" he demanded angrily, "exactly what sort of bloody measure you've used to judge our wisdom and ability to cope. What the hell makes you think that we are less capable than you are of coping with bad news?" Iain had been standing with his back to her looking out of the window whilst he'd been shouting at her. She was fuming, so very angry was she with him that she got up and moving quickly towards him she pulled at his arm harshly in order to turn him around and look at her full in the face.

And then she started. "Do you think I wanted to be the one to be told the details of all this horror? Don't you think that I would rather remember mum the way she was, not remember her fighting for her life?" Sheena was so fired up now as she continued, "Do you want to know why he told me and not you two, because it wasn't by accident you know?" She didn't wait for him to answer any of those questions because she was far too angry with him to wait for answers. But in the event. Iain was not showing any signs of apologising to her, or of answering her questions, in fact he just roughly pulled his arm away from her, he pulled it away in such a manner that it indicated clearly that he didn't want to know her right now, didn't want to speak to her.

But after a few seconds spent composing himself, he said sarcastically, "Okay, you seem to know everything else, so tell us why he picked you to give all this information to, tell us exactly what *you* think makes you so special." There was so much vitriol in his language that Sheena was in danger of being reduced to tears, but she was determined to push the tears back, she couldn't break down now, and so she pulled him round again to face her before starting her tirade again. She told him now in a steadfast manner that he'd picked her because he's a Bastard, he'd picked her because he 'gets off' on humiliating women, he'd picked her because he wanted to hurt and embarrass her. She added that he probably would have expected at the very least a punch from either, or possibly both of them if he'd told them, and so he'd picked her. Then she went on to tell them that he'd planned it all from the very beginning, and that it was in fact pre-meditated murder that he'd committed.

She had to do her utmost now to keep those tears at bay as she went on to tell him, "'Big Sid' had made sure that I went to see Mum the night before she died, and he'd done that purely to give us time together, time together for me and mum to say goodbye to each other, and while we were supposed to be saying that goodbye to each other he was sitting skulking in the kitchen secretly laughing to himself about it. And yes," she added with venom, "he was laughing at us, he was laughing at mum and me behind our backs, because *we* didn't know that we were supposed to be saying goodbye, only he knew that. *I* didn't know that I was supposed to be saying goodbye," she added, "and all the time he was 'getting off' on it."

She couldn't stop now she was so angry, so she added, "Tom and 'him' were sitting there in the kitchen discussing what it was like to have sex with me, and yes you heard me right, Tom was happily telling him what it was like to have sex with me. Should I have told you that too?" She demanded. She told them in no uncertain manner, that she'd asked him when he was breaking her heart by giving her all that information, she'd asked him to let her bring them both into the room. "So that you could listen too," she explained, "so that you wouldn't think that I was some sort of mad woman, because that was precisely what you first thoughts were when I told you both that he'd killed our mother.

That's what you thought, and you can't tell me that I'm wrong in thinking that," she added finally. She was running out of breath, she was shouting at him and accusing him of being thoughtless, but Iain still wasn't finished. His anger at it all, at his father, at life, and at her, was such that he just didn't seem to be able to calm down. But Sheena was now totally exhausted and so she'd sat back down heavily on to the sofa. While Graham for his part had stayed silent throughout it all, just looking constantly from one to the other of them.

Then Iain said rather quietly, looking again out of the window, "Whose car is that you've come here in?" That question puzzled Sheena, because she'd been fully expecting an apology, she couldn't understand of what importance her car was. So she told him, a lot more calmly now that it was Iain's car, because, she explained, when Tom left he took their car with him. But the response from Iain shocked her even more. Iain cut her to the quick when he said extremely hurtfully to her, "Don't you think you should have at least waited for your bed to get cold before you put another man in it?" Then he added even more cruelly, "There's probably more than our father and Tom who discusses your sex life."

Sheena gasped and looked at him dumbfounded for a moment. This was her brother speaking to her, a brother that she loved dearly and that she had thought, at least up until that moment, had also loved her equally dearly. But it was too much for her, much too much, and it had elicited a strength of venom in her that she hadn't even realised she possessed. She got up again and standing as tall and proud as she could she again physically turned him around to face her full on, and then with all the strength that she could muster, she slapped him hard across the face, so hard in fact that within seconds she could clearly see his cheek turning red.

Her immediate instinct then was to apologise, to beg his forgiveness and to offer him some form of comfort. But from somewhere deep inside her, something was holding her back, some inner strength, or hidden power, was telling her to hold back, telling her that he'd deserved that slap, and telling her to be brave and to continue standing up for herself.

It wasn't words being spoken to her, she wasn't going mad, but she did feel an inner strength coming from somewhere, and that somewhere, or someone, she believed was her mother. Her mother was giving her the strength to be bold, saying to her, don't let any man, no matter who, walk all over you ever again. She was suddenly reminded of that final conversation that she'd had with her mother the night before she died.

So she took in a deep breath before saying to Iain venomously, "Don't you dare judge me, don't you dare, or try to tell me what I should or shouldn't be doing." Her anger rising in line with the sound of her voice as she told him that one man or another had been telling her what to do, or what not to do, since she was a babe in arms. No one, no one ever again, she'd insisted firmly, is ever going to be telling her what she should, or shouldn't be doing now, and especially no man. Then she added harshly, "And as for that man that killed *my* mother," she'd emphasised 'my' now because she felt as though she was fighting a battle for her mother on her own, "you can call him 'father' if you want to, but don't ever call him that to me again, for he's no father of mine," she added, her voice now trailing off in frustration as much as in exhaustion.

She declared even more wearily now that he would never again be a father to her, and that all she was looking forward to where he was concerned was seeing him go to prison, hopefully for the rest of his life. And she added directly to Iain and with genuine feeling, that if he didn't have any respect or compassion for her, then he could stay out of her life as well. She hastily grabbed at her car keys and got up to leave. Iain had turned away from her again rubbing his stinging cheek, after she'd slapped his face and she wasn't about to get him to turn around again before she left.

But she stopped herself from leaving because she realised that there was something more that she needed to say. With this new inner strength that was now pushing her forward, pushing her to say everything that was on her mind, to hold nothing back she continued her tirade towards Iain by saying, "Do you want to know why Big Sid killed our mother; do you want to know what his main reason was for murdering her? Because he didn't murder her for nothing, he had his reasons, oh yes he had his reasons all right." She didn't wait for an answer, she couldn't stop now. "Well I'll tell you why," she'd said with her hostility towards him increasing all the time. "I'll tell you exactly why he killed her, he killed her for sex! Yes he murdered her for sex.

Yes," she added again with her heart beating ever faster and her temper rising all the time. "For that very same sex that you so easily denigrate where I'm concerned, that thing that seems to rule every waking thought of all men, well it was for sex. He quite proudly, and crudely told me that *my* mother," again she emphasised 'my', "wasn't only refusing to give him sex, apparently she'd had the audacity to refuse him sex frequently, weird sex, sex any way and any time he wanted it.

Well according to him, she refused him sex too often and he was no longer going to stand for it. He arrogantly believed that he had a God given right to demand any type or amount of sex that he wanted, any time he wanted it, and that as his wife she had the responsibility to provide it, regardless of her mood, or her health. That's the reason why after she died he didn't want any of us taking care of him, he was perfectly capable of taking care of himself, because all he needed in life was sex and now that he was free, he was going to get that sex anywhere and everywhere he could. So," she added finally. "Don't you dare deem to discuss, or even think about my sex life, because it has absolutely nothing to do with you? You men, she added indignantly, sex is all that's ever on your mind." She'd finished off by adding with as much sarcasm as she could muster, "And let me tell you this, sex is seriously over-rated."

But as she was about to finally leave, Iain did turn around, and she couldn't fail to see that he was crying, not just crying, but sobbing heavily as though it had all been too much for him. He'd dropped down onto the sofa and put his head in his hands and he was crying like a baby. She wasn't sure whether to console him or not because she was still so angry with him.

But he'd looked at her, his eyes pleading with her for forgiveness as he beckoned her, silently, to come closer to him. She was still angry, furious in fact, but she loved her brother and couldn't turn her back on him, no matter what he'd done, for in truth they all needed each other right now. And so she relented and sat down next to him and despite herself, despite her anger, she held him, she comforted him as he buried his head in her shoulder and said repeatedly that he was sorry, so very, very sorry.

He said that he didn't know where all that vitriol had come from, but he just couldn't bear to think of 'Big Sid' doing those things to his mother. He said that it was the vile pictures that had trespassed into his mind that had made him say those things. It was images that he didn't want to see, and he added much more contritely now, that he now understood her, understood why she hadn't told them all those terrible things, because if their situations had been reversed, then he would have kept that sort of information from her, he would have wanted to preserve her memories in the same way that she had obviously tried to preserve his.

Sheena's anger had finally subsided, and she was crying with him now, but she was still feeling proud of herself for standing up to him and not buckling under pressure, and so she kept telling him that it was all right, and reassuring him as best she could, that everything was all right. Graham then finally broke into the conversation by saying that they all needed to calm down a bit, that it had been such a shock for Iain and himself to hear those things, but he understood why Sheena had not told them, and he added, his voice also full of remorse now, that if he were completely honest, if she had told them on the day of the funeral all those terrible things then they probably *would* have thought she had gone mad. And he reminded Iain about how distressed and confused Sheena had been on the day of the funeral and that he'd also have to admit it, if he was being truthful, that he wouldn't have believed Sheena either, he'd also have thought that she was delusional.

Iain was doing his best to compose himself, but he was still rocking back and forth, hugging his knees and still crying, but somehow he managed to nod in agreement. Sheena thought hard about Iain, and although he was supposed to be this tough soldier, having served time in Northern Ireland at the height of the 'troubles', he was at heart a sensitive soul, some might even describe him as a mummy's boy. And she didn't mean that in a bad way, but it was true. He'd only left home and joined the Army to get away from 'Big Sid' and he was only sixteen, still very much a child. And now fifteen years on he was now an officer in the Army, but at heart he was still a mummy's boy. And there was no shame in that, Sheena thought to herself.

When Iain could finally speak, he explained that he'd been angry, jealous even, jealous that she'd been the one to spend the last hours with their mother, that he'd been so far away when his mother had needed help, and he added that he hadn't meant any of the things he'd said, especially about Phil, because he knew only too well that Tom had been a bastard, maybe not as bad a one as 'Big Sid' he said, with a nod to Sheena and trying desperately to get her to smile, but a bastard all the same. Sheena agreed with him about that, but she thought to herself that if he'd known just how much of a bastard Tom was then he would again be shocked, but she wasn't about to tell him any of that.

Then Graham said to Sheena, and not in a sarcastic manner, but in a complimentary one, "I'll tell you what kid." Graham being seven years older than her had always called her 'kid' or 'sis'. "You've changed, yes, you've certainly changed. And I can't tell you how proud I was to see you give this one here a slap. If ever anyone needed a slap it was him and it was then." He pushed his brother playfully as he said that. Then he added that it was so good for him to see her standing up for herself for once. "For," he said determinedly, "one thing that you said when you were so angry, really made me realise just how badly you've been treated during your life, and I am not only talking about just now, not just over all this, but all your life. Because you're right, all your life you've had to do what you were told, and you were always being told what to do by men. So yes kid, I'm proud of you." And, he added, somewhat complimentarily, "If Phil doesn't do the right thing by you and make you happy, I know that you'll show him the door. Yes, I've no need, no, *we've* no need to worry about you, not now, and that's good."

Everything between them all had finally calmed down but Sheena knew, especially in the light of all that had happened between them that she had to say more. She felt very strongly that she ought to warn them that there may well be some other things that may come up during the trial that could be even more distressing. So she did tell them that, and she added that there could be things that she herself wasn't aware of, but she hoped that they would all go together and do their best to support each other.

They both told her not to worry, but Iain especially hugged her tightly and said again that he was sorry, sorry for not only what he'd said, but how he'd spoken to her before and that of course they would all go together and help each other to get through what could possibly prove to be the worst time of their lives. He then clarified that with the indisputable fact that knowing your father has murdered your mother is bad enough on its own, but having to be told how and why he'd done it was something much more difficult to cope with.

Sheena left them finally feeling much happier. She had told them both that as soon as she'd been given a date for the trial then she would let them know. But she thought long and hard about what Graham had said regarding the fact that she'd changed, and she had changed, although she hadn't fully realised until then, how much she'd changed. But she knew that what she'd said about never again being ordered about by a man she meant every word of. She could never imagine Phil attempting to order her about, in fact he was just the opposite, he was helping her to stand up for herself, and she could feel herself changing and she liked that, she liked being a bit more in charge of her own destiny.

CHAPTER 23

Sheena was getting agitated, it had been almost a week now and still they hadn't been told the results of the post-mortem she'd asked Phil to find out, if he could, exactly what was happening. The funeral had been arranged because they had been given permission for that, but she was extremely anxious to know what the results of the post-mortem were. But Phil didn't come back with any good news. The post-mortem had in fact been completed but the Pathologist had sent the results directly to the coroner, which apparently is quite normal he added, and the coroner won't be releasing any information on the post-mortem until the trial,, which apparently is the way these things work, so unfortunately they all had to wait for the details until then.

Sheena was disappointed, of course, but she knew that if there had been any way to illicit any information prior to the trial then Phil would have found that way, for now she had to concentrate on the 'real' funeral for her mother which was to be the following day. But she did think, and not for the first time given recent events, that was that the wheels of justice did indeed move extremely slowly. She had informed both Graham and Iain of the new information and they had all agreed that there was nothing to do but wait.

During the last few days, and with Phil's encouragement, she had built on the confidence and change in her that Graham had noticed. She'd had her hair styled in a much more modern fashion and she'd been shopping for some new clothes, not that she had a big budget to spend, but she'd managed to save some money from when Tom was still living there, and she was using some of it to update her wardrobe, and she had to admit that looking the part, went a long way towards acting the part. And she was very much enjoying feeling her confidence growing daily. She had changed so much from when she was with Tom that when she looked in the mirror now, she didn't see an old woman looking back at her, an old woman covered in bruises, but a young woman, a young woman who was looking good and happily, excitingly looking forward, forward to a completely different life, and that pleased her greatly.

It was the morning of the funeral and this time it was departing from Sheena's house, not from her mother's as before. The manager of the funeral parlour had called to see her a few hours before the funeral to check that everything was okay. Sheena felt sorry for this man as he was obviously still extremely upset by his error over her mother's previous funeral. She had tried her hardest to ease his worried by letting him know that it wasn't important, in fact it had been a good thing for them, but he was worried that his business would be damaged if people got to hear about them mixing up bodies! He'd said that his family had been in this business for over fifty years, with his father running it before him and that nothing of this kind had ever happened before.

But he promised her that no expense had been spared for her mother, that everything would run smoothly and that he was sure that she wouldn't be disappointed with his choice of coffin. She didn't really know what she could say to him, she'd let him make all the arrangements, and to be honest she was glad of that so she simply told him, in a gentle and heartfelt manner, not to worry.

Phil accompanied Sheena to the funeral and along with Graham and Iain they all went together. When the hearse drew up outside Sheena's home, her heart skipped a beat as she realised that her mother was lying in there, inside that box, but she was calm this time. This time she knew that her mother truly could rest in peace, this time her murderer was behind bars, and hopefully staying there.

Aunt Joyce and other members of the family were there, having travelled all the way from Scotland, and it was truly good to see them all again. Sheena chatted with her Aunt Joyce for some time, filling her in with all that had happened and all that had yet to happen. She still couldn't believe how much Aunt Joyce hated 'Big Sid' and always had, but she very much enjoyed talking to her especially as she had a lot to say about her mother's younger years that Sheena had no idea about.

At the funeral Sheena suffered none of the outbursts that she had first time around, she was very calm and comfortable in her manner this time. In fact as the coffin passed her on its way down the church isle she kissed her finger tips and tapped them on the coffin as it passed her, and whispered silently, "Rest in peace now, mum, rest in peace." And as the coffin was being lowered into the ground she placed a single red rose on it. There were still tears; of course there were still tears, but no hysterics this time and no murderer around either!

After the funeral all the mourners returned to Sheena's house this time where she'd lovingly prepared some food and drink for everyone and Sheena along with both Graham and Iain had thanked the undertaker, they told him what a lovely coffin it was, and it was indeed a lovely coffin, and for a man who was so devastated by his mistake he went away pleased with the final outcome.

Iain had made a point of taking Sheena to one side and complimenting her, both on her supply of food and drink and more importantly he'd said, he was so pleased to see her looking so good and so confident. He did, however, show his nerves as he asked her if she truly forgave him for his attitude the previous week. Sheena gazed at him lovingly for a moment or two before embracing him warmly, there was no need for words between them, for they both knew instinctively that all was forgiven.

After all the mourners had left, Sheena and her brothers discussed the up-coming trail. It was to be the following week, and they all said that they were ready for it; in fact it couldn't come quickly enough. Sheena again gently reminded them that it would undoubtedly be upsetting for all of them. Sheena told them that she'd received a letter informing her that she would be called as a witness, she added somewhat bewildered, that she had no idea as to what she was supposed to be a witness to; but just that she had been called to give evidence and that it unnerved her somewhat. She had asked Phil if he knew the reason as to why she'd been called as a witness and he'd told her that it would be to put forward the details of her mother's supposed ill health just prior to her death, but it could equally be about anything. Apart from that then he was none the wiser on that matter than she was, but he did know that once you were called as witness, you couldn't refuse. It wasn't a request, even if it was worded as such, it was a legal requirement. That statement had only worried her more.

Graham and Iain both told her that she would just have to answer whatever questions they might ask as clearly and as truthfully as she could. She wanted to know from Graham in particular if he'd been called as a witness as he'd arrived at their mother's home on that dreadful day before she had, but he'd said that he'd quite simply received a letter informing him of the date and nothing else.

They were all looking forward to seeing 'Big Sid' get the comeuppance he truly deserved when he went to court to face trial, and they were all intending to be around for that. Sheena and Graham were worried as to whether Iain would be able to get any more leave from the Army to attend the trial, but he assured both of them that he'd have no problem with the Army giving him leave under the circumstances, but he would have to return as soon as possible after the trial.

They'd both asked Sheena if Phil had given her any idea as to what his sentence might be, when he was found guilty, because they weren't going to even think about any other outcome. Unfortunately she had to tell them that Phil was no wiser than her on that matter, he'd done everything he could to find out as much as he could, but there were no hard and fast rules and it would very much depend on the outcome of the post-mortem and what the Pathologist had listed as the cause of death.

CHAPTER 24

A fair amount of time had passed now since the funeral, and the trial was now planned for the next day. Sheena knew that she needed to talk to Phil about the issues that were worrying her regarding their own relationship. And although Phil had spent many nights now at her home she had always avoided the subject, and Phil had never put her under any pressure, but with the trial so close she really needed to discuss things with him, things that could no longer be put off, she'd already put them off more than she really should have.

Sheena had fully intended to talk to Phil that evening, but he wanted to take her out, wanted her to relax as much as possible before the trial and so they'd gone out for a lovely quiet meal. She asked him if he had any idea as to how long the trial might take, or what the order of things might be, but all he could do was support her as always, and as he'd never been to one himself, he had absolutely no idea as to what they involved.

She couldn't believe how easy and comfortable she was with Phil, it was as though they'd been together for years, so relaxed were they with each other. She'd also noticed that when they were out together, she was completely free to speak to whomever she wanted to. Even when Phil was close by and watching her, and he did watch her, his eyes were in fact on her all the time when they were out amongst strangers, well strangers to Sheena at least, but she knew without a doubt, that he was watching her because he was so proud of her, he actually *wanted* everyone to notice her, and what's more, Sheena actually *liked* the way in which he watched her, the way he couldn't take his eyes off her!

Whereas on the rare occasions that Tom had taken her out, well he was watching her because he was jealous, he'd always presumed that everyone she'd spoken to, especially if they were male, were speaking to her to arrange some kind of secret assignation. By contrast, she felt so liberated when she was with Phil, she was truly free to do what she liked without being chastised for one reason or another, and whilst that feeling was a very satisfying one, it was at the same time a scary one, because it was so difficult to get used to, so difficult to accept that Phil wasn't suddenly going to morph into Tom.

She laughed to herself when she even voiced those thoughts inside her own head, never mind out loud, because she realised how ridiculous they would sound to any normal human being, but the fact was that she had never really realised just how restricted Tom had kept her, how he'd controlled her every move, her every conversation, until Phil showed her that life isn't really like that – not for normal people anyway. And she enjoyed that freedom very much. And she hoped and prayed that nothing would ever alter between them.

Whilst they had been out that evening though, there had been a lot on Sheena's mind, and it wasn't only about the trial the next morning. No, there were things between the two of them that she had to confront and she'd decided that she was going to confront them that very evening, before the awfulness of the trial enveloped her completely.

She had received a letter from her solicitor that morning informing her that her divorce was going ahead without any objections from Tom, it was going to go through quickly because it was uncontested, she hadn't really expected any objections, not given what she had confronted him with before he left, but she was still surprised that it was going ahead so soon and she hadn't as yet told Phil, so she resolved to discuss it that evening.

Other aspects of their relationship were also on her mind, and no matter how hard she tried to push them to the back of her mind; they kept coming repeatedly to the fore. Phil had now spent many nights in Sheena's bed, and true to his word he had never tried to have sex with her, or to attempt to coerce her into having sex with him, but she knew well enough that he wanted sex with her, she knew that to be a fact, if only by the number of times she'd felt his erect penis against her body and it was, she decided, totally unfair of her to expect him to continue in that fashion, not if she was looking for a long-term relationship with him anyway.

And she did want a long-term relationship with him, she loved him, she loved him so very, very much that she just could not contemplate life without him now. She was also well aware that Phil loved her children and also that they, in turn, loved him back, they were so relaxed and well behaved with him, it was, thought Sheena, quite extraordinary for them to behave so well. And their approval was so very important to her, more important than anything. The more she thought about their relationship, the more she knew that there were almost no negatives, almost, she added again silently to herself, for the one *big* negative that remained, she intended to resolve that very evening.

And accordingly she had arrived at the difficult decision that she would have to let him have sex with her. She loved the feeling of his bare skin touching hers, and she loved the feeling of his big manly hands softly and gently caressing her body. And so she had come to the conclusion that surely he wouldn't be rough with her, or cruel, surely he would just 'do it' swiftly and gently. She hoped so anyway.

Maybe, she reasoned, she could let him have sex just every now and again; maybe he wouldn't want it every day, or even twice a day, as Tom did. And so although it terrified her, her mind was made up and so she had resolved to let him now, finally, have sex with her. She'd reasoned that it wouldn't take long, and that it would please him, and she so wanted to please him. All men wanted sex, *needed* sex even, and although she could happily live all her life without it, men she knew, couldn't. She just hoped and prayed that it wouldn't change him, wouldn't turn him into a demanding brute of a man.

CHAPTER 25

Since Phil and Sheena had arrived back home that evening, Sheena had been particularly quiet and that fact had not escaped Phil, and he was duly concerned about her. He wanted to know if the worried look that was etched all over her face, was about the trial the next day and so he'd put his arm around her in an reassuring way, in an effort to help calm the nerves that he could clearly tell by her very demeanour, were coursing through her body. But Sheena assured him that she wasn't worrying about the trial, or not only the trial anyway, no, she was worrying about him. Phil was perplexed by that and asked her why on earth she was worrying about him, surely, he'd asked, everything was good between them.

So Sheena, sitting forward and holding both his hands looked into his gorgeous blue eyes and smiling happily at him, she told him that she had been thinking very seriously about their relationship, and she added, quite sincerely, that she loved him, that he must realise just how much she loved him. There was a look of worry now showing on Phil's face and as Sheena became aware of it, she laughed, somewhat nervously, and tried to sound really happy and pleased about what she was going to say. "Don't look so worried, Phil," she'd assured him, this is something good, and more than that, it was something she was sure he'd be pleased about.

"Okay," Phil said, his face now breaking into a, still nervous, smile. "Tell me what it is. Tell me what's causing your face to look as though the end of the world is nigh!" He was simply trying to lighten the mood, but it was having no effect on her, and so he waited patiently, but worriedly for her to enlighten him. So Sheena told him about the letter, about the fact that her divorce was going to be finalised without complications, and finalised very soon. Phil was thrilled for her. "That's great Sheena," he said. "It will be a good feeling for you to finally be rid of him, to finally be yourself." And then he took her in his arms and smiling at her warmly he added with a huge grin on his face, "It will be good for both of us, we can start to look forward to a real future together."

Sheena was so elated by his response; it was more that she had hoped for. And so she told him that there was some other good news that she wanted to tell him. Phil could see that she was excited, but he couldn't imagine what could be better news than that, unless she'd heard something about the up-coming trial, so with his voice matching her own excitement he said, "Well come on then tell me, don't keep me in suspense."

Sheena, feeling that everything was going well, and prepared for the fact that she would now be able to cope somehow, she excitingly told him that she'd decided that he could have sex with her that night. That if he was able to.. to stay overnight that is, and of course *wanted* to stay overnight. She was babbling now and she knew it, but she had to continue, and so she added with as much forced excitement as she could muster, that he could have sex with her.

She was smiling and excited and looking very pleased with herself, she had told him, she had got the worst part over with, surely the rest would now be easy, and she fully expecting Phil to share, if not exceed her excitement. But the smile just fell from his face, worse than that he looked shocked, hurt and appalled. He quickly, and somewhat harshly, let go of her hands and standing up now he paced up and down the room for a few minutes, quite clearly deep in thought.

Sheena couldn't understand what was wrong. She asked him what was wrong, had she said too much, too soon. She told him that she'd been sure that he'd wanted her, and she added that she could tell how much he wanted her when he'd spent nights in her bed, and that she could *feel* that he wanted her. She was herself now distraught and begged him to tell her what was wrong. What had she done?

Phil, having calmed down a little, came back to the sofa and again sat down next to her, and looking very sombre and serious he took her hand again and started to explain to her exactly what was wrong. As he looked into her eyes, he could see her pain; he knew that his reaction had hurt her and the last thing he would want to do in this world, would be to hurt her. But he himself was feeling incredibly mixed emotions. He was feeling pain and sorrow for her in equal amounts. Pain for the way she had worded her thoughts, and sorrow for what must be the terrible way that this wonderful woman must have been treated in the past to address their first time of making love so.

He needed to make himself clear, he needed to make her understand, and he needed to do all that without hurting her any further. Because he knew that she'd had no intention of hurting him, but hurt him she had. She had totally disregarded his love for her, in what was basically just one sentence. He drew in a deep breath, and he told her, as gently as he could, that nothing, nothing at all had changed for him since the last time this subject came up, that he didn't want to have sex with her then, and he didn't want to have sex with her now.

Sheena now felt humiliated, embarrassed and angry; she immediately stood up saying that she was sorry, before adding that they obviously wanted different things, and that she'd patently misunderstood him. She tried now to give him an easy way out that would be the least embarrassing for both of them, and so she said that perhaps it would be better if he just left. Phil, smiling now at Sheena was totally amazed by this woman's lack of knowledge, lack of knowledge of real love, and he loved her all the more for it. So again gently taking her hand he told her, quietly and lovingly, to sit down while he explained something to her.

Sheena had absolutely no idea what he was going to say now, and she still wasn't sure if she wanted to hear it, but she sat down still feeling very hurt and embarrassed. "Listen to me carefully, Sheena," Phil said, "because what I am about to tell you will apply I hope, for the rest of your life. And that is that you must never, ever, 'let' anyone, anyone at all, have sex with you because as I've told you previously, I don't want to have sex with you." Sheena let out a deep and heavy sigh of frustration, before he continued. "But. I *do very much* want to make love to you, and let me tell you darling, there is a world of difference between having sex and making love. So never, ever 'let' anyone have sex with you."

Sheena was so confused, and she told him that she didn't understand, that she thought they were one and the same thing having sex, or making love. He smiled at her and held her tightly before saying, "Oh, my love, they're not. I promise you that they are not." He kissed her passionately with his soft lips devouring hers, and he held her tightly as he did so. And Sheena, despite feeling so embarrassed a few moments ago, couldn't help but respond. She so loved his kisses, she so loved the way that they seemed to go all through her body, and that they excited her in such a way that was so new to her.

Phil then gently released his lips from hers, and gazing into her huge, now tear-stained, brown eyes, he asked her if that was the sort of kiss she was used to getting. He looked at her then in such a comical way that his look was saying, 'don't you dare say yes'! For an answer Sheena just shook her head, as she too was now smiling, and she was lost for words and so very much in love. "Thank God for that!" Phil said laughing. "You made me wait for that answer didn't you? Well," he said. "When you are ready, and not before you are ready, we will make love."

Phil led her upstairs and they got into bed, both of them naked apart from their pants. Phil slowly pulled the covers back and gazed at her beautiful body, and he told her that she was beautiful. He found it so hard to believe that she had never been told that she was beautiful, because her beauty, to him, was ethereal, but to his great sadness he knew that she had never been told that simple, but true fact. Sheena turned towards him and wrapping her arms around his neck she kissed him, and she kissed him hungrily, she wanted him to know that she wanted him, but didn't know how to say it now, she was too nervous to say anything. She'd believed him when he'd said that there was a difference between sex and making love, but she still couldn't imagine what it could be, so she was trying to say with her actions, with her kisses, that she wanted him.

But Phil gently released her hold and told her to relax. "Just totally relax, sweetheart. I'm not *ever,* ever, going to hurt you." He asked her if she trusted him not to hurt her and she'd said that she did. "I'm going to help you to relax," he said. "But I'm not going to make love to you until you want me to, until you tell me that you want me to make love to you, all I need you to do is to relax and let me make you feel good, okay?" Sheena nodded, but her heart was beating fast just with him looking at her the way he was.

He'd repeated very slowly and firmly again, that he wasn't going to hurt her, and he wasn't going to make love to her until she wanted him to. And he made her promise that she would just say stop, if she wanted him to stop. He assured her that saying stop was okay, more than okay he'd added, smiling at her. Then he asked her once more if she trusted him and believed him. She smiled at him, but it was a nervous smile, she did believe him, of course she believed him, but she was lying there almost naked, and it left her feeling fully exposed. She tried so hard to relax, but the truth was that she was terrified and trying hard not to show it, to push her terror to the back of her mind. Phil had told her that he only wanted to please her, to make her feel good, but that reminded her too much of Tom. For it was with her lying in this very same position and so exposed that he had promised to give her the 'orgasm' of her life, and that then turned out to be his 'special'. So with her heart beating ever faster she closed her eyes and begged her mind to trust him, to trust him as much as he wanted her to trust him, and so she nodded again.

But Phil looked at this woman he loved, and he saw the terror on her face. Her body was physically shaking and her teeth were clenched tightly together, with her hands practically gripping the sheet beneath her. He could see that she was trying so hard for him, but he could also clearly see that she was terrified. He sighed heavily, for his heart ached for her, for what terror was lying behind those tightly closed eyes. He could only imagine what had been done to her to instil this very real fear in her, and in that moment he wanted to commit murder for her, he wanted to murder the man who had abused her so badly.

She wasn't ready. And he didn't want her to 'suffer' his kisses and caresses, and perhaps for the first time, he really realised what she had meant by 'letting' him make love to her, or as she herself had worded it, have sex with him. He gently pulled the sheet back over her, and lying now beside her, he kissed her eyes, then her cheeks and finally, he kissed her lightly, but with enormous love on the lips, and he told her that everything was okay, that he wasn't going to do anything, because she wasn't ready. He reassured her that she didn't have to worry about anything. He wasn't angry with her, far from it, and again he told her how much he loved her, for he did love her, now more than ever.

Sheena finally let her breath escape from her body that she'd been holding in so tightly, and she looked intently at Phil. She needn't have worried, she knew that now. She knew by his reaction to her fear, that she had no need to worry, and suddenly she wanted him even more, suddenly her confidence in him, in what he was saying, and how all of his intentions towards her were so full of care and love, was now soaring. She turned towards him, and as he was now lying prostrate on the bed, she sat up, fully aware that she was now openly displaying her breasts to him as the sheet had slipped back down, but she was surprisingly unconcerned about it.

She leaned forward, kissed him gently at first, then with much more passion, and her kisses were returned eagerly. She now sat astride him, his eyes clearly admiring her body, and she liked that feeling. She placed his hands on her breasts and smiling at him she said clearly and without any nervousness now, "I love you, Phil, and I want your gorgeous hands caressing my body, I trust you completely. I was nervous before, but I'm not now, I want to know what it is like to be truly loved, and I want you to show me."

Tears of love were escaping and silently falling down her face, but Phil could see that she had in fact changed, but he was himself now nervous, nervous of hurting her, of rushing her, and so he asked her again if she was sure, because, he'd added that he was more than happy to wait until she was totally sure, it didn't have to be tonight. For an answer she lay back down and pushed the sheet away herself, before smiling happily at him and saying she was sure. She loved him, she trusted him, and she was very sure.

"Okay then," he said gently. "But please promise me that you'll just ask me to stop if you're unhappy, or at all unsure."

Smiling at him and letting out a deep breath of contentment, she did now totally relax, she wanted to feel his hands gently caressing her, and she was absolutely certain that he would stop if she asked him to, she was absolutely certain that she had no need to fear him, and so she said simply "– I promise." Then with her eyes now just lightly closed she felt Phil's hands caress her body while he showered her with soft, slow, tender kisses. He kissed her neck, her face, her shoulders, and then he kissed her stomach. All the while his hands were caressing her body, all over her body. She had smiled to herself at the feeling of disappointment she'd felt when his kisses had bypassed her breasts, for with each kiss and each touch her body was reacting as though it was totally separated from her mind.

She had no control over it, and when he gently lifted the elastic on her pants to kiss her lower stomach, her body flinched, but it wasn't a flinch of fear this time, it was a flinch of excitement, and again the slight disappointment when he merely released the elastic for it simply to ping back into place, without him going further, she couldn't believe how good he was making her feel, but more than that, she couldn't believe how much she *wanted* him to make her feel so good.

Her heart was beating ever faster, but she felt like a duck on the water: her body serene and calm above the surface, to the naked eye, but underneath she was paddling like mad just to stay afloat, such was her excitement. They had lain together almost naked on many occasions, but they hadn't looked at each other's body, they'd touched held and caressed each other many times, but somehow they'd never looked at each other's bodies. She really ought to have felt embarrassed by the fact that she now knew he was looking at her, that she could *feel* him, *see* him in her mind's eye, looking at her, but she didn't, she simply felt pure joy.

And Phil *was* looking at her, he was admiring her beautiful body, he marvelled at the fact that she was so unaware of her beauty. And, of course, that just added to it, to his love for her. He loved her so deeply, so very, very much, and he was not about to hurt her. He knew that time and love would eventually bring them together in the right way. But he also sensed that she was now totally relaxed, totally trusting of him. He knew she was enjoying his touch, and he loved that.

He also knew that there was no hurry and he had to make her feel that, to know that. But she'd been right about him wanting her, because his body, and his heart were simply aching for her, but he had to bring his body and his needs under control. He was determined to make any enjoyment that night to be just about her, just about her pleasure, and he so hoped that he would be able to do just that. Talking to her quietly and lovingly he told her to just feel what he was doing. "Just let your body be aware of all the different sensations, and just enjoy yourself, this is all for you, not for me." Although he had to admit that he was loving the act of pleasing her, and of her reactions now to that pleasure. "Just let me please you," he said, "let me show you how much I love you."

Whilst he was talking quietly to her, Sheena was very well aware of the sensation of him. His hands were playing with her toes one minute, he was kissing her legs the next, and then his very manly hands were moving slowly but firmly up her legs. His kisses were warm on her legs, then on her thighs. His hands were tenderly caressing her stomach and her sides, the whole of her body, and as she let her mind drift freely, she felt as though she was floating on air. She quickly drew in her stomach however, as his kisses were high up on her inner thighs, close to her vagina, very close, but not touching it, and it reacted to the nearness of him, to the very thought him, it reacted by throbbing in such a way as she'd never before experienced. She thought that she still had her pants on, but the way she was feeling she couldn't actually be sure of anything any more. His lips were warm and soft as they reached her stomach, then his hands were finally caressing her breasts.

Her heart was beating faster and faster, she was hot and sweaty, and her body was trembling, trembling with excitement now. She no longer needed to *force* her body to relax. Then when his lips gently sucked on her nipples she moved her hand to reach for his penis, she wanted to touch it, to feel it, but he stopped her, and whispered to her quietly again, "Just for you, darling, just for you." His tongue played with her nipples now and they duly rose to attention, and at the same time her vagina was throbbing, pulsating, desperate for him, all in reaction to his tongue on her nipples. Then his hands were again stroking her body. Oh, his hands felt so good, his lips felt so good, *she* felt so good. Her body was tingling, pulsating in response to his touch.

Then his hands and his lips were all over her body, so much that she was losing touch of where he was, or where he was going next, and she didn't care, she just didn't want him to stop. Then she felt his kiss so very, very close to her vagina, but she didn't flinch this time, this time she wanted him to touch it, she so, so wanted him to touch it. Then she realised that she did in fact still have her pants on, because she felt him slowly but surely remove them, and she didn't try to stop him, in fact she raised her body to make it easier for him. And then his fingers were inside her and his touch was like electric, he touched her in such a way, in some special way, that made her body arch, and soft involuntary moans escape from her mouth, such was the pleasure she was feeling.

What had he touched? She wanted to know, what was he toying with that was making her feel like that? The touch of his fingers inside her was stirring her up in a way that she'd

245

never experienced, and she liked it, oh God, she liked it, it felt so wonderful that it amazed and astounded her. Then whilst still with his fingers playing inside her, stirring every sense in her body, he moved up and kissed her on the lips, full hungry kisses and oh how she responded, how hungry she was for him.

Then there was a sudden rush developing inside her, and as she felt that rush get stronger and stronger, and again she let out such a moan of pleasure, she couldn't control it, she couldn't control her body, she didn't want to control it, she wanted to let this wonderful feeling take over her, to control her, she couldn't kiss him hard enough, she couldn't get enough of him. Their bodies, their arms, their legs, even their tongues were entwined together.

She wanted him now. Oh God, she more than wanted him; her body was aching for him. She whispered to him, begged him, to please make love to her. He stopped kissing her for a moment, to look closely at her, to be sure she was sincere, but as she opened her eyes to look at him, he could see the undoubted pleasure in them, her eyes, like her body they were moist with pleasure, and he could clearly see how happy and hungry for him she was, and he knew that she really wanted him now, truly wanted him, but still he wanted to be sure, he still needed to ask, to hear her say that she was sure, really sure, for this beautiful woman of his was never again going to do anything that she didn't want to do, didn't want to do willingly. She answered frantically, while laughing giddily, "Yes, yes I'm sure, I'm sure," she panted.

And so he finally entered her, and only a moment or two after he did so, she again felt this rush through her body, only stronger now, like a power surge making her whole body throb with excitement, and again her body arched towards him as the surge coursed through her, like a wave of excitement rolling from her legs to the top of her head, and seemingly then bursting out through the top of her head, and she gripped his back tightly as she moaned again so loud, over and over again, but she couldn't stop them, her moans were moans of pure pleasure.

But still Phil hadn't stopped; still he was thrusting wonderfully inside her. And then Phil himself moaned a sort of deep guttural moan, and with her heart beating ever faster and her legs trembling, that wonderful rolling surge of excitement again coursed through her body, and again it appeared to go right to the top of her head and out again, until finally he stopped.

He lay on top of her for a moment of two, seemingly exhausted, before moving gently to the side of her, and resting on his arm whilst gazing into her eyes, he asked her sincerely if she was okay. If he'd hurt her at all or rushed her too much. There was so much love in his eyes as she now looked at him equally seriously, because she didn't want him to leave him in any doubt about how she felt, and so she told him that there had never been a truer statement said to her than the one he'd said before they came upstairs. And she said that she could truly and honestly say to him, and she could, that she had never, ever, been made love to before.

Then as she lay with her head resting on his chest and his arm wrapped around her, she had a question that was puzzling her, and so she tentatively ask him if she could ask him one question. "Ask me anything, my darling", he'd replied. She wanted to know how he could do 'that' twice without stopping. He didn't know what she meant by 'that'. So he told her that she'd have to explain what she'd meant by 'that'. And so with more than a little embarrassment she told him that she was sure she'd felt a rush inside her that was him coming to climax, and yet he'd continued and came to climax seemingly for a second time. She added that until then she hadn't thought that was possible to continue without a break. Her embarrassment was making her babble and she knew it.

He laughed out loud at her, whilst kissing her, and holding her close to him again, and told her, that it wasn't him the first time, it was her. "That first 'rush' as you call it, was you having an orgasm," he said, delighted at her naivety. But he looked at her quizzically and slightly bemused, as though she was trying to fool him, trying to be coy. He had no doubt, absolutely no doubt at all that she'd been treated cruelly in her life, but surely some of the time life had been good to her, surely in the beginning that swine had loved her. And so he questioned her, "Surely you've had an orgasm before?" he said, laughing lovingly at her.

She sat up sharply and asked him if he was sure about that, because she'd always believed that a female orgasm was a myth, a myth put about by film and script writers. The look on her face was one of absolute disbelief, but he smiled at her and said that he was sure. He was positive that the feeling she'd described to him was in fact an orgasm.

"Well!" she'd said matter-of-factly. "There's only one thing to be said about that."

"And what's that," he enquired, still smiling at her. She replied with just one word 'WOW'! She told him with absolute certainty that it was exactly as she'd already said, that she'd never been made love to before, so she answered him in such a precise manner that it left him in no doubt as to the truth of what she was saying, and that was, that if she'd never been made love to before, then she would probably have had an orgasm, and, she repeated again, she'd never had an orgasm before, so she'd obviously never been made love to before.

They laughed together and they both knew that it wouldn't be the last time that she'd experience an orgasm. But although he never said as much to Sheena, his heart was aching for this woman whom he loved so deeply. To realise that at the age of twenty-eight and with three children who she clearly adored, had never in fact been made love to. That was so sad to him, but knowing that her father had been charged with her mother's murder, it wasn't perhaps so strange. For she'd evidently been brought up never to experience any love between her parents, so why should she expect that love-making was something wonderful between two people very much in love. He promised himself then, that as long as Sheena was with him, and he hoped it would be for a very long time, then she would never again be hurt, either physically, emotionally or sexually.

Sheena lay quiet to contemplate what had just happened between them, her legs were still trembling and her body still tingling from his touch, and she wanted to enjoy, that feeling for a while longer. Then lifting her head towards him, and looking straight into his gorgeous blue eyes with a wicked look in hers, she toyed with his fingers for a while, remembering the passion that they'd stirred in her with them, before adding teasingly, that she didn't know what he'd been doing with those fingers of his, but he certainly hadn't been looking for keys! Phil looked bemused, puzzled and feigning mock, shock and horror, he demanded an explanation. But she just laughed at him, and tuning over now, she pulled his arm over her body to put it in her favourite position – cupping her breast.

CHAPTER 26

When Sheena got up the next morning, Phil had already left for work and as she was making her bed she found her mother's cardigan still beneath her pillow, and burying her head in it for a while, to devour the aroma of her mother that still lingered on it, she spoke quietly to her mother. She told her that she was happy now and that she had no need to worry about her any longer.

She also told her that she was so, so sorry that she'd never experienced love the way that she now had. And she vowed that she would make sure that 'Big Sid' paid a very dear price for what he had done to her. Sheena folded the cardigan carefully and placed it in her dressing table drawer, she felt strong enough now to take it from under her pillow, but she would never, ever, part with it completely.

The trial was due to start at 10.00 that morning and although Phil was working he'd arranged to meet up with her at lunch time. She'd been glad about that, because although she'd obviously have the support of her brothers, Iain had again returned home for the trial, she preferred to have Phil close by. They had no idea how long the trial would last, but they'd been told that it would probably be for a week or two.

Sheena, Graham and Iain were sitting outside the courtroom waiting to go in when the barrister who was leading the prosecution came to see them. He told them that he'd just been notified that their father intended to say in his defence that there was no case to answer. His argument was quite simply that their mother had not been murdered by anyone, but had in fact committed suicide.

Graham stood up and was pacing angrily and shouting at the barrister, "I knew it, I bloody well knew it. It's always been glaringly obvious to me that he would use that as his defence, because who can contradict him, he was the only one there, and we know from his own admission that she'd taken an overdose, but the difference is that he *made* her take that overdose." Sheena tried to calm him down, but he was extremely irate and not about to be calmed down.

Sheena wanted to know if that meant that there would now be no trial, or if it meant that it would be more difficult to try the case against him. The barrister laughed and said of course the trial would go ahead, whatever he pleads, whatever his excuses, he assured them, he was still charged with murder, and he was still going to be tried for murder. The barrister said that his new plan was quite simply a last ditch effort to try to get the trial cancelled, or at least to introduce an element of doubt for the jury. But he told them to keep calm and keep faith. He told them that there would be too much evidence for that plea to stand.

None of them understood what the barrister had meant by that, by *too much evidence*, and although Sheena knew that there were details to be unearthed during the trial in regard to the fact that he'd raped her mother and forced her to take the tablets, she couldn't understand how they could prove 'rape'. She wondered how they would distinguish between 'rape' and normal sex within a marriage. She also wondered how they could prove that her mother had been forced to take tablets, rather than have taken them of her own free will, it was all so very worrying.

Sheena then wanted to know from the barrister what reason 'Big Sid' had given for suddenly using suicide as his defence, she still couldn't call him father, not even to the barrister. Surely, she reasoned, if he'd wanted to claim that it was suicide then he would have done so long ago, when he was first charged. The barrister replied that he'd apparently not said anything earlier because he hadn't believed that it would get this far, and also that he'd wanted to protect his children from having to know that their mother had committed suicide, to know effectively, that she'd decided to end her life without telling them.

Sheena simply couldn't believe the arrogance of the man. To use that as his defence when he'd bragged to her about killing her mother, well it was simply beyond belief. Surely the jury will see through that, she just had to hope and pray that they would, that was all any of them could do, just pray that he wasn't slimy enough to convince the jury, that he didn't act the part of devastated husband too well.

However, Sheena, along with her brothers was seriously scared that this new plan would in fact see 'Big Sid' get away with murder. But she couldn't contemplate that thought too seriously; she wouldn't contemplate that thought at all, for that would surely drive her mad. He *had* murdered her, so he *had* to be found guilty. Surely there was no other option. British justice would just *have* to win through. Graham though was convinced that he would get away with it. And he lost his temper with Sheena when she reasoned that because he *was* guilty, then he would be found guilty. "Get real," he'd shouted at her. "People get away with murder all the time. No, he said firmly, he's going to bloody well get away with it." He then added ominously, that if he got away with it, it wouldn't mean that he would be able to live the life of a free man, not if he had anything to do about it.

Sheena was terrified that he was right, but she had to stay focused, she had to believe that justice would prevail. She told Graham that he was talking nonsense, and that the barrister would not have been so confident in what he'd been saying if he'd been in the least doubtful. She was at the same time trying to convince herself of that too, and she was far from sure that she even believed it herself. As it was now nearing 10.00am all that was left for them to do was to hug each other and pray that justice would prevail. Graham and Iain went into the courtroom and Sheena had to wait outside as she was going to be called as a witness, and apparently she would be the first witness.

CHAPTER 27

Sheena stepped into the witness box feeling extremely nervous, but she was determined not to let her nerves get the better of her, she was determined to help in any way she could to get justice for her mother. Looking around the courtroom she saw 'Big Sid'. He was looking at her and smiling, she couldn't believe he was actually smiling. She quickly turned away disgusted.

The barrister for the prosecution asked her to tell the court in her own words what had happened with regard to her mother in the days leading up to her death. So she explained about the christening and about how much her mother had been looking forward to it. She also told them about mother and daughter shopping together and about her mother's excitement.

He then wanted to know why her mother hadn't in fact attended the christening, to which Sheena replied that 'Big Sid' had called her to let her know that her mother wasn't well enough to come to the christening after all, but she added firmly that he'd been lying, because her mother wasn't ill at all. The barrister repeated to her, somewhat bemused 'Big Sid'? Sheena apologised and explained that she could no longer call that man 'father', she told him that as far as she was concerned, and indeed the rest of her family, that man in the dock was no longer her father, she informed him curtly that he'd lost the right to hold the title of father. She couldn't help but notice her brothers' smile of approval towards her when she'd said that, and she was glad that she'd been able to say it because *'he'* had also heard her. However, the barrister said that perhaps she could in future refer to the accused as Mr Williams if it made it easier for her. Sheena agreed to do just that.

Sheena was then asked when she last saw her mother alive, and in what circumstances. She told them that Mr Williams had asked her, demanded of her, to visit her mother the night before she died, and she added that he'd informed her that her mother was very ill. But, she emphasised strongly, that when she arrived at her mother's house, her mother wasn't ill at all, she was in fact very well and in fine spirits. She went on to explain, somewhat reluctantly, that her mother had told Mr Williams that she was ill because she didn't want to have sex with him, not the type of sex he was demanding anyway, and therefore to her mother, being ill was the only time he left her alone, so she explained, it wasn't unusual for her to say that, for her to feign illness.

Sheena had hated having to say that, having to talk about what she had not only considered to be a *private* conversation between mother and daughter, but it was also a very intimate conversation, and, of course, it had been her final conversation with her mother. She hadn't wanted to give the details of that conversation in open court, because that was the one conversation that she had wanted to retain, to keep for herself as something very special. But she was also very much aware of the fact that the prosecution would need every bit of ammunition that they could gets for that reason, and that reason alone, she was telling them those very personal details.

When she was asked what happened next, Sheena thought that she was about to faint, she didn't know if she could say what happened next because it was so awful. She suddenly and instinctively held on to the sides of the witness box, she'd held on to them to prevent herself from falling, to prevent her from collapsing, because that was what she was in very real danger of doing.

For she was suddenly transported back to that morning, that very morning when she was sitting on the sofa nursing her darling baby daughter, when she could feel the warmth of her baby's body close to hers. She even, in open court, absent-mindedly placed her hand onto her right breast, in order to 'feel' her baby's tiny fingers softly and lovingly caressing her breast, so strong was that memory. She'd looked into her daughters eyes that morning, blissfully unaware that this would be the last time that mother and daughter would enjoy such intimate contact. Blissfully unaware that her life as she then knew it, was about to cease forever, and blissfully unaware that her whole world was about to come crashing down around her.

And that intimate contact with her daughter being lost for ever had broken her heart, and her daughter was not immune to this pain either as she was suddenly thrust into the strange and unwanted new life of being weaned, of never enjoying being breast fed again. For her daughter would never accept a substitute breast, she would never accept a bottle with a teat; she had in fact suckled for the last time.

All of this, all of these changes, neither Sheena nor her daughter had wanted or expected. Her mind couldn't stir from that day; her memories were too precious, too important. She desperately wanted to go back to that morning, and for the rest of the day not to have happened. She didn't want this horrible reality.

But the barrister apparently still pressed Sheena for an answer to his question, his question as to what happened next, he seemed unaware that Sheena was unable to focus on his questions, unable to answer his questions because her mind was elsewhere. Sheena was trying desperately to remain focused, to answer his questions, but only a very small part of her mind was registering that she was expected to answer, and so in a barely audible whisper, she answered that her life changed forever. But from somewhere, somewhere that seemed to be very far away, someone was shouting, "Mrs Miller. Mrs Miller," the voice repeated loudly.

The shouting of her name caused Sheena to be suddenly and violently jolted back into reality, back into the real world and she realised that is was in fact the barrister who was now shouting even louder, and he was shouting repeatedly at her, "Mrs Miller. You need to answer the question; you need to tell us what happened next." And so from somewhere deep in the depths of Sheena's soul, a voice boomed out, a voice so huge, so loud, that it stunned Sheena. And it said that: **'The phone rang',** the words that had tumbled uncontrollably out of her mouth were full of extreme hatred and venom, and whilst those feelings were truly justified, she didn't want to present the court with a vision of a vitriolic and neurotic woman. So she sucked in a deep breath, and stood tall, proud and confident.

First of all she apologised for her outburst, then she went on to say; "what happened next, sir, was that my world changed forever, nothing that I knew up until that time stayed the same." She went on to explain that she had just finished nursing her five-month-old baby when the phone rang and 'he', she pointed directly at the 'Bastard', for in her mind now he couldn't even be called 'Big Sid', Sheena liked the term her Aunt Joyce had used better, "'he' uttered ten words to me, ten words that were cold, calculating and cruel." Ten words, she emphasised with precise heartfelt clarity, that he'd used in such a manner as to cause her as much pain and distress as possible, "And those ten words, sir," she added with as much aplomb as possible, "were; *'I'm just ringing to tell you that your mother is dead'."* *That,* she said crisply but defiantly, "Is what happened next."

She went on to tell him how those words and the manner with which they were delivered, had changed absolutely everything about her life, absolutely everything about her. The shock they delivered, she informed him, meant that the feed that she had just finished giving to her darling baby daughter was in fact to be her last feed, the last time that she could nurse her, because the shock of that phone call took her milk away. So not only did her life change forever, but her daughter's did also. It felt strange; it felt somehow to be a betrayal of her private thoughts, to now have to say those thoughts, out loud in open court.

And then Sheena, feeling exhausted and weak from the strain of attempting to remain completely composed, and still holding on to the sides of the witness box, now struggled to remain upright and so the judge ordered that she be given a drink of water and some time to recover. Sheena wanted to thank him for his kindness, a little kindness shown to her in this world of horror that she now found herself living in, but she was no longer able to speak, however, her eyes spoke to him, and they conveyed her heartfelt thanks.

After a few moments and that drink of water Sheena had calmed down, but now it was the turn of the defence barrister, but before he started to speak she glanced up and saw that Phil had arrived, he was sitting there smiling at her, silently encouraging her, and that boosted her confidence again.

The defence barrister tried to twist what she'd said, tried to say that her mother had in fact been ill, and not only ill but severely depressed. Sheena immediately thought that this was where he is going to suggest suicide, so she stood as tall and as confident as she could under the circumstances, and told him quite firmly, that he was wrong. She told him in no uncertain terms, how her mother had played 'ride-a-cock-horse' with her elder daughter and that she would have needed to be fit and well to play that particular game, that it would have been impossible for her to play such a boisterous game if she had been either ill or depressed. Her mother, she said sharply, had been happy that night, happy to see her, and happy to both see and play with her grandchildren.

She also told him that her last words were words that were in fact designed to say goodbye to her, and, she added succinctly, that it was only much, much later that she'd realised that those words were her mother saying goodbye to her. Sheena added, with silent, and unstoppable, tears sliding repeatedly down her cheeks, that it had pained her beyond measure when she'd realised that, when he'd told her that, because she hadn't said goodbye, she hadn't known that she was supposed to be saying goodbye, and as a result she left her mother that night feeling extremely annoyed that she *hadn't* been ill, annoyed because she knew that she would get beaten by her husband for her insistence that they visit her sick mother.

She stared at the dock where *he, the Bastard,* was sitting, whilst smirking unforgivably at her hurt and distress, *"and"* she added, trying desperately to wipe away her now abundant tears frantically with both hands, "I will never forgive him for that as long as I live, whether he is found guilty in this courtroom, or not, I will never forgive him, because *I know* he is guilty." And what's more, she stated clearly, and with more outward confidence than she truly felt, her mother had been saying goodbye to her because Mr Williams had informed her that if she ever refused him sex again, which she had done over the weekend of her granddaughter's christening, then he would kill her."

"He," she pointed again to the 'Bastard'. "*He* told me himself that my mother was fully aware that that evening was to be her last. Her mother though, had only known that his

259

intentions were to kill her that evening, when she'd realised that he'd gone out of his way to make sure that she visited her that evening, knowing, as he surely did, that her visit to her mother at such an odd time, and in seemingly desperate circumstances, would cause mayhem between herself and her husband. Then her mother knew her fate.

Sheena wasn't about to be silenced now, not now that she was in full flow, so she told the barrister that Mr Williams had planned it all, she told him defiantly, that Mr Williams himself had told her all this in his confession to her after what they all had thought had been her mother's funeral, after *he'd* thought that he was 'home free' so to speak. Finally she added that he'd admitted all this to her, his daughter, which she stressed, he not only told her, but he happily bragged about it. He'd also told her that he wasn't at all worried about whom she repeated their conversation to, because he'd believed that he couldn't be prosecuted for her mother's murder because there was no evidence, no body; he'd firmly and arrogantly believed that he'd committed the perfect murder and that he would get away with it. At last, with her ordeal now over she was able to go and sit next to Phil, to get some comfort from him, some much needed support, to enable her to listen to the rest of the trial.

Her mother's doctor was the next person to be questioned and his answers shocked Sheena, because they clearly demonstrated how lax he'd been as a doctor. Apparently her mother had never been hospitalised over any heart condition, she'd never actually had a heart attack, he'd never actually seen her suffer a bad attack of Angina, and she didn't have a temperature or any signs of a heart attack during any of his final visits to see her over her last weekend, although he did say that she'd had a raised heartbeat!

The barrister then belittled the doctor by saying sarcastically that his visits weren't entirely wasted then. He then asked him why he'd changed the cause of death from

'Heart Attack' to Suspicious Death. Sheena was more than delighted when he confirmed the reason for the change was a conversation that he'd had with the victims daughter in the days after her death, that the things that she'd said to him had made him think again, made him think that it might perhaps be better to err on the side of caution. Again the barrister was sarcastic in his humiliation of the doctor, when he'd said 'well, thank goodness for that then'.

CHAPTER 28

The court had broken up for lunch and all four of them went out to eat together. They were all excited to know what it was that Sheena had said to the doctor to make him change his mind, and why she hadn't told them. Sheena had been thrilled to know for certain that it was her conversation with the doctor that had changed his mind, and so she eagerly told them about her visit to see him, about how she'd played on his obviously huge ego to elicit sympathy from him. But she added mischievously, that he probably wished that he hadn't changed his mind now, after the grilling he'd just had in there.

"Well! Sheena," Graham exclaimed, with his joy and elation extremely evident. "You certainly did some good there. We would never have reached this stage at all if it hadn't been for you." Then he reached over to shake Phil's hand, and he told him that he was clearly the best thing that had ever happened in Sheena's life, for a long time, possibly for ever, he declared. "I'd noticed the change in her when I last saw her, he told him, but seeing her today, well anyone can see how much her confidence has grown, it shone through in there and no mistake," and he added, "with a great deal of pleasure, I believe that change in her is down to you Phil. Sheena,"

Graham added warmly, "played that doctor at his own game and she won, so keep on doing whatever it is that you are doing, and you'll always be a welcome visitor in my home."

Iain also shook Phil's hand and added his agreement to that. Sheena was so pleased to hear Iain particularly, speak so warmly regarding Phil, especially after his last comments regarding him when he'd spoken so disparagingly about him on his previous visit home. Sheena smiled happily at Phil and gripped his hand tightly. But they had to remember that there was a long way to go yet, there still didn't appear to be any real evidence to convict him, not anything that they could say was 'beyond a reasonable doubt'.

They were all concerned about that, about reasonable doubt, they had all been thinking it, but it was Graham who voiced their thoughts. Sheena told them that although what the pathologist would have to say would be hard to listen to; it was in fact their final hope of convincing the jury. They couldn't think of anything else that might help. The pathologist was going to be their final chance.

Going back into the courtroom for the afternoon they were all now able to sit together and support each other, for now it was time for the pathologist to discuss his report. The defence barrister asked him if there had been any barbiturates in Mrs William's system when he examined her. The pathologist confirmed that there indeed had been a large amount of barbiturates in her system. The barrister seemed pleased with that remark, as did 'Big Sid', but that news was not what the rest of them wanted to hear.

The defence barrister seemed so satisfied with that information that he didn't feel any need to ask any further questions. So it was left to the prosecution to ask for more details. Sheena was holding on to both Phil's and Iain's hands now, terrified of what was coming next, and yet wondering how they were going to contradict the evidence of the barbiturates, because of the obvious implications that that entailed.

But they were all extremely distraught at what they heard next, because the pathologist described their mother's injuries, and it was just too horrific. She had severe bruising to her legs and vaginal area, which he said was consistent with severe and repeated violent rape. She also had similar damage to her anal area, but there was also tearing there, again he said, this was consistent with severe, repeated and violent rape.

Sheena felt herself go weak at the knees listening to these horrific details, but glancing at her brothers, they were clearly in a much more distressed state than she was, because she had already listened to that Bastard, she couldn't even say 'Big Sid' now, tell her word for word what he'd done to her. What Sheena had been worried about was being able to prove the difference between a rape and marital sex, but she could see now that that was clearly not a problem.

The Pathologist went on to describe how some of her fingernails were broken and that skin was found underneath the complete fingernails that remained, suggesting that she'd fought valiantly for her life. Iain had buried his head in Sheena's shoulder, unable to listen, but unable to walk out either. He still needed to see the 'Bastard' squirm, and as yet he was still sitting looking smug.

Finally the barrister mentioned that it was being suggested that Mrs Williams in fact took her own life by taking a huge overdose, and he asked him what his opinion of that statement was. The 'Bastard' had sat forward to eagerly listen to his answer, his expression still very much a gloating one. But the Pathologist said that suicide was definitely NOT POSSIBLE. There were cheers all round when he said that. But the barrister, waited for some calm, and then asked him to explain exactly what he'd meant by that, given that he'd already stated that there was a huge amount of barbiturates in her system.

And so the Pathologist explained that the barbiturates had been taken over several hours, possibly eight or ten, because some of them were completely dissolved in her system whilst others had not yet even reached her stomach. She had, he said, been systematically fed them over a period of time, and in his experience, if someone intended to commit suicide, they do not rip their nails out fighting for their life, and they take the tablets in one go, very often, he added, with alcohol.

Finally the barrister asked him what, in his expert opinion, was the cause of death. He told him that she had in fact died of a heart attack. Sheena was extremely shocked and quite worried by that. Would describing her mother's death as a heart attack mean that it was a 'death by natural causes'? Would 'he' the 'Bastard' now get away with it, her heart was racing, and by the look on her brother's faces, they were thinking the same thing.

The barrister then went on to clarify what the Pathologist had just told him. So, he said, finally asking the question that they were all scared of the answer to, "Does that statement mean that Mrs Williams died of natural causes?" The 'Bastard' was grinning now, grinning directly at Sheena. But the Pathologist replied firmly, "No, her heart attack was brought about by the violent nature of her death, if she had not been attacked in the way that she was, then she would not have had a heart attack. Her heart," he said, "was in fact incredibly strong; she fought for her life for a very long time." And he added, "Summarily, that if she had survived the violence, then the barbiturates would have killed her before long, as there was a huge amount in her system. So the answer to your question Sir is that Mrs Williams was murdered, and murdered in a cold, calculating and heartless manner."

So the barrister then turned to the jury and said that in effect, the description of Mrs William's death was exactly as described by her daughter earlier, and that she in turn had heard that very same description from the mouth of the defendant. There was then a lot of hustle and bustle as the 'Bastard's' barrister had a conversation with the 'Bastard' before finally stating to the judge that his client wished to change his plea to guilty.

The smug satisfied grin, had finally been wiped from the 'Bastard's' face, and that pleased all of them. In fact there was uproar and elation from everyone. They all hugged each other, their pain at listening to their mother's horrific injuries temporarily forgotten.

But then Sheena stood up and letting go of Phil's hands she put her hand over her mouth as she gasped in shock. She was shaking, trembling and couldn't get any words out, she just stood there shaking her head. So Phil, now also standing up and taking hold of her again, repeated what the barrister had said again, more slowly and more clearly. "Sheena, look at me, listen to what I am saying, love, he implored her. 'Big Sid' has pleaded guilty to murdering your dear mother, your worries, fears and sheer dread that he was going to get away with that murder, is now thankfully all over."

Sheena started to weep and at the same time she was gasping for air, desperately trying to suck in enough air to stay conscious. For in her mind at that moment she was back in her mother's living room, and she was on her knees, her head gently resting next to her dead mother. She could still feel that her mother was cold; she could still see her eyes staring into nothing as her own eyes searched her father's face, for at that time she still thought of him as her father, for answers. And she'd *believed* those answers. At a time when her pain was at its highest, she'd believed those answers. She'd believed that he felt her pain; she'd believed that he'd loved her mother and she had believed that he'd gently nursed her in her last moments as she lay dying.

But now she knew the truth, now she knew that he'd not only been lying to her, he had been laughing at her. And far from nursing her in her dying moments he had in fact been responsible for those dying moments. In her mind's eye the picture that she was now faced with, was that of her mother lying beneath that 'Bastard' and she was fighting, kicking, and screaming at this big brute of a man with all the effort her tiny, weak frame could muster.

And that after his very brutal and disgusting raping of her she had been so drained of all her energy, brought so low with despair and pain that she finally, willingly, took the barbiturates that he'd been trying to force her to take, for she had known that the only way out of her nightmare was to now take those tablets. She had taken them knowing that then her nightmare could finally end. And all these thoughts, these terrible distressing thoughts, were in danger of bringing her to the point of collapse. It was too much for her. She had waited and prayed for this moment and now it was here and it was too much for her.

Phil held her tightly to prevent her from collapsing altogether while they all made their way out of the courtroom. Sheena's mind started to wander incoherently, inanely, in haphazard directions. Her mind just kept skipping to silly things, stupid unimportant things: was her home tidy enough? Had she remembered to put the dustbin out? And she wanted to know who was calling her name, who was shouting at her? Her mind was quite simply in a state of total confusion, she literally couldn't think straight.

But it was Phil, Graham and Iain that were calling her name, they were congratulating her, they were telling her over and over again that it was all over now and she could relax. Then Inspector Jeremy Loughton came to congratulate them, but it was they who wanted to thank him. He just smiled at them and told them that their father would be going to prison for the rest of his life. He would never again see the light of day. His murder of her mother, he explained, was cold, calculating, pre-meditated and cruel. He told Sheena that she should feel proud, that they all should feel proud, as her mother would truly be proud of them, because their determination, and their belief, and especially Sheena's, that their mother had been murdered, was what had brought all this about.

But Sheena said that luckily the 'Bastard' had been the author of his own downfall. Because he'd been so arrogant in his belief that he could get away with murder, that he couldn't help but brag about it. He'd also bragged about how he'd 'conned' the doctor, all Sheena had done she insisted, was to bring his own words back to haunt him.

Feeling much better now, even slightly euphoric, her mind came back to the reality of the moment, and Sheena was truly pleased with the outcome. She was glad when Phil suggested that they all go for a drink together to celebrate, and she was even more pleased when her brother's agreed. Phil bought a bottle of champagne, which Sheena thought was a bit extravagant, but he said mysteriously that there was more than one thing to celebrate.

So with everyone watching him he went down on one knee, and with his gorgeous piercing blue eyes beseeching an answer from her, he presented Sheena with a diamond engagement ring, he then asked her if she would do him the honour of marrying him. Sheena was more than a little shocked, but unable to stem the huge grin that was quickly spreading across her face, teasingly she looked to her right, and then to her left, as though he might be speaking to someone else, before finally pointing to herself and saying, "Me?"

But Phil, picking up on her obvious humour then added in mock distress, "Please don't make me wait too long for an answer, darling, and please don't say no!"

Sheena stood up and wrapping her arms around him, said, "YES PLEASE." She remembered the excitement of their previous evening, of her delight, of her passionate response to his lovemaking and she knew without a doubt that there was much more love and excitement ahead of her. For the first time in her life she could look ahead to a world completely full of happiness.